DRINK THIS

By Eileen Dewhurst

DRINK THIS
DEATH CAME SMILING
AFTER THE BALL
CURTAIN FALL

DRINK THIS

EILEEN DEWHURST

PUBLISHED FOR THE CRIME CLUB BY
DOUBLEDAY & COMPANY, INC.
GARDEN CITY, NEW YORK
1981

All of the characters in this book
are fictitious, and any resemblance
to actual persons, living or dead,
is purely coincidental.

Library of Congress Cataloging in Publication Data
Dewhurst, Eileen.
  Drink this.

  I. Title.
PR6054.E95D7   1981   823'.914
ISBN 0-385-17457-8

Library of Congress Catalog Card Number 80-2320
Copyright © 1980 by Eileen Dewhurst
All Rights Reserved
Printed in the United States of America

To R. H. R.

CHAPTER 1

I

When the day of Pentecost was fully come, they were all with one accord in one place.

Across the chancel Tony's eyes met Ginger's. Held them. Challenged them to falter.

And suddenly there came a sound from heaven, as of a rushing mighty wind, and it filled all the house where they were sitting.

Ginger gave in and blinked. Tony mimed his triumph then looked away, turning his head just enough to see along the choir stall. White shoulders. Hands. Books. Fidgeting. The pattern broken at the end by the vicar, his seat a little forward of the stall, his plump white hands clasped motionless in his lap. Opposite the vicar the curate, his head thrown back, his eyes blazing across at the lectern. Being everything thoroughly and now looking thoroughly devout.

And they were all amazed and marvelled, saying one to another, Behold, are not all these which speak Galileans? And how hear we every man in our own tongue wherein we were born?

The tongue of John Arkwright, lay reader, was stern and solemn. Tony could hear him but not see him, the lectern and half the congregation were hidden by the carved canopy above the vicar's chair. But he could see to the left of the nave.

John Arkwright's wife and daughter in the fourth pew. Janet the daughter gazing raptly at the curate. She had a crush on him. Tony thought Mr. Arkwright scowled at the curate as he swept back to his place behind him, he was certainly scowling at the back of the curate's head. Everyone knew he disapproved of Janet thinking she was in love with him. Perhaps he thought the curate was in love with her. That would be a crazy idea, but Mr. Arkwright was the sort of person who might have crazy ideas. Janet had lately begun to serve in his greengrocer's shop, and was sometimes mean in her efforts to be efficient. Thinking about the cherries Mr. Arkwright was piling up these June days in his window, Tony bit down heavily and received a cuff from the senior chorister behind him for his protest at the pain. But he hadn't got used yet to being minus four back teeth and having a tight metal band with a plastic top in his mouth. It didn't feel like his mouth any more. If he remembered not to do what he had just done it didn't hurt too much, but the whole time it was outrageously uncomfortable and it ruined eating. He sucked on his teeth vigorously, then felt round his lips with his hanky to see if there was any blood, but the wounds, a week old, were almost healed.

Jesus said unto his disciples, If ye love me, keep my commandments . . .

Tony tried to concentrate on the Gospel (and it was easier to concentrate standing up), but he saw his sister Annabel's pale face in the third pew, beside their father, and his thoughts drifted towards her on a wave of excitement . . . his sister, wife of Benjamin Quillin, big-time criminal, man in the news, who had eluded the police and disappeared after successfully masterminding an enormous London bank raid which one of the newspapers had described as "breath-taking." Benjamin Quillin. His brother-in-law.

Tony shivered, still not easily believing such an extraordinary fact. He had never seen much of Benjamin but he had always felt uneasy in his presence, despite the lavish gifts, at the same time as he had felt vaguely excited, vaguely menaced . . . Benjamin had come with pale silent Annabel on rare short visits, and then all at once it was Annabel alone, paler and more silent than ever, day after day reading through the stack of newspapers piled up on the floor beside her chair, and Tony a rather sheepish but not altogether unwilling celebrity among his peers.

"Today, Whit Sunday, Pentecost, we celebrate the presence in our world of the third part of our one God, the Holy Spirit . . ."

The Gospel had turned into the sermon, and the curate was preaching. The vicar preached the best sermons, even Tony didn't stray too far or too long when the vicar preached, but the vicar was generous about letting the curate preach and even, round about holiday times and at Evensong, John Arkwright.

Tony's view of the Reverend Malcolm Darcy was now in profile. He really was magnificent in the pulpit, tall and fair and handsome, with a ringing voice. He wasn't married. Perhaps if he had been in the parish before Annabel met Benjamin . . . Tony looked beyond the curate at his sister. He half thought that she might not have been suited as a clergyman's wife, but he didn't really know. He didn't know much about her at all, about what made her tick. It was funny, now he thought of it, to know so little about your own sister. People had been very sorry for her, when the business broke about Benjamin, and the whole idea was dreadfully pathetic, the wife ignorant of the husband's criminal activities, and then being abandoned when he successfully skipped. Tony supposed he was sorry for her, too, only he didn't really know if she was unhappy, he supposed she must be, but even before Benjamin had disappeared she had never been exactly cheerful or forthcoming, it wasn't her style. She had always been kind to Tony and even rather spoilt him with his favourite foods and letting him off things, but he sometimes thought it was a form of laziness. Although he didn't know. Funny . . .

And now to God the Father, God the Son, and God the Holy Spirit . . .

He hadn't meant to let the whole of the curate's sermon slip away, he truly hadn't. He put up an inarticulate prayer of apology as he rose to his feet. It was easier to concentrate for the Creed because when he turned towards the altar he could see only the white-robed back of the server and the gleam of silver vessels on the credence table in its niche in the south wall. When old Bedlington Byrne served he turned a full few seconds after everyone else, gustily sighing. Tony, from his seat at the altar-end of the choir stall, was always waiting for him to fall down the shallow steps or to drop one of the vessels. Although he was so fond of the old man he found the sung Eucharist less nerve-racking when Bedlington Byrne was glaring from his pew in the front row of the congregation, and someone else, as today, was handling the Elements. BB had told him, furious, that the vicar had suggested it was perhaps time that he ceased to serve.

Almighty God, who has promised to hear the prayers of those who ask in faith . . .

John Arkwright was kneeling in the nave, leading the intercession. Bedlington Byrne was not in his pew, which meant he was not in church, he would sit nowhere but his self-appointed place. Tony felt a twinge of anxiety. BB might be ill, or at least what everyone called, in his case, "unwell." BB had confided to Tony, leaning wheezily towards him and encircling his arm with nails sharp enough to hurt, that it was his heart. Well, after the service he would go and see. And if he didn't go, no one else would. Oh, the vicar would eventually, of course, as he would go and see anyone he feared might be in trouble, or Mr. Darcy, but they might be too late. And if anything happened to BB there were the cats and the rabbits and the monkey . . .

> Lord in thy mercy
> Hear our prayer.

Old Corrigan wouldn't go and see if anything had happened to BB, that was for sure. Even though he was his cousin. One of them at each end of the front pew. That wasn't very Christian, for a start. It must bother the vicar, the obviousness of those two cousins ignoring each other. Tony looked at Mr. Corrigan through his fingers. When he said "Hear our prayer" old Corrigan really *said* it, his lips moving as if he was issuing a command, his head up, staring in his haughty aristocratic way at the altar. It must be how his face was made, even old Corrigan wouldn't choose to look like that at the altar. He was a bit like an eagle, with his hooked nose and long neck. When Tony moved slightly (suffering another prod from behind) he could get old Corrigan's head against his own family memorial on the north wall, a brass halo. It commemorated three eighteenth-century Corrigans, and they too had all been churchwardens . . . Tony started automatically to turn his head again, but he knew he couldn't see Mr. Naylor, the other churchwarden; he always sat to the right of the nave, and a long way back. If old Corrigan was proud, Mr. Naylor was humble. One tall, the other short. Funny how people . . .

Tony was nudged to his feet by Goody Gordon on his left. John Arkwright had come back to his seat behind the curate and the vicar had moved to the altar. The server was hovering by the credence table. The candle-bearers and the crucifer were going along the nave to escort the members of the congregation bringing up the collection and the bread and wine. There was always a procession on high days, otherwise the Elements of the Eucharist were put ready beforehand on the credence table. Whit Sunday . . . This would be the next to last procession until the Church's year began again on the first Sunday in Advent. Mike Adams had said to them at their last practice, with his earnest lisp: "You must not think, boys, that because there are no high Sundays in the summer there is no need to strive for perfection. Every Sunday is a day of celebration."

Tony raised his eyes, above the cross as it slowly climbed the chancel steps, to where Mike's surpliced figure swayed on the organ stool. *Holy, Holy, Holy, Though the darkness hide Thee* . . . He realized that they had reached verse three of the offertory hymn, and that he had been singing unawares. Funny, how you could do so many things at once without noticing, including breathing. But if you thought about breathing you began to get breathless and that wasn't a good idea while you were singing . . . With a slight shock Tony remembered that his two solo lines would be coming next. While the congregation were communicating he would begin the anthem.

Little Mr. Naylor, handing up the offertory plate, stumbled on a corner of the carpet so that the plate went rather hastily into the vicar's outstretched hands. Tony and Ginger pulled faces across the chancel. Mr. Naylor had passed the vicar's wife on his way up, and Tony and Ginger were convinced he was in love with her, the way his face went pink whenever he saw her. It was pink now. Of course, she was very beautiful, almost as beautiful as the picture of his mother Tony could conjure up at any time for his comfort.

You certainly got a good view from the front row of the choir stalls. His Aunt Helen had the ciborium, and mad Miss Catchpole and Goody Gordon's fat father each had a silver jug of wine . . .

Almighty God, our heavenly Father, we have sinned against thee . . .

"I'm sorry I keep wandering off, honestly I am."

Old Corrigan was still staring at the altar. So was Annabel, but her eyes didn't look as if they were seeing anything.

God so loved the world, that He gave His only-begotten Son . . .

These words were all mixed up with the picture of Jesus on Tony's bedroom wall, with squirrels and birds on his hands and arms, and the words written underneath. Nice words, he would concentrate on them, and on what was happening. Mr. Groome was at the altar all the time now, talking to God rather than the congregation. But bits of singing kept breaking in—*Holy, Holy, Holy, Lord God of Hosts, Blessed is he that cometh in the name of the Lord, O, Lamb of God* . . . There was a lamb in the corner of the picture of Jesus, looking up at him.

The vicar made his Communion, and gave it to the curate, Mr. Arkwright, and Mike Adams. Then the choir. He put his hands on the heads of those who had not yet been confirmed. Tony knelt down again in the choir stall, the organ ceased to idle, he was prodded to his feet and in mild surprise heard his solo voice float up to the rafters.

How beautiful upon the mountain
Are the feet of them that bring glad tidings.

The other voices wrapped warmly round his single reed. The four places in his mouth still told him when he drew in air. In one other place the band was rubbing. How much longer would his voice climb high like this, and when it changed, what would it change to? Extraordinary thought, that it was bound to change . . .

The vicar and the curate were drinking up the remains of the wine. Tony made himself not watch them, trying to say a prayer while a few minutes remained. Phrases floated in. *Almighty God, we have sinned against thee . . .* Benjamin had sinned against God and against Annabel and against—well, against the bank and everyone else, really. He couldn't *feel* sinful, or he couldn't have done it. He had stood there, on the piece of carpet where Tony's eyes fell when he opened them, promising God to love and cherish Annabel. What did Annabel think about it, or about anything else?

And the blessing of God Almighty, the Father, the Son, and the Holy Spirit, be amongst you and remain with you always.

Tony could see through his fingers that both Annabel and Janet Arkwright, on their knees, were feeling for their handbags.

II

Tony came out of the choir stall, met Ginger, inclined his head, and walked with him the length of the chancel and into the choir vestry. Ginger passed him something uncomfortably sticky among the camouflage of the combined surplice folds. It was a freshly sucked toffee, which Tony just managed to transfer to his mouth before the clergy, and choir drew up for the vicar's final blessing. As the little formation dispersed Tony found that the toffee was sticking to his plate, and when he put his fingers in his mouth to pull it out the plate came with it.

Ginger had challenged him, he must have known that Tony couldn't manage toffee with his mouth in the state it was. Tony put the plate carefully on the washbowl before turning to wipe his fingers ostentatiously on Ginger's surplice.

They grappled silently in a corner, and when everyone else had gone they grappled, grunting, round the room. Eventually Ginger slipped on the polished floor and they fell apart. They looked uneasily at their crumpled surplices as they removed them and hung them up.

"We needn't lock anything," said Ginger, pulling ineffectually at the creases, "Mike's still here." Faintly from within the church came the discordant strains of a modern piece for organ.

"Just shut the outside doors, I suppose." Tony put his head into the main vestry, where the outside door was already pulled to. They shut their own door behind them and scuffled down the path.

"I'm not going home yet," announced Tony, with a parting thrust at Ginger's ribs. He turned right, the way eventually to BB's cottage, feeling carefree and invigorated. He passed the Red Lion at a gallop, then stopped abruptly half way down the hill beyond. He knew, even as the sensation drained out of him, why he was feeling so good. His instrument of torture was lying on the washstand in the choir vestry.

Tony took a few feeble steps forward, then stopped again. Aunt Helen had made him promise to keep the plate in at all times. More compellingly, so had the dentist.

Reluctantly, heavily, Tony turned round and plodded back up the hill, going slowly enough this time to hear the voices through the open door of the inn. He went up the deserted church path and round to the twin vestry doors. Both were still shut but he could hear the organ. He went inside the choir vestry just far enough to reach out and retrieve the hated device, and was inserting it in his mouth when his eye was caught by a movement in the main vestry. Beyond the connecting door, in profile, the vicar's wife was standing, and in front of her, staring at her, was the curate. The curate's fair hair had fallen over his forehead and as Tony looked, not wanting to look but unable to turn away, he saw the curate's long pale hands rise from his sides and cup Mrs. Groome's face. It was like watching something in slow motion, and in slow motion Mrs. Groome's hands also rose, took the curate's wrists, brought his hands down so that she was holding them at her waist like a bunch of flowers. The curate's face was flushed and anxious, as if he might cry, Mrs. Groome had a kindly smile. She stood smiling at the curate, holding his hands, and the organ soared overhead. The sudden sharp cry, just beyond the main vestry door into the church, was as startling as a gunshot. One of the shadows on the main vestry floor jerked and disappeared. Mrs. Groome stiffened, and Tony's power of movement came back to him. He turned and fled away down the path, not slackening his pace until he had reached the lane and run far enough along it towards home to be out of sight from the church.

He stopped beside the Small Green, to get his breath back and also to try and collect his thoughts, which were churning about in an almost painful way. He knew everyone loved Mrs. Groome of course, but he'd thought they loved her like he did, as a sort of goddess that you put offerings in front of, like people did with statues in places like Siam. Even when he and Ginger joked about Mr. Naylor, they never thought of him *touching* her. Mrs. Groome!

And something else was mingling with his discomfort. It took him a few moments to recognize it as a sort of fear. The main vestry door into the church had been open, the sound and the shadow had both come from the church. Someone else had stood frozen to see what he had seen, and had been shocked to so basic a cry he didn't know whether it was a man or a woman.

Staring at his solemn face in the hall mirror, Tony was glad his father and Aunt Helen had not yet returned. She at least would have noticed his strange look and asked questions. He would not have answered them truthfully, but he would have had to say something. As it was, by the time the three of them sat down to lunch he knew his appearance was back to normal.

III

"So you're off on holiday on Friday," said Detective-Inspector Neil Carter's Chief, musingly.

"Yes, Governor."

"You'll be going away of course."

Neil Carter shrugged. "I haven't thought."

His senior leaned forward with the heavy eagerness which in the early days of their association had twisted a cord in Neil's stomach.

"What? No package tour? No neat stack of passport, tickets and foreign currency waiting on the hall table?"

"None, Governor."

"But—you're not going to stay in London the whole fortnight?"

"I don't know what I'm going to do, Governor, but that isn't likely."

The Chief leaned back in his chair. "Playing it by ear, eh?"

"You could say that." Neil grinned. "No, actually, I fancied this time being free to see what gave. I'll take a few days somewhere. A country pub perhaps."

"I know a superb example."

The Chief was almost covering his desk with the heavy upper part of his body. He must have leaned forward this time by stealth. Not reassured by his open smile, Neil watched him carefully.

"Yes, Governor?"

"Red Lion at Bunington. Look after you, feed you, house you, like royalty. Owner-occupied."

"You've stayed there, Governor?"

"No, Neil, I haven't. But my information is good."

"Bunington? I seem to remember . . ."

"Heart of the country, but only five miles off the motorway," said the Chief, a shade quickly. "Another five miles from Latchford, which is a good little market town . . ."

"Benjamin Quillin," said Neil, without expression.

The Chief sighed heavily, leaning back. His smile changed, became knowing, and met Neil's. The atmosphere eased.

"Mrs. Benjamin Quillin," said the Chief, "which makes a rather more savoury prospect. Wronged daughter of George Chapman, solicitor, Latchford, sidesman and pillar of St. Leonard's, Bunington, widower . . ."

"I know."

"Of course you do," said the Chief genially. "It was only your involvement in the Delaney affair that kept you out of it."

"Yes, Governor?"

"Quillin has disappeared," said the Chief thoughtfully. "Went on a business trip to Germany and never came back. Well, it was easy, no one was looking for him. No one knew for another vital day that he had organized the bank raid of the century."

"Mrs. Quillin apparently didn't know, either."

"We're as sure as we can be, without incontrovertible proof, that she did not, Carter. She didn't even seem to believe us, at first—either about what her husband had done, or that he wasn't coming back. It was very convincing. She told us nothing. It was finally decided, by the Fraud Squad and all, that there was nothing she could tell us. She's been under surveillance continuously since Quillin hopped it and she's made no suspicious moves. Quillin never conducted any of his shadier business from home—never any of his business, for that matter—and it would have been quite possible even for a young wife as intelligent as Mrs. Quillin to have believed his import/export label. There were a few showy sops to throw around—the Nigerian deal, for instance, and his French connections. And of course the famous art gallery. Extraordinary why an able fellow like that takes the risk of turning to crime."

"Because it pays him."

The Chief glanced quickly at Neil. "We'll see."

"What is it you wish me to do, then, Governor?"

The Chief sighed again. He sometimes wished Carter would let the game peter elegantly to its natural close, instead of cutting it off so abruptly.

"If you went next week to stay at the Red Lion," he said flatly, "you could have a talk with Mrs. Quillin. A last talk."

"But I thought the last talk was the last."

"Officially, yes. Unofficially . . ." The Chief leaned forward very slightly. "I'll be frank with you, Neil. We're satisfied that Mrs. Quillin is one of her husband's innocent victims, and we've gathered that things weren't too warm between them of late. But we've gathered it from other people rather than from Mrs. Quillin herself. Truth to tell, Neil, the lady is a bit of a cipher. We haven't found what makes her tick. We can't hope for that final and incontrovertible proof, of course, because it isn't that sort of situation. But I'm not thinking so much now of Mrs. Quillin herself. If you—gain her confidence—she may tell you things she either didn't want to tell the rest of us, or simply didn't realize she knew. Some vital small thing."

"You want me to go incognito?"

"As far as anyone outside the Chapman family is concerned, yes. A young man on holiday who works in an office in London. But in fact I shall personally ask Mrs. Quillin to receive you, the very last of your line. We're actually calling off the vigilantes this weekend. She'll be resistant, but we'll get the worst part over first. She won't want to see you, but when she does . . ." The Chief's eyes passed over Neil, with rare overt approval. "Be relaxed," he said, "be almost lazy, you can tell her you're on holiday. You'll have a good time anyway, in Bunington, and with an attractive companion . . ."

He realized he was sorry that Carter was going on holiday, he would miss the verbal stimulus. He must be getting old and soft, to be affected by so small a prospect, he would have to watch it.

"You'll call on Mrs. Quillin, then, Neil?" asked the Chief, lumbering to his feet.

"If you tell me she agrees to see me."

"I'll tell you if she doesn't agree. She will."

"And my accommodation will be booked at the Red Lion?"

"It will. Half pension?"

"That should do very well."

"When will you go down?"

"I'll go down on Sunday."

"Good lad. I'll have the file sent through to you this afternoon. Thanks, Neil."

The file was on Neil's desk when he got back from a job at tea-time. Inside, on the top, was a note to say that Mrs. Quillin expected him at her father's house at eleven o'clock on Monday morning. Also that accommodation had been reserved for him at the Red Lion, provisionally for a week.

CHAPTER 2

I

In the first half of the week Tony promised himself each day that after school he'd go and see if BB was all right, and in the second half he told himself that he'd see BB in church on Sunday and, if BB wasn't there, then he would go straight to the cottage after the service, as he'd intended to do the Sunday before. He tried not to think about why he hadn't after all seen BB the Sunday before. He was helped by the news that a senior officer from Scotland Yard was coming to talk to Annabel. The exciting thing about this visit was that he, Tony, was to take part in a deception wherein the detective was to be explained as an old friend of the family.

BB wasn't in church the next Sunday morning either, and without lingering in the vestry after the service Tony set off for the old man's cottage. Outside the Red Lion a dark, youngish man was sitting behind a pint of ale. He matched Tony's inquiring glance as Tony cantered by. He looked interesting, and Tony hoped he was the Scotland Yard detective. By tomorrow night the Scotland Yard detective would know more about Annabel than he did. He couldn't imagine Annabel talking to anyone, confiding in them, but she had agreed to talk to the Scotland Yard detective. If they talked in the drawing-room, and if he didn't have to go to school, he might have managed to hang about in the hall or under the window . . .

Tony skidded to a halt where BB's tidy hawthorn hedge took over from the waving fronds which edged the next-door field. BB was standing motionless in his small immaculate garden. Tony called out, looking at the back of the familiar shaggy grey-brown head, the powerful shoulders and arms as brown as the tattered shirt. BB didn't turn round, or even move.

"BB!" he called again, louder.

"Come in, boy."

BB still didn't move. There was an odd note in his voice. Tony ran along to the gate and plunged into the garden. BB was looking down, at something small and brown and still which lay at his feet. Tony was almost upon it before he realized, with a shock which for a few seconds made him feel sick, that it was the body of the monkey. It was stretched out in a quite natural way, but he knew it was dead. A rust-coloured stain was on the grass beside its mouth. He and BB looked up at one another at the same moment.

"He's dead," said BB, still with that extra throbbing note. He moved his mouth exaggeratedly, and still moved it, pursing, relaxing, pursing, when he had finished speaking. Waves of alcohol reached Tony, the veins in BB's cheeks and nose shone brilliantly in the sunshine, his eyes were wet and as he and Tony stared at one another a tear escaped and wavered down into the red.

"What happened?" whispered Tony. He put out a hand towards the old man, with a vague instinct of leading him away. BB ignored it. He might have been rooted to the spot.

"Found him this morning."

"There? I mean, where he is now?"

"There. Haven't touched him."

"Was he ill last night?"

"Not a bit of it." BB offered a hiccup. He brushed at his tear as if it was a fly. Flies were hovering near the monkey's body. Occasionally one alighted for an instant on the staring open eye.

"We ought to bury him," said Tony, still hushed. "I mean, he's . . ."

"Ought to bury him, yes."

BB was less drunk than Tony had sometimes seen him, and far more upset than he had ever seen him before. This time Tony let his hand fall on BB's arm, and gently push.

"I'll bury him for you," he said. "Let's go inside and you can find me a box."

BB's fierce eyes wavered, fell again for a moment on the monkey's body, looked angrily back at Tony.

"People . . ." he said.

Tony felt the shock again. "But surely . . . nobody did that! I mean, he looks . . ."

The old man shrugged. "Don't know. Don't want to know. Come inside. See what we can find."

He started to move slowly towards the cottage door. Tony walked beside him. He glanced back in the doorway to see the flies now settling down on the monkey's body.

"I'll do it right away."

The sickly smell of BB's neglected home came unpleasantly to his nose. He always got used to it within a few minutes, and he always felt annoyed with himself that it hit him as a rebuff, it made him feel soft. But his stomach, on impact, persisted in disliking it. It was hard to believe that the cottage and its garden belonged to the same person. All BB's effort went into the garden. Every two or three months, when they had called and been nauseated, the vicar or the curate persuaded a good woman of the village to stem the tide of dirt. She did it on the pretext of a home-made sponge cake, for which BB had a weakness, and, once inside, once having cleared a space for the cake on the kitchen table, she overcame the old man's objections.

Tony registered, unwillingly, the fact that Mrs. Mason had not been in for some time. BB tipped one of his sleek cats out of an old shoe box.

"This all right?"

"It's super."

Tony went to take the box out of BB's hand but met resistance. BB shambled over to a large cupboard and pulled it open, still clutching the box. Various things fell out on to the floor at once, then more as BB started rummaging. He brought out a fairly clean piece of cloth.

"This all right?"

"Gosh, that's great."

BB put the shoe box down on top of the cupboard and carefully laid the piece of cloth inside. He turned his wet eyes on Tony, balancing the overlap of cloth on his hand.

"You can wrap this over him."

"Yes, I will."

BB slowly held the box out to Tony.

"You stay in here," said Tony, being allowed now to take it. "Just tell me where you want it."

"Under the—under the magnolia," said BB, hiccuping again. "Behind it, close t'the hedge."

"Yes. Have you got a spade?"

"Leanin' by the rabbits. Get on with it, will you? Don't want— don't want the flies."

Tony went unhappily out into the garden. The flies were a cloud over the brown mound and he went straight to it so that they dispersed. He tried to close the bright eyes, but they were set immovably wide. The body was limp, still warm, perhaps from the sun. Tony could hardly see it as he put it gently into the box, from a sudden rush of tears. Beppo had always been so alive, his muscles rippling out of your hands. He folded the cloth over the body, tucking it in. He put the box in the shade of the magnolia tree while he went to find the spade. The spade was where BB had said it would be, against the cottage wall beside the rabbit hutch. The rabbits, gleaming with health like the cats, stared at him impassively. Tony remembered BB's face, distorted with rage as he recounted how John Arkwright had suggested he should turn them into a little business, cashing in on their flesh and fur. He took the spade back to the magnolia and started digging behind it. There wasn't much room and the soil was dry and hard from days of fine weather, but he worked savagely, working something off, and got a good deep hole. He lowered the shoe box into it and laid the first covering of soil with his hands. When he had finished he put the spade back by the rabbits and went into the cottage. BB was sitting forward in a sagging armchair, a whisky bottle and an almost empty glass on the table beside him. There was a can of Coke and an empty glass beside the other chair.

"Thanks," said Tony, sitting down and pouring. Dust rose round him, released by his weight. Another of the cats came and rubbed against his legs. "It's all right." He took a long drink. "Just where you said. D'you want to tell me?"

"I told you," said BB irritably. "Came down this mornin' and found him there. There was a bit of froth on 'slips. Notice?"

"Yes. But I think he looked—well, sort of asleep. You have to be thankful for his sake, that he didn't suffer." Aunt Helen tended to say that, to people shocked by sudden deaths. In these circumstances it seemed quite appropriate.

"How d'you know he didn't suffer?" challenged BB scornfully. One huge grey-brown eyebrow drooped over one fierce bloodshot eye. "Nobody liked him—oh, except you, boy—everybody said: "Damned old menace, with his damned unsuitable pets." Shouldn't be surprised if somebody hadn't seen to it."

"Oh, I don't think so!"

"What *you* know about it?" BB drained his glass. Tony found himself trying to count the ring stains on the table. "Doesn't matter, anyway." BB set the glass down so near the edge it fell off on to the floor. "All that matters is that I'll miss him. Miss the little fellow. He was a friend, glad to see me . . ."

BB broke down in tears. He was obviously drunk, but he was deeply distressed. Tony thought he heard the words "innocent creature," then was sure he heard BB telling him to go home. "C'again soon," said BB, not unkindly.

"All right." Tony drained his glass and got to his feet. He picked up BB's glass and set it back on the table. "Do please come to Evensong tonight," he said.

He went slowly out of the room and out of the cottage, stopping in the garden to wipe his eyes and comfort his beleaguered tongue. He looked at his watch as he went out through the gate. Still half an hour to lunch. He went more slowly this time past the Red Lion. The stranger was still there, talking now to Jim Bates the landlord. The man and the boy looked even more curiously at one another.

II

It might have been the fact that he had not drawn his curtains properly on Saturday night which sent Neil off to Bunington so early on Sunday morning. The sun found the triangular gap, shone across the room on to his face, and wakened him before seven. It was already hot. The only green he could see from the windows was his own window box, the petunias already wilting. All at once it was nothing like enough. He watered the petunias, had a small beakfast, packed a small case, left a key and a note for his neighbour, and set out for the country.

He caught the summer traffic only in the last half hour of his journey, and arrived at the Red Lion, Bunington, before eleven. He was impressed to find that his room was ready. He met the landlord, approved the room, deposited his case, and immediately went out again.

Bunington is one of England's finest remaining examples of picturesque and unspoiled village and Neil Carter, stepping out of the Red Lion to face across the Big Green, found himself at once at the heart of it. The Big Green is true to its name and includes a pond with ducks, thinly fringed by willows. A low white iron rail with large gaps in it defines the Green, and opposite are a few well-kept small Georgian houses, forming with the older and humbler cottages which intersperse them a continuous and attractive crescent behind a frieze of well-stocked gardens.

Neil saw lanes winding away to left and right, and after standing for a few moments in the road outside the pub, grinning to himself at such uncharacteristic indecision, he took the lane that led left.

The village was only an incident in the countryside. Already, as he turned the first corner, the hedges were shoulder high and crammed at their foot with wild flowers and grasses. There were smells both floral and farmyard, and now and again Neil heard sheep. The hedges broke and lowered to both sides as he walked on, to reveal cottages and small houses. The biggest break came round the third bend, exposing a small church with squat Norman tower and delicate-windowed, Early English nave, strangely proportioned as a result, interesting rather than beautiful as a whole. The door recessed in its ribbed Norman porch was open and Neil heard singing and an organ. The church path was marked by yew trees, and the tidy grass around it was stuck about with sparsely set, crazily leaning and very old headstones. Beyond the church, round another sharp bend, was the Small Green, lacking the dimensions of the Big Green and the pond, but no less charming. Neil stood for a few moments looking across at three Georgian houses which were the major events in another, smaller, crescent. In one of them lived George Chapman and, for the time being, his daughter Annabel. There was no sign anywhere of life and Neil, after looking round approvingly on the general scene, retraced his steps.

The sun met him grillingly as he left the lane and came out on to the unshaded forecourt of the Red Lion. He glanced at the four tables set under gay umbrellas against the pub's pink-washed walls but kept on walking, into the lane which wound away on the other side. Here again, intermittent branches from the high hedges tempered the glare of the sun. Neil strode easily downhill, aware of

health and strength, of things new and probably strange, of antici-
pation . . . He quickened his step, putting a hand out and running
it along the leaves and twigs as he went by. A sourness which had
been on his life, he all at once admitted, for perhaps months, seemed
to dissolve and disappear.

The only sign of human life was an old man with a lot of untidy
hair standing contemplating in a cottage garden. He seemed unaware of Neil going by. The lane led to a fork which promised, on
the left, a burrowing even more close and intimate into the heart of
the country and, on the right, the commercial centre of Bunington.
Neil pursued the right fork past facing rows of small shops made
from cottages, and a post office whose other half was a house with a
garden extending beside it. Beyond the shops the road straightened
and widened and continued out of sight in an attractive interchange
of houses and hedges.

Basically, he had seen Bunington. Neil came back up the hill
rather more slowly. The old man in the garden still stood rapt. This
time Neil sank without hesitation into the shaded seat next to the
pub door. Jim Bates the landlord was with him instantly, and clearly
would have lingered to talk if some of the people beginning to come
out of the lane from the church hadn't turned into the pub and
needed serving.

Neil watched them keenly, not seeming to. He knew that he had
this knack, because he saw it working, making people study *him* less
warily than they would otherwise have done. Everyone looked at
him on the way by, those that brushed against him as they went into
the pub, and those who dispersed round the Green by car or on foot.
Neil felt he had gone back in time. He had never knowingly been
in a community where every resident was so firmly registered that
every stranger became an event. He nodded to the few men who actually said good morning. Front doors opened across the Green, and
some of them stayed open on to the sunny prospect. One of the
earliest people to go by was a boy with brown skin and fair hair,
looking purposeful. But it was obvious that he put his purpose aside
for a moment as he passed Neil. Neil let him see that he was looking back at him. He knew the boy was tall for his age, from the photographs he had seen in the file on Annabel Quillin. He didn't
smile, as he had done in most of the photographs, but it could be
that there was something odd about his mouth. Neil watched him as
he entered the lane on the right, accelerating out of sight. Jim Bates
came out and stood beside him.

"How come no one sits outside?" inquired Neil.

"There's a lot of habit about here, sir." Jim Bates leaned against his wall. A rich, warm smell came from him when he moved. "You see, it isn't so often hot like it is just now, and they're used to going through into the bar. Want their beer quick, too, sir. And then, when they've got it, and had a few swallows and come up for air as it were, then they see the garden behind, and they go out into that. There's a few of 'em out there now. More tables and brollies too. This evening when it's cooler, they'll hang about out here, and there'll be visitors and all by then, it being such a fine Sunday in June."

"Can you come, Mr. Bates?"

There was a suggestion of hysteria in the thin female voice. Mr. Bates retired inside his inn, and Neil sat peaceful and relaxed, counting the ducks on grass and water and watching the figures which came and went in the gardens across the Green. Mr. Bates joined him when he could. He was talking to Neil when Tony Chapman came back. The boy stared harder this time, and so did Neil, noticing the flush and the agitation.

"Who was that?" he asked Jim Bates, when the boy was out of sight.

Jim Bates gave him a quick look. "That's Mr. Chapman's boy Tony. Nice lad. Gets a bit excited sometimes but he means well. Bit of an afterthought. Reckon he cost his mother her life. The family's had a rough time lately, as you'll maybe know."

"Yes, I do know," said Neil, meeting the keenness of the landlord's gaze. "In fact I know the family. Or my father did. I don't think I've ever seen the boy."

"Is that a fact, sir?" He and Neil stared at one another, and Neil was glad when the landlord was distracted by the arrival at the pub door of a middle-aged couple who he had been vaguely aware were crossing the Big Green.

"Good morning, Mr. and Mrs. Naylor, then," said Jim Bates cheerfully, "you had a good walk?"

"Excellent, Jim, excellent!"

Mr. Naylor had a pleasant smile, the most positive thing Neil found himself able to note about the man, beyond the fact that he was small and thin. Otherwise he was unremarkable. He had an unfamiliar slow way of speaking which Neil decided must be local. His wife, although without style, was pretty rather than not. She gave Neil no opportunity to compare her voice with her husband's.

"Won't you sit down with Mr. Carter here?" suggested Jim Bates to the Naylors. "Mr. Carter's on holiday from London. Mr. Naylor is one of our churchwardens," he explained to Neil, as the Naylors rather diffidently took seats at Neil's table. Neil guessed that Mr. Bates had just obliged them to break a habit. He tried to look welcoming. It was quite impossible to catch Mrs. Naylor's wandering, anxious blue eyes, but Mr. Naylor smiled again, the smile spreading over his neat sharp features.

"I'll just have a shandy," said Mrs. Naylor, to the umbrella above her head. She had a slight London accent.

"And half a pint of draught for you, Alec?" suggested Jim Bates.

The churchwarden nodded and Mr. Bates retired, after noting Neil's indication of his own empty glass.

"One of our churchwardens," repeated Neil after what felt like a long pause, concentrating on the husband. "I should have thought, in such a small parish . . ."

"Not so small as it appears. It takes in Little Bunington as well," said Mr. Naylor proudly.

"Little Bunington?"

Mr. Naylor's smile grew apologetic.

"It sounds silly when you say it." Jim Bates reappeared and transferred three glasses from a tray to the table. He went inside again. "Little Bunington was only a half dozen cottages and some flat fields, and they built it up. Bunington is protected, you see, and Little Bunington's all of three miles off. Built it up in quite a big way. Light industry too. Latchford's protected as well, so they built Little Bunington up to take people from Latchford as well as people who got jobs in the new factories—"

"Factories and a new town three miles from here!"

Neil felt shocked, but Mr. Naylor said, as eagerly as his flat slow voice would allow,

"It's all right, though. You see, it saves Bunington and Latchford. The area's done its bit, and they won't worry at it any more."

"I hope your optimism is justified. But there's no Anglican church in Little Bunington?"

"There was going to be. Then someone said—'

"One of them at the top!" interposed Mrs. Naylor sharply, making Neil jump. She looked crossly at him for a few seconds, before resuming the restless journey of her eyes.

"One of them at the top," agreed her husband, regarding her thoughtfully. "There was one of those economy campaigns and they

said they'd better wait and see how full the old church got at Bunington. That's this church. St. Leonard's. Which would have been
the mother church of any new church, and shared the clergy and
officers. They appointed a curate, and when the people's warden retired they invited a successor from Little Bunington." He smiled,
self-deprecatingly. "I was happy to accept the nomination. I was
born a free churchman, Mr. er . . . , but I was attracted to the Anglican persuasion. The historic foundation of the ministry . . . This
is an active parish, with a fine vicar." There was sudden colour in
the pale face. Neil recollected reading somewhere that fanatics
tended to be made out of converts. "Forgive me," said Mr. Naylor
apologetically, "I'm talking too much."

"Not a bit of it!" said Neil. "Have another drink?"

"Thank you, but we'll be getting back." Alec Naylor got to his
feet. "To conclude my story as far as it goes," he said, putting his
hand on his wife's shoulder. Neil noted how her eyes came immediately to rest on the table top in front of her. "The congregation at
St. Leonard's has not, I regret to say, grown sufficiently to warrant
the new church."

He took his hand from his wife's shoulder and she stood up. He
held it out and Neil got up too and shook it. Mrs. Naylor made no
acknowledgement of him and the two of them went over to the
small car which Neil had noticed when he first came out of the inn
after his arrival. Jim Bates was standing beside him as the Naylors
drove past the inn and took the lane which led to the shops and,
Neil now knew, to Little Bunington which had grown so big.

"Nice little feller," said Jim Bates. "Not a bit like the other one."

"The other one?" Another smell, from inside the Red Lion, was
eclipsing Jim Bates's personal aroma. Neil realized he was hungry.

"Christopher Corrigan, Esquire, of Corrigan Hall. He's been
churchwarden here since he was quite a young man, I'm told, and
he's an old 'un now. Stiff-necked bastard I'm sorry, sir." It was clear
that Jim Bates had conceived his last sentence in one piece.

"I'm only booked in for an evening meal," said Neil, "but can you
do me lunch?"

"It's ready when you are," said Jim Bates.

Neil realized that he had been sleuthing, unconsciously and from
habit, all the time he had thought he was relaxing over his beer. He
really did need a holiday. All he had to do was to find out anything
he could about Annabel Quillin. It was absurd to imagine that the

Naylors, Jim Bates, or Christopher Corrigan, Esquire, could be privy to her counsel. After lunch he would go to sleep.

III

After lunch, which was heavy and good and eaten in the company of two itinerant motor-cyclists, Neil read the paper and had a prolonged coffee under one of the garden umbrellas. He then walked along the lane which led to the shops and took the left fork into the immediate shade of trees. He didn't go very far before turning off again from the last semblance of pathway, and when he went to sleep he chose a glade beyond a belt of trees, half way to some water meadows, under a speckle of shadow and sun. He slept heavily and when he awoke he lay still for another half-hour listening to fragmented bird song and lazily reviewing the recent past as if it was a film of someone else's life. It had an interest of technique if not of content—perhaps because since his arrival in Bunington he had been so agreeably aware of the simple technical fact of being alive, moving and looking and listening. He walked for the rest of the afternoon, up and around the nearest hill, finding every small thing agreeable to do, even going upstairs back at the inn and lying on his bed reading *The Hand of Ethelberta* with the window wide open over the Big Green. It was hearing the church bell through the open window which prompted him to go to Evensong, and he reproved himself for not having thought of going without the nudge of the bell, for having relaxed too far.

The church was more beautiful and harmonious inside than out, all pale stone delicately carved, the windows pale too and intermittently coloured, with the austerity of pre-Victorian glass. The only Chapman present was the boy, who was in the choir and not observable by Neil during the service because, unknowing, he had sat to the right of the nave, on the same side of the church. He had chosen that side after a lightning look round and the discovery that the only people of obvious interest were the two old men at opposite ends of the left front pew—two tall, proud, picturesque old men, the one (who Neil thought was the man he had seen motionless that morning in a cottage garden) like a degenerate version of the other— redder, untidier, more blurred in outline. It was the other one who presented the offertory plate. Neil assumed that the cleric who accepted it was the vicar, a man of about forty-five who preached with

a spare clarity which held Neil's attention for the fifteen minutes of
the sermon. The vicar's voice, light, clear, quietly but radiantly
confident, the calm authority of his bearing, belied his appearance:
small, stout, unhealthily pale, sparse of hair, facial contours lost in
flesh. Nature had dealt the man a poor hand.

It was so long since Neil had been to church he hadn't known
that Evensong was no longer read from the Prayer Book. The new
version in the booklet handed to him as he went in was a bewilder-
ing mixture of the familiar and the strange—and though he had
stayed away for so long, there was no doubt what was familiar, the
phrases he had once known without a catalyst flooded back word-
perfect from the catalyst of re-reading. During the space for private
prayer he felt a bit unprotected and uncomfortable. It would have
been easier if he had deliberately stopped believing, *decided* not to
go to church . . . He was relieved when the vicar's voice resumed
the ordained words.

All that Neil really observed in the end, by going to Evensong,
was his own reactions. In the porch afterwards he introduced himself to the vicar as a man on holiday.

CHAPTER 3

I

Neil began the week with a courtesy call on Divisional headquarters
at Latchford. Even though it was only nine-thirty he was shown
straight into the Detective-Inspector's office.

"How's divisional crime?" asked Neil.

"Pallid. Or so it seems, since the Quillin affair."

The tall fair Inspector made no attempt to conceal the fillip
afforded him by Neil's unheralded arrival. Neil liked him right
away, and his obviously undogmatic approach. His name was John
Oliver, and he could have gone straight on and played the juvenile
lead in a dramatization of P. G. Wodehouse.

"Annabel Quillin's family live in Bunington," said John Oliver, "but you'll know that."

"Yes. In fact I know the family." Neil said his piece.

"You haven't been involved on the case at all?"

"Not personally, no. And now I'm on holiday. But if the shining hour showed itself capable of improvement . . ."

"Every time," said Inspector Oliver. He had a charming smile.

"People always being so ready to put two and three together," went on Neil, "I've not said anywhere in Bunington what I do for a living. The Chapmans know, of course, of old."

"I'm certain you're wise. Do you think you could come for dinner while you're here? I'd like it and I'm sure Jill would, but you must see what you can manage."

There would have to be a jarring note somewhere soon. Neil drove back through the hot sunshine with his elation at being in Bunington taking on an edge of apprehension. Perhaps at the thought of the imminent presentation of his person, rather than of his mission, but he didn't analyze his feelings. When he got back to the Red Lion he went upstairs to his room, already restored to order, and sat down with the Quillin file for a half-hour before setting out for the Chapmans'.

The last thing he did before leaving his room was to look at himself in the mirror and imagine he was being assessed by the Chief. A man tall rather than short, thin rather than fat. Wiry black hair, skin a little sallow, features a little sharp, good bones, keen eyes, intelligence. Lips narrow, mouth wide, canine teeth showing points when he smiled too fiercely, but smiles to one's own image were always mirthless. It was two minutes to eleven when he ran downstairs and out of the hotel.

The heat was intensifying and Neil walked slowly towards the Small Green. Two mallard ducks and a drake had come over likewise from the Big Green and were sitting in a small patch of shade. He took the stony path which edged the grass, where occasional branches tempered the sun. The gardens of the houses and cottages were checkered light and dark. The garden of Wesley House was attractively laid out and perfectly maintained, and there was a white seat under a tree of heaven. Neil forgot about both Chapmans and Quillins as he stood still with pleasure. He had spent his early summers under such a tree, and he hadn't seen one for years.

"It's a tree of heaven."

"I'm enchanted to meet it."

"Detective-Inspector Carter?"

He turned slowly round to the owner of that quiet, unextended voice. Annabel Quillin photographed accurately, but the photographs gave no indication of her positive lack of colour which was a colour scheme in itself: the cloudy black hair, the pearl pale face and creamy-pale arms, the exquisite brown outline of the lips, the brown eyes and lashes, the filmy pale dress like water under sunlight. The faint colour in her cheeks was merely a deepening of the pearl pallor. She smiled slightly at Neil as he looked at her and went on looking, and no more colour came into her face.

"It's too hot in the back garden," she said at last, "and I don't much like conducting my business in the public view. So I think we had better go into the drawing-room."

It wasn't so much that her voice sounded tired, rather as if she made the minimum of effort to use it. She seemed to float ahead of him into the dark cool hall. He said as he followed her:

"Conducting your business. You encourage me."

She looked over her shoulder as she opened a wide white door. "Oh, I don't think you should be encouraged, Mr. Carter." She had picked up the invitation of his ambiguity, he was certain, but he had no idea what she was making of it. They sat down beside the long window that looked on to the Green, and Neil imagined being under water, in the cool pale blue-green room. Annabel Quillin leaned back in her chair and folded her long pale hands in her lap. Her slight smile might be a rueful acknowledgement of the effect she knew she had. It was not the right moment for silence, but he had to make an effort to break it.

"You're exceedingly gracious," he said, "to receive me without a scowl. Even to offer me information about your father's flora. I appreciate it. You must have had policemen up to here."

He put his hand across his neck. Her neck, he noticed, was long and white. She shrugged.

"I thought I had, but the Chief Inspector was very . . ."

Neil knew how his Chief would have been, laying it on, almost as if he had heard him.

"Besides," she said, "I thought perhaps you might have discovered something . . . there might be something to tell me . . ."

He wondered if the very slight tremor in her voice was suppressed hope. She gazed at him. So that had been the Chief's tactics. Hinting at information received. Leaving it to his Detective-Inspector, when he had gained access and favour, to disabuse the lady. Well, he had gained access. It would be impossible to know what the lady was thinking, unless she chose to tell, and that, thought Neil, was unlikely. But he did know that she had put out a plea.

"No," he said quickly. "I'm afraid you'll be disappointed if you think that. I've nothing whatsoever to tell you."

He watched her keenly, but there was no noticeable disappointment, no annoyance, she merely gave a fluttery sigh which for a few seconds seemed to stir the whole quiet figure.

"No, well. It was stupid to hope."

"One must always hope," said Neil, on a rare pang of pity. "I'm sorry it can't be from me."

"What from you, then, Mr. Carter?"

"No, from you," he said gently. "Clues."

"Clues?"

"Things you might know—trivial things, things you didn't think could possibly be of any importance—about your husband and his associates. Things you've dismissed—but buried rather than forgotten."

"Burial. Or forgetting. Dismissing in one way or another. It amounted to the same essential process."

The reproof was as oblique as the plea, but Neil centred it.

"I'm sorry, Mrs. Quillin. I should have begun by saying that I was aware of the intrusive nature of my visit. I am very much aware of it, of course. And I have no intention of bullying you. Nor, I will tell you frankly, do I or my superiors consider we have any further right to demand answers to questions. You've satisfied all your questioners. But, frankly again, we've drawn an absolute blank and my Chief thought—"

"That you were just the man for a last despairing throw," she said as expressionlessly as she had said everything else, but with something briefly sparking in her eyes which brought a twist in his stomach.

"All right, if you like, that's probably it." He laughed, sounding false to himself, because he was feeling so serious. "You've already indicated," he said, "that you would not be deterred by loyalty from telling us—"

"Oh, loyalty!" At last an expression passed over her face, a flash of scorn. "You have to appreciate," she said, more openly reproving, "that I've been schooling myself to forget rather than remember."

"I appreciate," he said humbly.

"I didn't try to be obstructive," said Mrs. Quillin, fluttering a hand in the air. "I don't think I can remember anything. But at first —I had to think about myself. Now . . ."

"Now you're stronger." Someone like Annabel Quillin couldn't go on feeling betrayed and desolate, she was too well equipped (mentally as well as physically, decided Neil) to dictate events. "Look," he said, "I'm on holiday really, as my Chief will have told you, and there's no hurry. Take your time. In fact—" he smiled at her, aware of what his smile could do—"perhaps you'll agree to combine business with a little pleasure, in the shape of helping me to enjoy my holiday. I mean—we could meet next time over a dinner table. And you'll know a good place."

She smiled back at him, but no more enthusiastically than she had smiled on his arrival.

"All right," she said. A finger of sun licked the white sill beside Neil. He had no idea at all whether she was agreeing from boredom, from passivity, from curiosity, or because she would like to see him again.

"Tomorrow evening?"

"Very well."

It wasn't a bad start, from either angle. But he felt strangely subdued. Perhaps from the impact of her perfection. He got to his feet, not really reluctant to leave. Annabel Quillin too had got up, was floating already to the door. But she said to him over her shoulder:

"Hang on and meet Aunt Helen. Have a drink. I'll find Auntie." His attention was caught by a movement in the garden.

"Thank you," he said automatically.

She went out into the hall and quickly and quietly Neil tried the handle of the french window. It yielded, and in one movement he was in the garden and had dived into the bushes that grew against the house. He came out holding Tony Chapman's ear. The boy's blue eyes stared at him for a few excited seconds before dropping.

"You *are* the detective!" muttered Tony to the ground, triumph mingling with apprehension. He looked up at Neil again. "You won't tell them, will you?"

"Not at this moment," said Neil, "and if you tell anyone outside this house about me, I'll have your hide."

"Of course I won't!" said the boy indignantly.

"All right." Neil let go of the ear. "Come and see me at the Red Lion after lunch. Two o'clock in the garden."

"Yes!" squeaked Tony, and was gone. Neil turned back to the drawing-room. Another figure familiar from photographs was cross-

ing the floor. She and Neil looked at one another over the threshold.
Neil saw a tall, capable-looking woman with a good face and curly
grey hair. He knew Miss Chapman was one of St. Leonard's sacristans and presided over a number of committees as well as her
brother's household.

"You're looking at the garden?"

Neil shook the cool firm hand.

"With admiration and envy." He told her about the tree of
heaven as he stepped back inside. Immediately she closed and locked
the door behind him.

"I'm sorry," said Neil, "to have let the heat in."

"Don't worry. But it's as well to keep the door closed after eleven
o'clock and until six."

How competent she would be. Neil found himself studying Miss
Chapman with professional keenness, and made himself switch off.
However competent, it was ridiculous to imagine that she could
have anything to do with the criminal behaviour of her nephew by
marriage. Not that he had been imagining that, of course, it was just
habit. Could he never really relax?

Not when Annabel returned, either professionally or personally,
although he knew he was giving a good imitation of it. He asked
them about the boy, what his interests were.

Annabel didn't bother saying much, with her Aunt Helen there
ready to answer questions and keep a conversation going. Aunt
Helen told Neil that Tony liked animals and birds and food and,
oddly enough, history, and that he was off school that day because
he had wakened with a stomach ache.

"He's in bed, then?" asked Neil.

"He was until about half past ten. He hardly ever complains and
I let him lie in. Then he got up and said he was going for a walk. I
hope he keeps in the shade."

"Will he go back to school this afternoon?"

"I'll see what shape he's in at lunch-time."

When Neil left, Annabel strolled with him to the gate.

"You decide where you would like to go," he said, "and I'll collect
you at seven. All right?"

"All right."

"And—do what you can for me." He spoke and looked in such a
way that she could infer two meanings.

"Oh, I will try, now," she said carelessly, turning back into the
garden.

Neil walked round the edge of the Green. He noticed that the mallards had gone. He turned round at the top and saw her sitting under the tree of heaven. It was impossible to tell whether or not she was looking after him.

II

There were only two customers in the Red Lion, farmers said Jim Bates, both drinking pints of ale in the cool interior. The night before, after Evensong, the inn had been well patronized and the clients had spilled out back and front. Neil had sat in the open at the front again for most of the evening, attracted by the classic pose of a man outside an old inn by a village green. He had joined in a few conversations, and listened to a lot. Most of the people had been holiday-makers and there were as many cars as could be squeezed in parked on the forecourt. The only local man Neil had got into conversation with was Christopher Corrigan, who had marched in at nine o'clock for a half pint of beer. Neil was inside by that time, sitting in the open french window and looking down the garden. The proud eyes had raked the bar, swooping to rest on him, and the man had come over and sat beside him. It was more a monologue than a conversation, although Mr. Corrigan asked a few abrupt personal questions which Neil side-stepped. For most of the time he was in the pub the senior churchwarden talked about conditions on his estate and barked the odd condescending remark at Jim Bates and his more bucolic customers. Neil thought he behaved like a feudal landlord, then felt more inclined to understand him when he learned as the monologue progressed that Mr. Corrigan did in fact own a large part of the village. It would have been interesting to hear his opinion of the vicar and his fellow churchwarden and above all the Chapmans, but Neil restrained himself. The old man made his half pint last almost an hour, and went out as soon as he had drained it.

"Stingy bastard I'm sorry, sir," said Jim Bates, looking after him. His face brightened at Monday lunch-time, when Neil got back from the Chapmans'.

"Everything all right, sir? A pint of draught? Or perhaps a half?"

Jim Bates would probably be aware that he had spent an hour across the Small Green, and that refreshments must have been offered. This was one thing Neil knew he wouldn't like about living in a village. His life since he had grown up had always had compartments which must be kept separate and in ignorance of one another.

He said, swallowing on the effort, "I've been to pay my family's respects to the Chapmans."

"Of course, sir."

Neil had a ploughman's lunch under a garden umbrella, and a half pint of draught. He was finishing them as Tony Chapman came through, in the wake of a slight explanatory altercation with Jim Bates, which had drifted out on the clear air. Tony plumped down flushed on the other chair.

"What do you want to drink?" asked Neil.

"Coke?"

"Go and get it."

It was marvellously peaceful in the garden of the Red Lion. Bees droned in Jim Bates's hectically bright herbaceous border and a blue tit pinked. By and by he would sleep again in the glade, and there would be more to dream about . . .

"You were eavesdropping this morning," he said to Tony, as the boy flopped down a second time carrying a bottle of Coke with a straw. "Do you tend to be sly?"

"No!" The blue eyes bored indignantly into his, then dropped. "No," said Tony, apologetically. "It's just—all this business with Annabel. The papers . . . People . . . And you coming. I thought you'd come and go, and I wouldn't get a chance . . . I wanted to know if it was you. I mean, I saw you yesterday . . ."

"I saw you."

"I thought you did, and I thought you must be the detective, but I wanted to be sure."

"All right, all right. I can understand. Although you've dug into your credit a bit this morning, haven't you? What with telling a lie about feeling ill."

"I know. But I had *got* some credit. I'm never ill."

"So your Aunt Helen told me. She also implied she might send you back to school this afternoon."

The eyes dropped again. "I couldn't eat any lunch, which *never* happens."

Tony looked up at Neil, and they stared at one another and began to grin at the same moment.

"Go and ask Mr. Bates for what you want," said Neil, "and never, never do it again. By the way, in your photographs you smiled. Is it the thing on your teeth?"

"Yes. It looks so awful. And it feels worse." Tony bared his teeth briefly in illustration.

"Don't let it stop you smiling when you feel like it, really don't," advised Neil. "You won't have it on for ever. And you mustn't forget how to smile."

"All right." Tony smiled as he ran off. The movement did already feel slightly strange. He came back with a soft batch cake and a ham roll.

"I wish I could help you!" he said, through a mouthful.

"Perhaps you could."

Neil watched carefully but the boy immediately shrugged.

"They've asked me heaps of questions already," he said, "and I've tried and tried to think of anything which could help. But Benjamin hardly ever came to Bunington. He was always very nice to me, but in his way, if you know what I mean."

"I do indeed." It was a pity this boy hadn't been privy to anything, he'd have noticed and reproduced it as well as anyone could.

"I mean," went on Tony, "that he never answered any questions. Though I only realized this—afterwards. He asked *me* questions sometimes, to be nice, that was all, then when he'd had enough, done his little thing, that was the end of the conversation. You know."

"Yes. Your sister?"

"Oh, she's all right. But she's twelve years older than me and—well, I don't really know all that much about her."

"No, I suppose not." Neil wondered briefly about the dead mother.

"How long are you staying here?" asked Tony.

"You know, I think I'll stay over at least until today week." Neil made up his mind as he spoke, looking at the brother's face but seeing the sister's. When he focused on Tony's he saw that it had fallen.

"What rotten luck still being at school! We break up the middle of next week. No, I'll be well enough to go back tomorrow, honestly. But it's stinking luck."

"I'll take you for a drive on Saturday." This at least would not be going precisely over old police ground.

"That's another thing," responded Tony gloomily. "Saturday's the Summer Fair. St. Leonard's. In old Corrigan's big field."

"What time?"

"All stinking day. The choir have to help. Stewarding and organizing races and so on."

"Isn't there a rota?"

"Not for us. We've just got to be available. The whole time."

"All right," said Neil, "we'll have a run out on Wednesday night. Go for a meal somewhere and drive round. Would that be a good idea?"

"It'd be super!" The expressive face was radiant.

"Your sister and I are doing business over dinner tomorrow," said Neil.

"I know."

Tony studied Neil's face suspiciously, for signs of that sheepish expression which he had noticed was common to the widely varying types who succumbed to his sister's charms. There was no evidence of it, and Neil even gravely met his eye, but Tony was not entirely reassured. He had gathered from those of his contemporaries who had older brothers that Annabel was rather exceptionally attractive. Still, he hoped the detective wasn't smitten by her, it would be a weakness in him, and it would make him less than a good companion.

"Off you go, now," said Neil. "And just to remind you, you don't know who I am."

"If anyone asks," said Tony with dignity, "I tell them you're an old friend and work in London. Honestly, I—"

"Of course, of course. I've already realized you're intelligent. Now, you'd better go and lie down, and I'll do the same."

Tony sped away. Neil eventually lay down in the spot where he had lain the day before. The shape of his body still showed in the soft ferns. He didn't sleep so long or so soundly, but he didn't dream. His remembrance of the morning shimmered in an aesthetic, unsensual, aquamarine light.

CHAPTER 4

I

Most people can be articulate on the subject of themselves, given the right audience, and Neil Carter was no exception. The difficulty is finding that audience. People are either not interested, or if they are, it is for the wrong reasons: because they have nothing to say for themselves, or because they are as genuinely absorbed in us as we are, both of which make it less than entirely satisfactory to hold forth.

Annabel Quillin was the best audience Neil had yet encountered. Looking beautiful, not interrupting, clearly listening because during his pauses showing in her few words that she had taken his nuance, recognized his allusion, understood his angle. He had begun really with the intention of encouraging Mrs. Quillin to talk by his example, but she was so perfect a listener, it was so rare and enjoyable to hold flowingly forth about himself and his concerns, that he went happily on. It was only dancing with her which brought his near-monologue to a close.

He had wondered if Annabel might choose a restaurant with a dance floor. He had asked her to dance right away, as soon as they were shown to their table, but she had said "Later," and this was how he had got launched. Once he had danced with her he no longer wanted to talk, he wanted only to sit back and watch her, and listen to her answers to his questions. He would have liked her to offer information, as he had done, but he elicited a few things through asking. Not so far relevant to the Quillin inquiry (and he had already almost decided he was on a delightful wild goose chase), but about her likes and dislikes, and what she had done between school and marriage. She didn't sum anything up, she just told him precisely what he asked her, or less than that, and it was for him to come to conclusions, to deduce that she had been something of a misfit in Bunington at eighteen—a sullen, mutinous one, he imagined, until she had gone to London and got a job in an art gallery.

Benjamin Quillin had had the largest stake in it. Neil, again, deduced that she had been infatuated with him, although she didn't say so, she just told him the facts of meeting and marrying, and going to live in Benjamin's enormous house.

She was twenty, and it was four years later that her husband disappeared.

She had gone, as she regularly did, to the gallery after Benjamin went away on his final business trip, and she had found the place empty and the police in possession. Reading between the cold lines of the file before coming out, Neil had already made a picture of the pale young woman, wearing the water-coloured dress, sitting alone in the empty gallery, between empty walls, when the police had gone . . .

Tonight she was in pale green chiffon. On the dance floor they touched each other lightly and the contact was at the same time familiar and strange. They smiled at one another lazily. Being so near to her was incredibly sweet. When she said she didn't want to be late he answered "Fine," and felt no qualm, he was content that she should regulate their progress. On the way home, once, he put his hand for a moment against her cheek. She neither leaned towards him, nor away. When he drew up at the gate to Wesley House she was out of the car and standing beside his open window as he switched off the engine.

She leaned in slightly towards him and for an exciting few seconds he held his breath.

"Don't get out," she whispered. "Good night."

He didn't attempt to fix another meeting. He watched her flit up the path and open the door before he drove away. His was the only car now outside the Red Lion. He could see Jim Bates moving about behind the blind over the door, but he let his hand drop as he raised it to tap, suddenly aware of the mysterious charm of the night. He walked slowly away from the forecourt of the inn, and down the lane where he had just passed in the car.

II

Tony came away from choir practice in a restless, dissatisfied mood. He stopped in the lane by the church gate, kicking a stone and wishing the detective hadn't gone out with his stupid sister. He refused to let himself think that if it hadn't been for Annabel he would have had no access to Neil Carter at all.

"Aren't you going home?" inquired Ginger.

"I'm going to see BB."

"Hope you enjoy yourself," said Ginger, running off.

Tony began to walk slowly the other way. His enjoyment was always in inverse ratio to BB's internal store of alcohol. But that wasn't so important. He was the only visitor, and BB relied on him. He noted with relief that the old man was sitting outside the cottage. He was nursing one of the older cats, and the white paws of the other veteran could be seen protruding from a nearby leafy shade. The young cat, tortoiseshell Tim, was chasing his tail on the lawn.

"Good evening, boy."

"Hello, BB."

Tony flung himself down beside the canvas chair. The young cat came and pushed its head against his thigh, and he fondled it, watching BB. He always knew very quickly what stage BB was at. Tonight he was at the touchy stage, ready to respond exaggeratedly to flattery or slight.

"You been to choir practice?"

"Yes."

"That fool Groome wants me to give up m'serving."

"You told me."

"I only told you he suggested it. Now he says, 'At the end of the church year.'" BB had assumed an affected tone not in the least like the vicar's.

"I'm sorry."

"So am I, boy, so am I." BB gave a sort of growl, and then his face changed as his head turned stiffly to look at Tony.

"You came straight to me from choir practice, hum?"

"Yes."

There was so much whisker about BB's face it was difficult to divine his expression, but in the clear evening light Tony had no problem in seeing the old man's sudden moist-eyed satisfaction.

"Well," said BB, "we'll have a drink."

Tony thought a bit guiltily of how he would have been with Neil Carter at that moment, if he could have been. He jumped when BB said, struggling to his feet, "I thought the police had finished with your sister."

Tony helped him to find his balance, feeling for his own.

"They have," he answered, as casually as possible. This was not his first indication that BB was more interested in village events than he made himself out to be.

He followed the old man into the house. The smell was less and there were clean surfaces. Mrs. Mason had been in, and she was a friend of Mrs. Halliwell who did for the Chapmans.

"There's a stranger at the Red Lion been visiting your house. Must be a policeman. They always are, since Benjamin Quillin went off."

"Neil Carter's a friend of Dad's."

BB eyed Tony thoughtfully as he thrust a glass and a Coke can into his hands.

"Nobody'll believe that." He led the way outside again with his own glass and whisky bottle. "The whole sanctimonious, holier-than-thou lot of them, they'll all be whispering, and looking, and saying behind their hands, 'I know what *he's* up to!'"

"But he isn't!"

"All right, boy. I know that, and you know it." BB sat down, plonking glass and bottle on the misused table beside him. He poured himself a drink and downed it. "But the rest of 'em . . . Even the vicar, even the curate. 'By the way,' they'll say, turning to leave after dispensing spiritual comfort, 'I gather that Mrs. Quillin . . .'"

Tony poured his own drink, wishing BB would expend less energy on scorn.

"It doesn't really matter," he said.

He thought he glimpsed a smile.

"No, boy, it doesn't really matter. Timmy's growing up all right, eh?"

BB leaned forward, picked up the thin lithe body and held it on his lap. The young cat responded, luxuriating in every caress, preening its muscles each time the large gentle hands had passed by.

"You like animals better than people," observed Tony, and then wished he hadn't as BB began to think about people again, and to scowl. He put the cat gently to the ground.

"They're innocent," he said, pouring himself another drink. "The animals. The people know right from wrong, and they do wrong. They are strong enough to be magnanimous, but they are spitefully cruel." He took a long swallow. Tony remembered being told that years back BB had sometimes preached at St. Leonard's. For the first time he could imagine it, and believe that the vicar who had decreed it knew what he was doing.

"Have you had your supper?" asked Tony.

"Yes, boy, yes, I've had my supper," said BB irritably. "Don't fuss."

Tony wasn't sorry when he was told to cut along. He went home and upstairs without encountering anyone, and did his homework in his bedroom. When he had finished he opened his window and leaned out. It was still daylight, but the bright colours of summer had faded to pastel. It was warm now without being hot. He had a sudden idea of himself walking, running, walking, across the fields behind the house, while round him it slowly grew dark. There was already a see-through moon in the pale sky.

Aunt Helen's voice came up the stairs, hoping he was getting ready for bed. He went into the bathroom to clean his plate and his teeth in the persistent vain hope that he could make things more comfortable, then called over the banisters that he was ready. He kicked his shoes off, turned his bed down, and got in, clenching the sheet and blanket round his neck as he heard Aunt Helen on the stairs. She asked him, pulling at the blanket, if he really needed it.

"To start with," said Tony, hastily rebridging the gap, watching her undisturbed face and remembering that his summer shirt was almost the same blue as his pyjamas. She kissed his forehead, and when she had gone he lay listening for the sound of the drawing-room door. It didn't come, so he started thinking while he waited, wondering if Scotland Yard would ever catch up with Benjamin, hoping Mr. Carter wasn't especially enjoying himself with Annabel, imagining what fun it would be to visit Mr. Carter at Scotland Yard. He had to keep making an effort not to think about the curate and Mrs. Groome. Mr. Carter might be able to arrange for him to visit the Houses of Parliament. Local government was a sort of version of Parliament. His father was at a council meeting, he hoped he wouldn't look in on him when he got back, and see that he was missing. There'd be an awful row if he did. So far, the few times he'd sneaked out for a walk, he'd been lucky. Had he missed the drawing-room door? He couldn't risk it because if Aunt Helen was in the kitchen she could hear him and see him. But he must get out before his father got back. Oh, and Annabel . . .

Tony blinked at the oblong of the window. It was faintly silver. He heard an owl. There was, otherwise, profound silence inside and out. One moment he was utterly confused, the next he knew, on a wave of fury against himself, that he had fallen asleep. He turned his head on the pillow and the pattern of green dots on his clock told him it was half past midnight.

The heat had wakened him, of his socks and trousers and the blanket. He remembered Annabel, and got out of bed. He opened his door very carefully and looked out on to the landing. The only light to be seen anywhere was under her door. He went in his socks across to it and listened, and he could hear her moving about. It was a relief to know she hadn't stayed out very late with Detective-Inspector Carter.

He didn't want to go out himself any more, and he went back to his room already pulling at his belt. He shut the door quietly and walked over to the window, making a gap in the curtains with his hands. The garden in the moonlight was like a black and white film, and on the white seat there was a huddled black human form. Tony's heart gave a leap of shock, and at that moment the figure turned towards the house and he saw it was Janet Arkwright. Although he had jumped backwards as the head turned, she could have seen him. Ashamed of his reaction he parted the curtains again and waved. Then he fastened his belt, slipped into his shoes, crept downstairs and, after what seemed like long moments of fumbling, out of the front door.

Janet was still there, and he sat down beside her in silence. She turned and stared at him tragically, apparently without surprise. The moonlight glinted in two lines down her cheeks and as he looked at her fresh tears began.

"What is it?" he whispered, shocked. The Arkwrights lived over their shop, at the other side of the village.

"It's Father," she muttered.

"Your father?"

To his alarm Janet wriggled a shoulder and upper arm out of her skimpy blouse. There were two long weals in a bruised surround. They looked black in the moonlight, and in the centre of each of them black liquid oozed.

Tony stared, horrified, as Janet wriggled them back out of sight.

"He hit me. He said he was going to knock the nonsense out of me once and for all." Her voice was quiet, expressionless.

"The nonsense?"

"Because of Mr. Darcy." Her eyes glittered past him.

"What does Mr. Darcy think?" asked Tony, unwillingly accepting another piece of uncomfortable knowledge.

Janet looked at him with disdain.

"I don't know," she said. "That doesn't matter."

"But—your arm. That's awful." Although it was warm his teeth were chattering. "Your father—did that."

"I've told you. Not for the first time. But this was the worst." She stood up. Tony felt suddenly sorry for her. Although she wasn't ugly she was pale and ordinary, so different from Mrs. Groome. "I'm going home," she said impatiently.

"Why did you come—here?"

"It didn't matter where I went. I saw the seat." Janet looked calm, indifferent, but he suspected an unhappiness too deep for him to understand. His discomfort grew.

"But—your mother?"

"He told her to go away." She saw him, he thought, for the first time, and her face briefly softened. "Thanks for coming down, Tony."

"It's so late . . ." he began feebly, but she was already darting out of the gate. He stood watching until she was out of sight, then went slowly back into the house and upstairs to bed. The last time he looked at his clock before going to sleep it said twenty-five to three.

II

Neil walked slowly back up Church Lane, feeling consciously glad to be alive and well. The night was magically beautiful and mysterious, silent but for his own footsteps, the recurring tremor of an owl and the occasional animal shriek of dream or capture. The solitude and the dark fostered instincts and senses and discouraged thought—Neil kept only one thought in his head: that, for the sake of both his professional and his personal roles, he would not go back into eyeshot of Wesley House.

In the lane, the night hedges yielded up the whole essence of summer so that he felt drunk with it. He stopped for a few moments beside the church gate, looking at the shape of the building silhouetted against the pale night sky. He was intrigued rather than disconcerted when a dazzling gold oblong of light leaped out of the blackness alongside it. Within the oblong a figure was standing and it seemed to Neil as he blinked and stared that the figure, slender and female, was golden too, from head to hem. Even as he gazed, entranced like a child, arms went gracefully out and up, abruptly cutting off the golden picture. As his eyes adjusted, the shape of the curtained room was given back to him, a faint red glow in the surrounding darkness, then lost again in the headlights of a car which came out between gateposts only a few yards from where he was standing. Neil had reached it before it had started to turn, from a different sort of instinct.

"Good evening," he said through the open window.

Mr. Naylor the churchwarden stared at him as if confused, moistening his lips.

"The vicar keeps late hours," observed Neil. Mr. Naylor smiled gently, as he had smiled when they had met outside the Red Lion.

"He may do or he may not," he said. "I was not calling on him. I am on my way home, Mr. er . . . , and am merely saving myself a stamp by delivering a note."

"Of course." Neil wondered, vaguely curious, if Mr. Naylor had beheld the golden vision. He realized that his own presence, too, in such a place at such a time, called for an explanation. "What a night!" he said. "I just can't bring myself to go in to bed. It must be this country air."

"It is pleasant in Bunington. Good night, Mr. er . . ."

"Carter," said Neil, stepping slightly away from the car, as he had done in his early uniformed days to indicate that the questioning of a motorist was over and he was at liberty to proceed. Mr. Naylor smiled at him and drove away.

Still reluctant to go inside, Neil turned away again from the forecourt of the inn and made a slow circuit of the Big Green. The vision beside the church, vivid inside his head in all its bright detail, seemed as unlikely as the transformation scene in a pantomime. So did the anticlimactic appearance of the churchwarden. Grinning, Neil increased his pace from a stroll to a run, slowing down again when his circuit was almost complete and he was once more approaching the junction with Church Lane. He had stood stock still and started to concentrate his ears almost before he was aware of it. Footsteps were approaching the mouth of the lane, hastening, dragging, hastening. A girl of sixteen or seventeen with hair falling over her face and bare arms erupted at a sprint on to the forecourt, then walked slowly on towards the lane beyond. Her face was set straight ahead, and he heard her catch her breath. Concerned now rather than curious Neil followed her at a distance, down the lane, past the cottage where he had seen the old man in the garden, to where the shops began. He stood at the side of the road and watched her disappear without hesitation somewhere among the façades.

"Village life," thought Neil in amazement, as he turned round and walked quickly back to the inn, feeling for his key, suddenly very ready for the interior of a building and a bed.

CHAPTER 5

I

Neil had lunch next day in a pub in Latchford with Detective-Inspector Oliver, after his colleague had taken him on a cursory tour which showed Latchford to be as attractive an example of a small market town as Bunington was of an unspoilt village.

The two men discovered during their talk that they were twins. In his new unfamiliar Bunington frame of mind, a contrary mixture of passivity and readiness for the rich and strange, Neil took the coincidence as a pleasant matter of course. Inspector Oliver was openly delighted by it.

"I'll never forget your birthday!" he said.

Neil could see already that it was characteristic of the man to put it that way round. "Nor I yours," he offered.

"Do you think you'll be able to have dinner at home before you go?"

"Yes. May I ring you?"

"Do. Any night will suit, I've already checked. Have you gleaned any incidental intelligence from Annabel Quillin? I shouldn't ask you, of course."

"You should. It's your patch. But I really don't think there's any more the lady can tell me, or anyone else."

He was sure now there was not, at least in the current phase of their relationship, but to John Oliver he didn't qualify it. He rang his Chief when he got back to the Red Lion, letting him know he was aware of the false pretence by which Mrs. Quillin's consent to the audience had been secured.

"The lady was as ready to hope as I to deceive," said the Chief gaily. "Have you learned anything?"

"Nothing. I really am almost convinced there's nothing to learn."

"But you're looked upon with favour?"

"Not with disfavour," said Neil, after the briefest of pauses. "The lady is undemonstrative."

"That we know. Could do better."

"Would do better, if there was any kind of a chance."

"I know, Neil, I know. And if you end up with nothing, I'll be finally convinced there's nothing." The Chief paused, then said in a rush: "Not even a sign of the unexpected?"

"The unexpected?"

It was like a furnace in the closed-in triangle under the stairs which was the Red Lion's telephone kiosk. Neil kicked the door ajar.

"Mood reactions."

Neil thought the Chief spoke self-consciously, and suspected he had picked the phrase up from a subordinate.

"All as expected and already demonstrated. Going to London was an escape out of a prison. Marrying Quillin was an escape into a wide, wide world. Reaction now is the extreme of reaction then. Infatuation. Revulsion."

"She said this?"

"She said some things. I'm afraid I'm still having to translate. But she *did* say she would try and see what she could dig out. Implying that now she's strong enough and then she wasn't. Which might make for a change. Leave it with me."

"Oh, I'll do that. You'll stay over the weekend?"

"Yes. I'll see you or ring you on Monday. Ring you sooner if there's anything to say."

"Are you enjoying your holiday?"

"The weather's good." He relented. "And Bunington, actually."

"There you are, you see. It's sweltering here. What about the Division?"

"Friendly responses from my opposite number John Oliver. He's all right."

"That's about it then, Neil. Red Lion up to standard?"

"Thank you, Governor."

He went for a walk before ending up across the Small Green. Annabel Quillin was sitting on the white seat under the tree of heaven. He didn't know that she was *not* hoping to see him. She lifted an arm lazily as he approached the gate. She was in the centre of the seat and there was plenty of room to each side of her but Neil

thought most people would have made a token gesture of moving
up. Annabel remained perfectly still as he sat down. Her dress was
white, whiter than the seat. He sat as still as she, overwhelmingly
aware of her presence. He had never met a woman who gave him so
few clues as to what she thought and felt, her personal reticence perfectly matched her inability to help the police with their inquiries.
But the difference was, no doubt, that one was could not and the
other would not . . .

"What have you been doing today?" she asked at last, somehow
surprising him.

"Lunching with my opposite number in Latchford. It's a nice
town."

"Yes," she said listlessly, and he put his hand briefly and avun-
cularly on her arm. It was strange, how rarely he remembered to feel
sorry for her.

"Then I talked to my Chief on the telephone. Then went for a
walk."

"Leaning on you, is he? Your Chief?"

For the first time she looked towards him, and he towards her.
Life had come into her eyes, which could be a gleam of amusement.

"No. I rang him. Perhaps he was disappointed, I don't know."

"I could invent something, for the sake of your career?"

"I can't pretend that if I don't come up with anything it will
affect my career. Remember, the investigation as far as you are concerned is officially over."

That was true, but he realized his professional reaction was still to
try and put her off her guard. Contrary to his personal reaction,
which was that this was now as unnecessary as looking suspiciously
on Aunt Helen or Jim Bates.

"I should like to help you," she said.

"Well, you can help *me*," he answered cheerfully. "I'm still on
holiday. There must be another place, in another direction, as pleasant as the Frog. Or the Frog again."

"For weather like this," she said, "there's the Rose and Crown at
Ibthorpe."

"Dancing?"

"Yes."

"Tomorrow?"

"Very well."

She must have been enthusiastic sometimes as a small child, but it
was impossible to imagine.

"I'm taking Tony out tonight."

"I know. He's made up."

"He's a nice boy."

"I know that too. The trouble was, I suppose, that we were too far apart to do things together, and not far enough for me to . . ." She tailed off, not bothering, in the heat and her indolence, to put it into words. She would have been twelve when she lost her mother, and even if she hadn't found the baby brother a poor substitute . . . Some girls, of course, could feel motherly at twelve but not Annabel, he thought, not at twice that age.

"What time does he get back from school?"

"About five. He has to walk up from beyond the shops."

It was half past four and Neil decided to be gone when Tony arrived. Annabel walked with him to the gate. Neil watched a ladybird crawl up her arm and across her bare shoulder, make the climb on to the soft stuff of her dress. He felt the sight going permanently into his storehouse. She stopped too to watch the creature, and he was pleased when she put her finger beside it, waited for it to transfer, and then shook it gently off into the grass. She pressed the finger for a second into his shoulder.

"Have a good time with Tony."

Tony arrived at the Red Lion on the dot of seven. Neil was cleaning flies off the car windscreen. When he saw the boy he was glad he'd decided to put on a tie. Tony was wearing a smart blue one on his white shirt. His hair was damped down dark and his manner too was subdued, it took them both about half an hour to get back to their normal selves, the hair fair and floppy, the manner exuberant. Neil consulted his map, then set off in the direction suggested by Tony, and they ranged slowly along by-ways, under a pale blue settled sky. The good summer was bringing an early harvest, and a gold sheen suffused earth and sky alike. A few times, where the prospect was most sharply beautiful, Neil stopped the car and got out, calling a less eager Tony to join him in looking and listening. Neil started the evening by trying unsuccessfully to glimpse Annabel's features in her brother's, her voice in his, but came to accept the pleasure of Tony's company for its own sake. They ended up in the garden of an inn, having ordered grills and with long drinks in front of them.

"What did you do today?" Tony asked guardedly.

"Walked and talked and ate and read and slept and bought chocolate and razor blades," said Neil serenely, aware of scrutiny. "How did you get on at school?"

Tony told him, and told him too that in the autumn he would be going to boarding-school, and that at the moment he rather thought he would like to be a solicitor, like his father who had a super office in Latchford and lots of people to work for him. He had never known any grown-up person so easy to talk to, although he didn't say anything about Janet in the garden or what he had seen in the vestry. He told Neil about being in the choir, his recent dental sessions, BB and his animals and the death of Beppo. Also about the fact of not being allowed to have an animal at home because there was no one there all the time to look after it.

"Dad's out all day of course, and there are lots of days when Aunt Helen is too, and Mrs. Halliwell goes at lunch-time, and of course Annabel won't be there all the time."

He watched Neil again, but again there was no reaction. In any case, Neil at that moment was thinking about the brother rather than the sister, approving him for trying to see reason in the reasons put forward as to why he couldn't have a pet.

"I wish I *could* have a dog or a cat, though. Rabbits look nice but they're a bit stupid and they drop their doings all over the place. BB doesn't mind that but Aunt Helen . . . Well, I wouldn't have rabbits in the house, of course, but even so . . . Do you think I could ever come and see you at Scotland Yard?"

"I don't see why not."

Time went quickly and Tony didn't remind Neil over the prolonged aftermath to their meal that it was getting late. It was eleven before they were back in Bunington and Aunt Helen, although gracious enough at the front door in the face of Neil's apologies, didn't ask him in. There was no sign of Annabel.

He tried to talk business with her next evening over predinner drinks in the Rose and Crown at Ibthorpe, and over the main part of the meal, before they danced. He ignored the long opportunity to resume his monologue. He didn't get anything but he felt he had tried, had earned the subsequent pattern of dancing and sitting and looking and dancing again. There was a thunderstorm which they went out to watch from the verandah. Lightning stabbed the sky, thunder cracked and tore it open, heavy rain fell through to drench trees and plants and release their fragrances. When the storm was over the crickets maintained their relentless beat behind the quiet rhythm of the rain and Neil, the silent Annabel at his side, was

amused to find himself thinking about the more exotic stories of
Somerset Maugham. Once, just before they went inside, they turned
towards each other on the same instant, and he kissed her lightly,
with Maugham-like elegance. Again, she left the car swiftly when
he stopped outside Wesley House, but she had already told him she
would see him at the Summer Fair.

Maugham to Hardy! Annabel was only one element in the elation
with which he drove the few yards home.

II

Neil was beginning to feel he had spent the best part of his life in
Bunington, in two senses. The waking when he was ready, the lei-
surely inspection of sights and sounds through his window, the de-
scent to the sunny dining-room and lightly philosophic chat with
Jim Bates while his breakfast was freshly cooked, it was all deeply
and pleasingly familiar. The heat and brilliance were restored on
Friday morning after the storm, and he discussed with Jim Bates the
relative intensity of the decibels from their respective geographical
standpoints. Jim had some guardedly approving things to say about
the Rose and Crown. After breakfast Neil telephoned John Oliver,
taking Annabel's explicit mention of Saturday as an implicit warning that she would be unavailable on Friday, and accepted the invitation to dinner. He spent what he already described to himself as a
basic Bunington day: wandering and reading punctuated by lunch-
time and early evening sessions in the pub, talking a little and listening a lot, almost surprised, half disappointed, that there were no
more bizarre experiences. Tony popped in to thank him for the
night before, but didn't linger. Neil suspected this restraint to stem
from Aunt Helen rather than from Tony's inclinations but he let
him go, after promising to look out for him at the Summer Fair next
day (post meridianally), and patronize whatever activity Tony found
himself involved with.

He got the warm welcome he expected at John Oliver's converted
cottage on the far edge of Latchford. John's wife Jill had a little-girl
look and the two of them seemed absurdly young to be the heads of
a family of four. Two of the children were in bed but the elder two,
a girl and a boy, sat with the adults for the length of an orangeade
and behaved charmingly. A few outstandingly attractive and quite
valuable things struggled through the domestic clutter—Jill had been

a junior partner in an antique business when she met and rapidly married John. There was hardly any shop talked and the conversation ranged over all sorts of interesting eternal questions, interrupted as John or Jill anticipated each of his possible requirements. Neil enjoyed himself enormously. Really, the whole week in Bunington was drenched in charm, from every direction. It would cloy, of course, but not yet. Charm. Annabel on the white seat and Jill Oliver on her swinging hammock in the dusk. Ducks on the village greens and leaves soft on his face as he sought his fern bed in the glade. Tony's face lighting up and Jim Bates settling down for a chat. Flowers and bees and the soaring eternal stone of the church, and the sun and blue sky that he was tending to believe were exclusive to the Bunington area of England. George Chapman's cool blue-green drawing-room and John Oliver's cheerful living-room with a pot lid next to a Beatrix Potter frieze. Charm. Annabel not expanding towards him as other people did, but being prepared to be there. Neil knew on his drive home that he was not yet ready to leave.

Even the Summer Fair presented from a distance an appearance of charm. He didn't go near it until the afternoon, when it had been under way for several hours. The Corrigan fields were behind the houses on the far side of the Big Green and when he first saw the scene it looked tranquil, idyllic, clusters of brightly-clad figures drifting on a green base against a tree surround, booths like little houses shaded overhead by gay strips of fabric. But from close to he saw that it was furiously active. Little Mr. Naylor was lining up small boys for a race. Mr. Chapman, recognized from the Quillin photograph, was restraining some slightly larger ones who had to wait their competitive turn. The fringe of stalls buzzed with movement and voices. A tall fair man in a clerical collar was effectively barkering a bran tub. Neil paid his entrance money at the gate, into the hand of the dark man who had read the lesson at Evensong. He advanced cautiously over the rutted grass and started to wander along the lines of stalls, mostly staffed by middle-aged women, stopping to exchange remarks on the continuing fine weather. Tony, breathing hard, rosy-faced, found him quite soon.

"Aren't you working?" Neil asked him.

"I have been. I'm just going to."

"What?"

"Take over from Ginger at the bran tub."

"Lead the way?"

The Reverend Malcolm Darcy had a punishing hand grip. Tony

discreetly introduced Neil as mere Mr. Carter, and the curate, after a large automatic smile and an injunction to partake, resumed his vocal efforts. Neil gave the required sum to Tony, rolled his sleeve up, and sank his arm to the elbow in the soft yet scratchy bran. He came up with a gaily wrapped package containing a stuffed cat-shape covered in black plush. It had paste-gem eyes and a bow round its neck and he wouldn't have parted with it for the world. He tied the parcel's coloured string round his wrist, so that it dangled safe.

"Who's the man on the gate?" he asked Tony. "The good-looking dark one?"

Tony, to his annoyance, felt himself flushing.

"That's Mr. Arkwright. He's the lay reader and the greengrocer. You think he's good-looking?"

"He's not bad-looking."

"He sells super cherries," added Tony in fairness. Janet Arkwright was standing so close to the bran tub group that he muttered reluctantly, with a movement of his head, "That's his daughter, Janet."

Neil looked at the untidy pale dark girl hovering beside them, raising and lowering her eyes. He thought that her father, in a lull at the entrance, was looking at her too, although he was too far away to be sure, just as the girl he had followed a few nights before had been too far away for him to be certain she was Janet Arkwright.

"How's it been?" he asked Tony.

"All right, really. The worst thing's organizing the little ones for the races. I've done my stint at that. This is OK. Tea tent duty's a bit frantic too." Tony looked at his watch. "Three o'clock that starts."

"Meanwhile, what do you recommend for the idle onlooker?"

He had to make an effort not to find the continuing busy-eyed presence of Janet Arkwright disturbing.

"It's worth going round the stalls," said Tony judicially. "There are some quite good things. Oh, and you ought to let Miss Catchpole tell your fortune. She told me some fantastic things. Bit creepy, really."

"Miss Catchpole?"

He waited while Tony took four sets of money from four dirty hands.

"She's a sacristan," said Tony, sternly watching the little girls at the bran tub. "One at a time!" he told them, his own voice as high as their excited twittering. "Aunt Helen's one, and Miss Catchpole's the other."

"I must have known once, but I've forgotten what sacristans do."

"They keep the church vessels clean, and the cloths and so on." Tony dropped his voice slightly, although the curate was making more than enough noise to drown it at its normal pitch. "Miss Catchpole's creepy anyway. We call her mad Miss Catchpole. All skinny and old and piercing eyes. It's no wonder she tells fortunes, she looks as if she can see right through you."

"I must certainly visit Miss Catchpole. Where is she?"

Tony pointed across the field, apologizing as his stabbing finger met the vicar's jacket.

"That's all right, Tony," said the vicar. "Good afternoon, Mr. Carter. I'm glad to see you're still with us. You've met young Tony Chapman?" He looked at Neil in what might have been curiosity. Neil was impressed, as he fancied he would always be, afresh each time, by this man who almost nobly surmounted his appearance, and who had effortlessly remembered his unremarkable name.

"Indeed I've met Tony. My family and his are old friends." Neil smiled at the vicar, unable to think of anything else to say, and amused to find himself afflicted by a mild version of that sense of guilt which after leaving school and ceasing to attend divine worship he had felt whenever he had come across a member of the Anglican clergy.

The vicar turned to Janet Arkwright.

"Your father would welcome your help, Janet," he said quietly. She raised her eyes and stared at him for a few seconds before appearing to take in what he had said. Then she nodded with a quick anxious smile, and set off for the gate. Neil and the vicar both looked after her, and Neil saw John Arkwright set his hand on her shoulder and the girl draw swiftly back.

"All right, Malcolm?" asked the vicar. Neil realized that since the arrival of the vicar the curate had fallen silent.

"Of course, Ernest," replied the curate, as gently. Neil was aware that the two men were looking at one another, he could have imagined that they were testing an understanding. The vicar put out his hand and patted the curate's arm in a kindly way before moving on, and the curate continued silent for a few moments before beginning again to cry his wares. The vicar, reflected Neil, was an interesting man. More interesting than the curate, but that was perhaps to make too hasty a judgement. After telling Tony he would be sure and be served by him in the tea marquee, he moved slowly across the field towards the fortune teller's tent. He was starting to look out for Annabel, lazily as yet, and he didn't see her.

The small tent presented a pleasing appearance, gaily striped and decorated. A notice on a stake announced *Madame Anna: Fortunes*. There was a cluster of little girls outside who as Neil approached were routed by the woman behind the nearest stall.

"Go on in!" she encouraged him, and he entered the cool dim tent, smelling so strongly of grass it tickled his nostrils. The contrast with the brilliance of the field was great and for a few seconds he could see nothing but a vague outline behind a small table draped with a cloth. It told him, in a soft slow voice, to sit down. He had to feel for the chair but as he drew it to the table, aware under his feet of the damp grass which had been covered before the sun could draw up its dew, he made out the small white face under the coin-rimmed bandeau, almost lost in the folds of an unbecoming brightly coloured scarf which flowed each side of it. A few wisps of grey-white hair had here and there escaped confinement. The small mouth, the rather prominent nose and chin, the keen dark eyes, certainly did give Miss Catchpole a witch-like air.

"Madame Anna?" inquired Neil.

"Hand. Hand!" she demanded, and when he tentatively held them out for her to choose she grabbed both by the wrists and pulled them towards her. She bent her face over them so that for a second he felt her nose against a palm. She told him in the same soft expressionless voice that his life was moving to the close of a tranquil phase. The phase would end abruptly. Violently. "I see red," said Madame Anna. "Blood, it may be."

He was not much impressed, but he was impressed when she went on to talk about his character and propensities, of what he was and why. It was as if she knew him well, without illusion. It was by no means a pleasant experience.

"This isn't a fairground gimmick," he said with a grimace, as he gave her the money she asked for. He forced her to smile, as he could force most people if he had no involvement with them.

"Of course it isn't. I have second sight. Second touch, really. If I hadn't taken your hands . . . It isn't even the lines, so much, although I read them. All this . . ."—she made a disdainful gesture at her head—"the children like it. A last thought." She stared at him with undisguised interest.

"Yes?"

"Be careful with Annabel Chapman."

The shock made him shiver. He stared back at her.

"I've given you some constructive things, you know," she said at last.

"I do know. I'm hoping to remember, although I think I'd rather not."

He was glad to get out into the sunshine. Although he didn't for a moment think she was mad, she was a disconcerting old bird. He walked away from her tent looking round a little more keenly for Annabel. He wished they had arranged a meeting point, but at the time he had not wanted to pin her down. He glanced at his watch. Three o'clock already, and Tony would be on duty.

Neil made his way to the tea marquee. Helen Chapman was in charge of a small team behind a trestle table. She greeted him briskly.

"What's the form?" he asked.

"We'll give you a cup of tea," she said, "and the food will be brought to you. Sandwich, scone, cake."

There was as yet a mere sprinkling of clients. Tony followed Neil to a table, set the paper plate before him and removed its protective cellophane with a flourish. Then he flopped down in the seat opposite.

"Not much doing yet," he explained, "and she said I could sit with you until they really start coming in."

"Good. I only want the scone."

Tony attacked the sandwich, then groaned as he was reminded of the state of his mouth. "Did you have your fortune told?"

"Yes." Neil shivered deliberately, but it was an appropriate reflection of how Miss Catchpole had made him feel.

"I know. She tells you things. Hardly ever nice ones."

"No," said Neil a bit absently. A beautiful woman had just come into the marquee and was talking to Helen Chapman, the wrong answer to his growing longing for Annabel. Except for her height she could not have been less like Mrs. Quillin. Her beauty was in her colouring and her glowing health and bright golden hair and warm happy smile. It was impossible not to look at her.

"Who's that?" Neil asked Tony.

"Tony, come and look after Mrs. Groome!" called Miss Chapman.

"Don't you know? That's the vicar's wife," said Tony, getting reluctantly to his feet. Neil noticed he had flushed. "See you later."

Neil gazed in amazement at his golden vision. As a boy he had been taken behind the scenes after a pantomime, and the girlish princess had been a middle-aged woman. He had never forgotten his disillusionment. The vicar's wife was as beautiful off stage as on. And he could only think that added to her more obvious gifts of nature was that of perception. She could not have married the Reverend Ernest Groome for what met the eye.

All at once his longing for Annabel became insupportable. He pushed the remains of his scone away and got up so abruptly the chair fell over. She was standing beside him when he straightened up, as if he had summoned her. He felt an enormous sense of relief. They looked at one another.

"Have you had tea?" he asked her.

"No."

"Do you want some?"

She shook her head.

"Let's get out of here."

She turned and led the way to the daylight, waving a dismissive hand at her Aunt Helen. Mrs. Groome was watching her. How did they get on, for heaven's sake? Tony was at the other end of the marquee, filling sugar bowls. Neil smiled at Aunt Helen as he passed her, and she nodded in cool response. Outside he came abreast of Annabel and they crossed the crowded field.

The people they passed and sometimes greeted seemed a million miles away, they might already have been alone. When they were outside the gate she said:

"Of course you didn't come by car."

"It's at the pub."

They walked back in silence to the Red Lion.

"May I try the car?" she asked. "I'm a good driver."

He let her into the driving-seat. The car protested only once, as she first manoeuvred it. She drove past the church and past the Small Green, and they were in the country. She drove fast and very well. All he said, once, was "Annabel." She said nothing and stopped the car by a stone wall edging a network of small sloping fields skirted by woodland. They went through the gate into the nearest field and after a few hundred yards Annabel turned into the wood. Neil followed her under the abrupt gloom, shot through with sun shafts. They came out after perhaps five minutes into a small glade, an almost perfect circle. Annabel sat down and leaned against a tree. She held up a hand to him.

"It's convenient," she said, as he slowly sat down beside her, "that we are having a long dry summer."

CHAPTER 6

I

Beloved, let us love one another: for love is of God, and everyone that loveth is born of God, and knoweth God . . .

Neil shifted in the pew, taking his eyes from Annabel's beautiful half profile and looking towards the altar set with the mysterious green-cloaked objects of the Eucharistic feast. St. John was writing about *agape* and not *eros,* and his message ought to be a second setback to the Detective-Inspector's incredulously recognized half wish to share in the feast for the first time in more years than he could remember. The first setback was that, even as he was reminding himself that he was a confirmed member of the Church of England, he knew that if he went up to the altar it would be merely because of chance and following years of unrepented neglect. He was hesitant in the first place, in fact, precisely because he had been brought up in the Church, because he remembered certain things. *He that drinketh unworthily . . .*

To go up on a whim was a kind of unworthiness.

And now, in the Epistle of St. John, here was another check . . .

There is no fear in love; but perfect love casteth out fear; because fear hath torment: He that feareth is not made perfect in love . . .

He had never really known either kind of love, perfect or imperfect. The thing to fear, listening to John Arkwright read the Epistle, was self-examination. That was something he had tried to carry out, when he was about thirteen and preparing to be confirmed. Conscientiously, regularly, when there had been so little to examine, he had knelt down. It had all long since gone, but the sense of right and wrong hadn't gone, whether or not he translated it into words and deeds.

And this commandment have we from him, That he who loveth God love his brother also.

He almost never thought about God, and never about people in general except to dislike them. But he half wanted to go up to the altar. As the congregation rose for a hymn Neil realized that the other characteristic of this strange week, besides charm, was a willingness on his part to be led, if only in partial understanding.

The vicar was preaching on love, taking his text from the Epistle. He was even naming the two kinds of love, *agape* and *eros,* as Neil had named them to himself, and Neil shifted again in the pew.

"*Agape* is always the ultimate love, because it is into *agape* that the best of *eros* will eventually grow, and thus become no longer subject to the ebb and flow of human feeling."

Everything that small, almost ludicrously ugly figure said was powerful and lucid, informed with faith and common sense. Neil several times would have liked to clock out from the vicar's sermon, and found it impossible. He was relieved when it was over, but the recitation of the Creed muddled him even more over what he should do, because he could go no further in certain parts of it than acknowledge that he did not disbelieve . . .

The tall stern-faced John Arkwright had gone up the aisle and knelt down to lead the prayers. At last Neil wandered, thinking of Annabel Quillin and her relationship with her husband, something of the flavour of which he had now extracted from her on the plea of comparison—a very different appeal from the appeal of the police.

The intercession was drawing to a close. It might be his last chance to make some sort of preparation. If he was going up. He still didn't know, but he essayed a prayer for guidance.

Seeing we have a great high priest who has passed into the heavens, Jesus the Son of God, let us draw near with a true heart, in full assurance of faith, and make our confession to our heavenly Father . . .

The invitation was the curate's, that must be why he was wearing the impressive green garment which matched the coverings on the altar objects, while the vicar was merely in an alb.

He listened to himself saying the words of the Confession aloud. It was easier than trying to pray in his own words, the remembered childish formulae were no good and he had no others, no words at all to bridge a sudden leap from lapse to participation in the central act of worship. Neil found himself wishing he could ask the vicar what he ought to do.

The peace of the Lord be always with you.
And with thy spirit.

The curate had a fine voice, rich and resonant. The congregation rose for another hymn, during which a collection was taken. Christopher Corrigan attended to the left side of the church and Alec Naylor to the right, on which sat Neil next to the aisle. Neil noticed that the other old man, Tony's friend Bedlington Byrne, was absent from the front pew and that a tall unsteady figure, enveloped and girdled in an alb, hovered by the wall to the right of the altar, its face purple and scowling.

The curate advanced down the chancel and took Mr. Corrigan's proffered tray. Bedlington Byrne came down and took Mr. Naylor's. Recalling Tony's observations on the two cousins, Neil wondered if the less provocative of two possible arrangements had been decided upon, or simply allowed to happen. The churchwardens retired and Bedlington Byrne stood facing the altar, swaying slightly, waiting to hand the curate his tray. When he had taken it the curate then remained at the altar, and Bedlington Byrne returned to his place beside it. He tripped on one of the shallow steps and Neil, watching between his fingers, saw Tony's head for the first time as it dropped forward out of line, the face screwed up in worry as it followed the old man's uncertain progress.

The curate began the prayer of consecration and Neil covered his face.

Blessed is he that cometh in the name of the Lord.

Would he go up, or wouldn't he?

Neil parted his hands again, and saw the vicar standing beside the officiating curate, waiting to assist him. Bedlington Byrne wavered from the niche in the wall, carrying a silver jug, which the vicar took from him. The curate held out the chalice and the vicar poured. He poured again from the glass jug which the old man then brought him. The curate turned to the congregation.

Draw near with faith: receive the Body of our Lord Jesus Christ, which was given for you, and his Blood, which was shed for you; and feed on him in your heart by faith with thanksgiving.

Neil covered his face again. He recalled that the clergy took Communion first themselves, but the moment of his decision must be very near.

As he waited his concentration was broken by a curious bubbling, choking noise somewhere in front of him, which grew into a protesting roar that filled the church. Afterwards he remembered thinking that it was more like the bellow of an animal than a human voice. It came again, and then again, railing against the rafters. Neil, leaping to his feet, saw the curate turn, the chalice jerking from before his face. Wine splashed up and over, on to the vicar's white alb and his outstretched hand. Bedlington Byrne's shouting died on a rattle and he fell back against the choir stall and slumped to the floor. Tony stood up. The curate set the chalice back on the altar, wine slopping on to the hand which he now extended towards the vicar's. Both men stood motionless, as if frozen in the moment of attempted contact. Neil could see, even before he started running down the aisle, the dark burns spreading on both hands where the wine had fallen.

II

Neil ran straight to the altar and put his nose above the chalice.

"Don't touch anything!"

He didn't know whether the two priests had understood, or even heard him. He glanced at the heavily-breathing, unconscious Bedlington Byrne, beside whom Tony was already kneeling. He turned and cannoned into John Arkwright, who had left his place behind the curate's chair, almost knocking him down. Now Alec Naylor and two men he didn't know had come down the aisle and were lined up in front of him. Again, it was only later he remembered their expressions and realized that in their ignorance of his calling they were probably on their way to restrain him, thinking it was he, the stranger, who had caused the disturbance. But at the time he merely snapped at them:

"Organize a car to take the vicar and the curate at once to the nearest hospital, and ring the hospital to ask for a cyanide antidote to be available for the washing of affected skin. Get an ambulance for the old man, I don't think he should be moved except by experts. And please ring the Divisional police at Latchford." They stared at him, in company with Christopher Corrigan who had been the nearest and who had joined them last, and with an angry gesture Neil pulled out his identification and thrust it at their faces. "Hurry!" he said.

"It's all right, Alec, do what he says," called a voice from the congregation. Neil saw George Chapman and beckoned him up. "Will you take people's names as they leave, please. Get someone to help you. And will your sister go to the vicar's wife." He had been aware, early in the service, that Mrs. Groome was not in church.

The group, briefed, made its way to the door, and Neil turned back to the chancel.

Mr. Adams the organist appeared at the foot of his stairway, and Neil took hold of him and John Arkwright by their surplices.

"I don't want anyone to go into the vestries. Are there keys?"

The lay reader said, with injured dignity, "The doors are open in both the main and the choir vestries. The keys to the outside doors will be in the locks." His proud face grew suppliant. "What is it?"

"The wine was contaminated. Look, I'm sorry, but will you take the choir out with the congregation? They can leave their surplices in their seats."

The two men looked angry and bewildered, and Mr. Arkwright said, "For contaminated wine? Really, Mr. . . ."

"Carter. Detective-Inspector. Poisoned wine. The Latchford police will prefer it if no one has been in the vestries. I take it that the wine is kept in the main vestry? And prepared there?"

"Yes. I'm sorry, Inspector Carter, it's—a shock."

"Of course."

"We'll take the choir out through the church," said Mike Adams.

"If you would. Quickly and quietly."

He was back at the altar just in time to guide the priests away from its contents. "I'm afraid you mustn't touch anything. Potassium sodium cyanide is both lethal and incapable of getting into wine of its own accord."

He turned away from the pain in the vicar's face. The choir was struggling out of its surplices and leaving the chancel except for Tony, with whom John Arkwright was arguing across Bedlington Byrne's body.

Neil took a few steps. "Thank you for being so helpful," he said to Mr. Arkwright. "Tony can stay here. I can use him until the Latchford police arrive."

"Very well." Mr. Arkwright was stern and dignified again. He put his surplice on his seat and followed the choristers into the nave, speeding their progress. Neil turned back to the altar.

"It doesn't hurt," said the curate wonderingly, staring at his hand. His thumb and forefinger were a rich red, like the back of the vicar's hand.

"So, it doesn't hurt," agreed Neil, "but it must be treated."

"Allow me to dismiss the congregation," said the vicar.

"Quickly, please."

Neil stood aside, by Tony and the old man. The noisy breathing was still regular.

"My friends," said the vicar, quietly but in a voice which stayed the choir in its straggling progress through the congregation, and stilled the swaying heads of his flock, "something has happened which we do not yet understand. Our service this morning cannot continue and I send you forth." He raised his arms. The dark stain on his hand glowed in a sun shaft. "May the blessing of God Almighty, Father, Son, and Holy Spirit be with you and remain with you always." He dropped his hands and staggered slightly. "Please all go now," he said, "as quickly and quietly as you can."

Neil went back into the chancel. He heard impatience in his voice as he called up the nave. "Will someone please come and help the vicar and the curate to a car!"

Two men came up. Behind them the congregation were filing out, assisted by Messrs. Naylor, Adams and Arkwright, where they showed any inclination to linger or ask questions. The curate again put his hand out towards the altar, and it was the vicar who put his uninjured hand gently but firmly on the curate's wrist and guided it away. The curate was shaking his head, as if to shake himself back to understanding. The vicar's colour was even more deathly than it normally was and Neil saw him surrender his weight to the two men who had come to assist them.

"Two more men up here, please!" he called sternly across the church, and the vicar and the curate went away with two supporters apiece.

Only Neil and Tony and the unconscious Bedlington Byrne were left in the church. Tony was still beside the old man.

"Hang on there for a moment, there's a good chap."

Neil went quickly to the two small doors, side by side in the north wall, and through the first one. A key was in the outer door and he turned it. He noticed a bare table under a cupboard and reached out to the cupboard door, but let his hand fall without touching it. He went into the choir vestry through the unlocked connecting door. The two rooms were of identical size and shape, each with a door from outside and a door into the body of the church. A key was in the connecting door, on the main vestry side, and keys in the other two doors. Neil turned the key in the outside door, leaving it there. Then he went back into the chancel. He stood looking down on the large old man flat on his back, his mouth slightly open, his face suffused. There didn't appear to have been any change in his condition.

"Will he die?" whispered Tony.

"I don't know."

Neil found the boy had unfastened the girdle of the alb, and loosened the tie.

"He hates wearing a tie," said Tony. He surreptitiously wiped his eyes. "Thanks for letting me stay. What happened?"

"There was a deadly poison in the wine. But I shouldn't tell that to anyone."

"I won't. So if the curate had drunk it he would have died."

"If he had drunk the veriest drop." Neil found he too was whispering.

"So if BB hadn't warned him . . ."

"Yes."

"How did he know?" asked Tony, then as he stared into Neil's grave face his own face was suddenly bright red and his eyes flashing.

"Oh, no!" said Tony, whispering a shout. "No, no, no!"

"Don't get so excited," said Neil, feeling helpless, "the police will find out what happened."

"You're the police. Oh, gosh, listen, he may have been grumpy, but he would *never*—oh, no!"

"I know I'm the police, but this isn't my province. It belongs to the Division in Latchford. Sometimes divisions call in Scotland Yard eventually, but all the routine work belongs to them. As soon as the Latchford police arrive, that's it for me."

"I'll talk to the Latchford police, then!" hissed Tony fiercely.

"And they'll talk to you!"

"But," said the boy wildly, "I mean, you're here. Surely they'll ask you to help!"

Surely that nice-natured, pragmatic Divisional Inspector Oliver would do just that.

"It's a very unusual situation. Let's wait and see, shall we?"

"The animals!"

"What?" There were sounds at the back of the church, and Neil was taking his attention off Tony.

"BB's animals. Who'll feed them?"

"You will. Look, go down to the door and see who it is and if it's the police or the ambulance men direct them up here. Otherwise tell them to go away. Then go home."

"I don't want to go home!"

"Please. I promise you I'll come and see you as soon as I can. And as I don't expect to be needed here once I've handed over, that will be pretty soon."

Tony got up reluctantly and went so slowly he was passed by two men and a stretcher. Neil wrote down the details of the hospital where they were taking Bedlington Byrne. When they had removed him there was no one in the church but himself.

The quiet was somehow eloquent. A few drops of wine had burned the carpet. "I see red," said Madame Anna. Neil looked at the silver vessel on the table by the altar, and would have cautiously investigated it had there not been a silver lid to lift. As he turned back to the altar he acknowledged his sense of shock. It was intensified by that silence, by the peace and beauty of the church. Bars of sun lay across the altar steps, from a pale window. Wall monuments extolled the esteemed dead. Someone had made a lovely thing of the flowers.

Beloved, let us love one another. He was conscious, too, of irony. Should he, shouldn't he, go up to the altar? Well, he had gone. He found himself kneeling down on the spot where the old man had fallen, clasping his hands. "Lord, let the outrage pass from this place." He didn't know where the words had come from. When he heard sounds from the back of the church he got hastily to his feet. He explained what he could to John Oliver and the sergeant with him, and gave them Bedlington Byrne's address.

"It's yours now," he said, preparing to leave.

"Look," said John, drawing him out of earshot of the sergeant. "You said you were staying on here a bit?"

"Yes."

"Having you here's too good a coincidence to be wasted. Could I ask you, unofficially . . . you told me you've got the confidence of the boy. You even said he was an expert witness wasted! Can you fish around, Neil, still the relaxed chappie on holiday?"

Neil grinned at him.

"*That* image has taken a tumble! But yes, of course I can."

III

There were a few people in the churchyard, and round the gate. Some young girls were giggling together and one of them, pushed forward by the others, almost fell against Neil. It was Janet Arkwright. She looked as untidy as she had looked in Mr. Corrigan's field, but there was a spot of colour in each pale cheek. Her eyes faltered before Neil's stern look, but he took her by the arm as she tried to turn away from him.

"Do you want to say something?"

"I . . ." She suddenly looked hard at him. "Is Mr. Darcy all right?"

He could see a tic at work in her cheek. He said quite gently, letting her go,

"Both Mr. Darcy and the vicar are all right. I should go home."

"You're a policeman, aren't you?" called out one of the others, and Janet Arkwright was reabsorbed into the group as it shifted with resumed nervous mirth.

"Yes," said Neil, "but I'm on holiday. If the police are needed, the Latchford men are in charge." He started to walk away, but found he couldn't leave it like that, and turned back to them. They had fallen silent, looking after him. They seemed like decent girls, fourteen, fifteen, sixteen years old. "Look," he said, "the wine had got contaminated. And Mr. Bedlington Byrne had a stroke. There's nothing more for you to find out. Go home, like good girls."

He grinned at them and turned decisively away. Someone said the name of a TV policeman, briefly provoking his satisfied vanity, but there was no more giggling. He walked quickly down the lane. A lark was warbling overhead, and for a moment he envied it its location and its frame of mind. He stooped reluctantly in the dark doorway of the Red Lion. The bar was much fuller than it had been the Sunday before, and everyone fell silent as he entered. He picked out the attentive face of Alec Naylor.

"The Latchford police are in charge," he said quietly to everyone, since everyone was listening, "of whatever has happened. It was fortunate I was here this morning, but I'm on holiday."

He longed for a stiff drink, but not there. Knowing his smile was tight he went out of the bar again, ignoring a step towards him by

Mr. Naylor, went into the telephone kiosk and closed the door. Now he welcomed its sealed exclusivity. He dialled the Chief's home.

The Chief's wife was a zealous protector and he was glad the Chief answered in person.

"I'm sorry to disturb you, Governor, but there's been an attempted murder."

"In Bunington? The Chapmans?"

"In Bunington, but not necessarily to do with the Chapmans. In the parish church. Potassium sodium cyanide in the Communion wine."

Neil rather admired the Chief for hesitating so briefly.

"That's been confirmed?"

"No. It's not half an hour since the incident took place. It isn't very long either, you'll remember, since I went on that poisons course. 'The characteristic odour of bitter almonds.'"

"Which was why it was only attempted murder?"

"No, actually. I think only an expert—only someone who had studied the subject—would have detected it. Or at least realized its significance. It's all very strange, Governor, but an elderly alcoholic who was assisting at the service had a stroke, preceding same by a great deal of noisy shouting which unnerved the curate and made him spill the wine instead of drinking it. It burned his hand, and the vicar's hand nearby, and he put it down. They've been taken for treatment."

"And you've called in the local boys, of course."

"Of course."

"Well, well. The old man had an eleventh-hour repentance, then?"

"Unless . . . it certainly looks like it."

"However, it's not our worry, Neil. Not yet, anyway."

"No. But John Oliver at Latchford has come up as I thought he would."

"Yes?"

"He's asked me to keep eyes and ears open. Rather as I'm doing already in the other connection. The boy, for instance, is a keen observer of human nature, and a particular friend of the old man. Oliver knows I've got his confidence, and he's already told me he'd like me to stand unofficially by. All right?"

"You've got another week's holiday," said the Chief after a short pause. "You haven't come up with anything yet in the other connection. Just don't display any bad manners, Neil. Anything you do will be by courtesy. Keep a low profile, as they say."

"Yes, Governor."

"What a very extraordinary thing!"

"I don't like it. I don't think I've liked anything less, even where there's been a body. Mind you, having looked at the old man, there may well be one before the week's out."

"Which will probably be the tidiest thing. Keep in touch with me."

Neil came out of the telephone kiosk with his face as tight as when he had gone in. He felt a slight ache in his cheekbones. He went quickly out into the sunshine. A couple of figures in gardens across the Big Green straightened up. Without pausing he set off for the Small Green, crossed the grass and went up the Chapman path. Helen Chapman opened the door to him. She looked personally stricken, her face, he thought, somehow lopsided as if she had had a stroke.

"I'm very sorry," he said.

"It was good of you to come." She had already pulled herself back to normal. "I've seen Mrs. Groome and she's gone to the hospital. For goodness' sake come in and have a drink. You won't want to run the gauntlet of the Red Lion."

He followed her into the house. Annabel and her father were in the drawing-room. There was no sign of Tony. George Chapman jumped to his feet.

"What can you tell us?"

"Get him a drink," said Helen reprovingly, and her brother obediently turned away. "He likes gin and tonic," said Helen, still sounding reproachful. She passed a hand across her face. Annabel looked at Neil with a slight smile.

"What did happen?" she asked.

He sank gratefully into the chair which Helen indicated.

"Nothing, thank heaven. I don't mean nothing, of course," he corrected himself, as he took the cold glass from George Chapman. "Bedlington Byrne had a stroke, and the vicar and the curate were burned."

"*Burned?*"

The brother and the sister spoke on an instant. Neil found himself reflecting that even if one was aware that cyanide killed instantly, one might be ignorant that it could affect the skin. Annabel said nothing.

"There was potassium sodium cyanide in the wine. It burns the skin very severely. Doesn't hurt, which is an additional macabre hazard because the victim doesn't hurry for the treatment he needs."

"But how on earth did such a substance get into the wine?" George Chapman glared at him.

"I've no idea. Except that it couldn't have got there by accident."

He had almost cured himself, in the last lotus days, of being a detective, he had to make an effort to watch them keenly. Although, of course, it was hardly necessary. Whatever Tony said and felt, BB had surely condemned himself out of his own mouth.

There seemed to be no reactions beyond the expected horror, although Neil had the idea that once again, for a flash, Helen Chapman's face was distorted, as if he was looking at it in a fairground mirror. There was still no reaction from Annabel.

"The old man," went on Neil, "did all that trumpeting just as the curate was going to drink, which rather makes it seem as if he was having second thoughts, the effort of which brought on the stroke. At least he must have *known* what was in the wine, or it would have been . . . Anyway, it's not for me to speculate. I called in the Latchford CID as I had to and they're already on the job. The old man's been taken to hospital, and the vicar and the curate too, for as long as it takes to treat them for burns."

"How could anyone get hold of such a deadly poison?" asked Helen Chapman sternly.

"There's only one way for the layman, and that's not easy." The drink was going to the right place. His sense of shock, almost of drought, was being absorbed in it. "It's used to destroy wasps' nests."

Helen Chapman turned to her brother. "George!"

He said irritably, "I know, I know!" He turned to Neil. "There was a nest a month ago in the churchyard. A few people were stung and we decided to get rid of it. We got the stuff from the Latchford chemist—Corrigan or Naylor or Arkwright, I think—I remember we didn't get it too easily. Had to sign a book and then were told we were being given it only because we were who we were."

"And it was used?"

"Oh, yes. And worked."

"And what happened to the remainder?"

George Chapman's face had flamed red, as his son's had earlier in the church beside Bedlington Byrne. Guilt or rage? thought Neil automatically, before dismissing the question.

"I don't know," said George Chapman grimly. "But if some clot put it in the shed . . ."

"Don't talk to people about it," said Neil. "Not, I'm sure, that you need my injunction as far as that goes. It would be nice if the Press didn't come in. But I expect that's a vain hope. I'm sorry I'm blown, but we'll stick to our story—I visited you because I was a family friend. If I concealed my real status—well, people always rush to make connections."

There was further consternation among the brother and sister. This was an implication they hadn't realized for themselves. Neil inwardly was cursing his Chief.

"You'd better warn Tony," said Helen at last.

"I already have. He takes the point. Where is he?"

"Oh, at Bedlington Byrne's," said George Chapman, testy now rather than enraged. "Said something about the animals."

Neil felt a pang of concern for Tony, which was immediately swallowed up in another sensation. Animals! He found himself on his feet.

"Forgive me," he said quickly, "but I've just remembered something I should have said to my opposite number in the Latchford force. I don't want to go but I ought to find him." He had been drinking rather quickly and there wasn't much left in his glass. He drained it. The other three got up. There was enough of his attention unengaged to be pleased when Annabel said she would walk with him to the gate.

"Thank you for the drink," he said to the other two. "I'll still be at the Red Lion for another week's holiday."

"Can I see you tonight?" he asked Annabel on the path. "I need to." It was an exaggeration, but not much of one.

"Yes."

"At seven, if I can make it?"

"Yes."

He hesitated for a moment outside the church, then went up the path. The door was locked and, cursing, he ran round to the vestry doors and knocked on them both. The sergeant came out of the main vestry and Neil told him what George Chapman had said about the poison for the wasps' nest. Then he went on to Bedlington Byrne's cottage, walking more and more quickly. He nodded to the few people in the porch of the Red Lion, without slowing down. There were police cars in the road outside the cottage, and voices in the garden. When he walked through the gate Neil saw Tony standing in the doorway, holding a cat in his arms and looking defiance at a phalanx of police personnel whose equipment was spread about the lawn.

CHAPTER 7

I

"What's the matter?" asked Neil quietly. "Tony?"

"They want to go in!" Tony's eyes raked the group with fire.

"And so they must." But he would like to spare the boy the ignominy of weeping in front of the men. "And I want to talk to you. Come here."

After the dignity of a short pause Tony put the cat down. It ran across the lawn, skirted round the slender legs of some forensic equipment, and disappeared into the border. Tony walked slowly over to Neil.

"Yes?"

"I want to talk to you."

"So you said."

"All right." Neil nodded to the men. "Is there somewhere to sit?" he asked Tony.

"There's a bench in the yard."

"Lead the way."

The rabbits were still eating their lettuce breakfast. Tony felt the tears crowding closer. It wouldn't be so bad if they came now, but it would be bad enough.

"Why do they have to go into his house?" he asked angrily, as he and Neil sat down on the rustic bench which BB affected to despise but kept there because it was somewhere to take the weight off his legs.

"I think you know why. Police have to begin in the most obvious direction. And there's something else."

"What?"

Neil was silent so long Tony lifted his sulky face and looked at him.

"What?" he asked again, more urgent and uneasy.

"Can't you think?"

"I can't think of anything that will help you," said Tony mutinously. Before this morning, Neil could not have imagined such an expression on the boy's friendly obliging face, which was ridiculous, of course. He thought briefly of Annabel at eighteen.

"You've already helped me, although you'll wish you hadn't, until you really think about it. You told me about BB's monkey."

"So?" Tony stared at him, hostile.

"There may not have seemed any reason why the monkey died," went on Neil gently, regretful the boy was too old for an arm round his shoulder, "but he was BB's monkey, and it was BB who served the wine this morning and shouted a warning to the curate not to drink it."

The eyes dropped.

"I must tell the police," said Neil steadily, "so that they can exhume the monkey and find out why it died."

Tony was on his feet, backing away. Neil's heart sank, before the scorn in his eyes.

"Tony . . ."

Neil was on his feet too, putting his hand out and grabbing Tony firmly by the arm as he turned to run away. The arm wriggled in his grasp.

"Listen, Tony, you can't defy the law. You don't have to stay here, you can run as far and as fast as you like—but after you've shown me where you buried the monkey." The struggle was becoming disagreeably agitated. "If you don't tell us, we'll dig up every inch of the garden," said Neil, and Tony's arms fell to his sides, so that Neil's hand slid away.

He forced himself to meet the expression of contempt. It was extraordinary how expressive the brother's eyes were, and how unrevealing the sister's.

Tony turned and led the way back into the garden. He went straight to the magnolia and pointed behind it. That last Sunday morning, when he had dug the hole and buried the shoe box, seemed a million Sundays away. It was as if there was a fountain in his chest, trying to gush up and out.

"There!"

He knew he was being unjust to his friend, but he wanted to hurt him.

"And—where was the body?"

Tony hesitated again then walked into the centre of the lawn and stood glaring at Neil.

"Thank you," said Neil gently. "That's all, Tony. Come back and feed the cats and the rabbits, won't you? They'll be relying on you."

"You don't have to remind me about that."

"I'm sure I don't. Now I should go if I were you. I'm afraid the Latchford police will want to talk to you eventually. I'll come and see you as soon as I can."

"Don't bother."

Tony walked slowly and steadily to the gate and out into the lane, fiercely glad through his sense of nightmare that he had managed not to cry. Only when he had passed the Red Lion and the church and was half way across the Small Green did he quicken his pace, because the fountain had begun to gush. They were perhaps tears rather of rage than of unhappiness. It was even more obscene to think that BB had killed his monkey than that he had tried to kill the curate. His hands when he held a small animal! At those times, his face!

Neil followed Tony at a distance and met John Oliver at the church gate. He told him about the monkey on the walk back to the cottage.

One of the men was just coming out of the garden shed.

"Nothing," he said.

Work was still going on in another outhouse, and in the cottage itself. Neil indicated the piece of ground behind the magnolia, and he and John stood and watched the two men who started digging.

"We've made a rough test for the cyanide," said John, "and it's there. Must have gone straight into the jug, the opened bottle in the vestry cupboard seems to be clean."

One of the men had the shoe box in his hands, and was knocking soil off. He asked John if he wanted to see it.

"No. Have it taken as it is to the lab." The other man was restoring the earth behind the magnolia.

"Check the lawn," said John, indicating.

Someone else came out of the back door, breathing deep and looking up at the sky.

"Nothing so far, sir. But we haven't finished. Bit of a penance, this one!"

"Yes, Sergeant?"

"It's the smell, sir. Old man wasn't too particular, by the look and the smell of things."

Tony hadn't given Neil a hint of this. Neil already felt a sense of loss, when he thought of Tony.

"Occupational hazard," said John cheerfully and the sergeant, forcing a smile, went back indoors.

"Lunch with me at the pub?" suggested Neil. "I know we shan't be able to talk while we're in the dining-room, but we can go up to my room afterwards if you'd like to ask me anything."

He hoped, and he was almost certain, that John Oliver would want to tell him things as well as ask them, but at the behest probably of the Chief's warning rather than of his own instincts he didn't put that into words.

John looked pleased.

"I told Jill of course not to expect me home for lunch. What a splendid idea." His expression changed. "I'm sorry you've been rumbled in Bunington, Neil. I don't mean . . ." he added quickly. "But people being what they are, they'll swear you're here for a purpose."

II

Neil had already ordered lunch for one, and there was always plenty in Jim Bates's kitchen, so he didn't feel too bad, bringing a visitor in after one o'clock. Nor was Jim Bates put out, rather he appeared gratified. He ushered the two detective-inspectors into the dining-room, leading them quickly past the still active bar.

In the dining-room there were only two couples placed as far away from Neil's table as they could be. Neil didn't recognize either of them, and they didn't particularly look at him and John.

"Tourists," supplied Jim Bates, as they sat down.

"It's a nice place," said John, indicating the sunny garden, empty of all but Christopher Corrigan under an umbrella, a small glass of light brown liquid in his hand instead of his usual half pint of beer. Neil felt a shaft of interested surprise.

"With it all looking so open and shut," he said, "are you interested in uncharacteristic behaviour?"

"If you've been here long enough, and been observant enough, to spot any, you really are worth your weight in gold!"

"You are interested, then?"

"I must be."

Neil gestured through the window.

"That old boy is the senior churchwarden. Owns a lot of Buning-ton land. Memorials in the church to locally illustrious ancestors. Mean as muck. Comes in only in the evenings, and only for a half of bitter. Now he's sitting in the garden at lunch-time, drinking a short."

"He must have been put out."

"Yes, and you'd think if it had anything to do with him he'd have taken himself off home as quickly as he could, and steadied his nerves there. Not invited comment."

"So you would. But one files it away."

"Can I ask you what horrible thing you discovered in the church woodshed?"

"You can ask me anything you like, Neil, and if I can I'll tell you. We found nothing, nor any traces of the stuff. Now we must try and find what did happen to that wretched lethal bottle, find some-one to admit to actually putting it back in the shed after it had been used on the wasps. The trouble is, it was such a damn fool thing to do—if it was done—that the idiot responsible is unlikely to own up."

"And if he does—will it really help?"

"Probably not."

"And if the old man dies without speaking?"

"I know. But if ever there was circumstantial evidence . . ."

Jim Bates in person put their roast chicken and vegetables in front of them. Neil found he wasn't hungry and that his sense of outrage had left him with a slight sickness to which alcohol was more sympa-thetic than food. But he made himself tackle the heaped plate.

"This is good," observed John Oliver.

"It always is. Circumstantial evidence, as you say. The warning at the crucial second first and foremost, of course. But also the ani-mosity of the man, it appears, to the whole local establishment. And the vicar according to Tony Chapman had recently suggested to Bedlington Byrne it was time he retired from his duties at the altar. Perhaps he had baited his trap for the vicar personally and he cried out when his slow wits showed him it was going to be the wrong victim."

"That sounds quite likely. And if the monkey was poisoned . . ."

"Yes. John . . ."

"What is it?"

"Look . . ." Neil, half way through, gave up and pushed his

knife and fork together against the rest of the food. "If the monkey's poisoned it would seem like additional proof. But from the attitude of the boy—Tony—it should point the other way."

"What on earth do you mean?"

John had left nothing but a clean bone. It was disconcerting how one week in a place could make the difference between being able to eat and being too queasy to manage it.

"To the boy—the idea that this old man could have planned to murder is—well, it's obscene. And that he could have tried his idea out on an animal is even worse. All week the boy's been prattling to me about the old man's huge bark and tiny bite, and his fanatical love of animals. The boy's highly perceptive . . . Oh, heavens, John, this isn't counter-evidence, I know, but I've got to know the boy. I'm glad this isn't my pigeon, I can tell you."

John Oliver said slowly: "Children even more than adults, I think, tend to believe what they want to believe. My James lost a few bits and pieces at school—coins, pencils, a book or two. So did some of the others. Suspicion fell on the laddy whom James had appointed his best friend. James swore black and blue it couldn't be his friend Rodney. He *knew*. Then Rodney was caught *in flagrante delicto*."

"How did James take it?"

"Not very well, I'm afraid. And it wasn't the sort of lesson I particularly wanted him to learn—at that stage, or ever. We had to work very delicately to heal the breach."

"Yes. I suppose it must be the same story. But you'll take your own impression from the boy. I have an idea he'll be the only one to speak up for the old man."

"Why so friendly?"

"I think it's a protective instinct, although this is very rough and amateur psychology. The boy lost his mother at birth and was brought up by what I think is a rather preoccupied and short-tempered father, a hyper-efficient aunt, and a sister too young to be motherly and too old to be a pal. He could have been short on compassion, but he went the other way. He simply sees himself as the old man's only friend, and that's quite a realistic view."

"Yes. What astounding luck that you were here!"

"I'm not so sure. Oh, I'm not thinking of my own point of view—although I certainly am *not* sure about that! No, what I was meaning is that I may fog a clear issue. Any news of the old man or the clerics?"

"I haven't asked for any yet."

He looked at Neil and Neil said: "The boy has fallen out with me, of course, but I'll try to run him to earth this afternoon and take him to the hospital."

"If you would. I suppose if anyone could coax the old man to speak, it would be the boy."

"Without a doubt, I should say."

"I've sent someone to wait by the old man's bed, of course, so even if he rambles we'll get it."

"I'm not hopeful, somehow."

"Neither am I."

III

When John had gone Neil wandered up to his room, still preserved by the geography of the house from a bar which was continuing to do fair business. He lay on his bed, staring through the open window, thinking about what seemed, for the time being at least, the complexity of his association with the Chapman brother and the simplicity of his association with the sister. He thought of the infinite number of remote possibilities in connection with the morning's outrage and the one apparent certainty, and his thoughts eventually merged into the sense of outrage itself, making him realize it was his dominant emotion.

It decided him what he was going to do next, and he got up and went out. He walked along the lane to the church, noting almost with surprise that it was still benignly hot and sunny. He left the lane to read the notice on the church door, an announcement signed by Christopher Corrigan that there would be no service of Evensong. The transformation scene in the light of day was a large plain window through which he could see, as he walked up to the vicarage front door, a sofa and a plant. Mrs. Groome opened the door to him. Neil had seen her radiance as evidence of an abundant, perhaps slightly ingenuous, delight in being alive, and its slight diminution now, a comparatively subdued quality in the movement and the manner and even, it seemed, in the brilliance, made him think for a moment of a sensitive creature whose questing antennae had been bruised and drawn in. This image, allied to the real but painfully summoned smile of welcome which held, he thought, a general compassion, strengthened his impression that she was as good as she was beautiful. All this he was aware of before either of them spoke.

Mrs. Groome said, as her smile reached its warm zenith, "How good of you to come, Mr. Carter!"

"I hope your husband is home again."

"He is. He's even had a little to eat. Come in and see him, will you?"

Her voice too was beautiful, low and soft and warm.

"I only came to inquire . . ."

"Nonsense, you must come in. He isn't ill."

His reluctance didn't really stem from politeness, it was that he didn't want to see that look of pain again, or watch the vicar struggling with his sense of outrage. The thought of it made his own feeling seem like an impertinence. But he had to follow her, across the hall and into a large room with an open door on to the garden.

The vicar, in a short-sleeved shirt and old flannel trousers, was sitting by the door, his feet on a stool. His right hand was bound. Neil went slowly over and stood looking down at him. He said, "I'm so very sorry."

The pale eyes looked back at him, in apparent serenity. But with the Reverend Ernest Groome, it was the voice which was the window of the soul. A window shrouded, now, against the possibility of curiosity or embarrassment.

The vicar said calmly: "Thank you, Mr. Carter. And thank you for doing all you did. It was mercifully fast and efficient."

"Mercifully?" He had repeated the word before he knew.

"I must thank God for his mercy this morning, rather than upbraid him for his terrifying leniency."

"Surely you upbraid—whoever it was—for his terrifying outrage!"

Again, Neil had spoken before he knew. The memory of his schoolboy reaction to clerics was no longer inhibiting.

"I grieve for him. What agony of soul! And if he dies without contact . . . They told me at the hospital that the prognosis was poor."

"You mean Bedlington Byrne?"

The spiritual situation was obscured by his detective's reactions, like the sun by a sudden mean little cloud.

"I'm afraid I do."

"Tony Chapman won't have it," said Neil, forcing both a lightness of tone and his slight smile.

"It's a cruel lesson," said the vicar, "and not one he needed to learn." Neil thought of what John Oliver had said about his son. "But if Tony was right . . ."

"If he was right?" Neil felt a tingle in his spine.

"Think of the implication, Mr. Carter!" There was sweat on the pale forehead. The vicar got a handkerchief out and touched his temples. He looked dangerously tired and unhealthy.

"I must leave you now," said Neil.

"I regret . . . I didn't ask you to sit down."

"Not at all. I merely came to find out if you were—all right." He said the last two words reluctantly. They were insultingly wide of any possible mark. But the vicar smiled.

"Thank you, I am. And Mr. Darcy. We'll talk again, Mr. Carter. Are you having anything to do with—the inquiry?"

"No. It belongs to the Division in Latchford. But I have another week's holiday in Bunington."

"Good. I shall look forward to seeing you again, for a longer meeting." He made a move to rise but his wife came forward energetically from the doorway.

"Don't get up, Ernest. Mr. Carter won't expect it. I'll see him out."

"Goodbye, then." A little of the old sense of shortcoming had returned. Without reciprocating Mr. Groome's expectations of further contact, feeling clumsy, Neil followed the vicar's wife to the front door.

"I'm glad he's all right," he said to her.

"He is. He could even take that. But he shouldn't have to!" The flash across her eyes showed that she did not share her husband's acquiescence. She smiled again. "Thank you so much for coming."

The house was homely yet elegant. There didn't seem to be any evidence of children. He would have to ask Tony. If he still could.

Neil quickened his pace at the vicarage gate, and went on over to the Small Green. He was glad to see Helen Chapman in the garden and not, at that point, Annabel.

"Tony?" he asked, leaning on the gate.

"He's back at the old man's cottage, bothering about the animals."

"That's nice of him."

She stopped digging and straightened up.

"Yes, it is."

"I've just seen the vicar." He watched her hand holding the spade. It trembled noticeably, but the more dramatic effect was the brief whiteness of her high-coloured face.

"He's—all right?"

"He appears to be. A strong character."

"Oh, yes, Mr. Carter." She made a token jab into the earth.

"There's something Tony'll want to ask you," said Neil. "Your answer will be important to him."

"What is that, Mr. Carter?" asked Tony's Aunt Helen, it could have been ominously. She had recovered. She could not be crossed. She could probably not be told. He wondered for an uneasy second if he was going to make things worse rather than better. But he had to go on. Perhaps he could help his case by appearing to ask a great deal and then retreating . . .

"I gather Bedlington Byrne is unlikely to recover. Even if he lives it's hard to see him ever being other than pretty helpless. He won't be able to see to his animals. There are three cats, and two hutches of rabbits."

She gazed at him sternly.

"Really, Mr. Carter, haven't you already put me to enough inconvenience!" He gazed back at her, and saw her immediate regret. "I'm sorry, I shouldn't have said that and I didn't mean it, but if you are suggesting I should invite Tony to transfer Mr. Byrne's menagerie to this house . . . I would very much appreciate it if you will not take it upon yourself to encourage him!"

He heard himself laugh. "Oh, no, Miss Chapman, I wouldn't be so impertinent. All I was going to say—to you, and not to Tony—was that there is one very young cat which Tony seems to be particularly fond of. The old cats are creatures of habit and sleep in their boxes most of the time. As long as there's a plate of something to eat they'll be all right. The young fellow though will roam about with no one in the house, perhaps get himself run over. Tony will be miserable." She was still staring at him. "He's miserable enough now," said Neil.

"He's often miserable," said Aunt Helen, getting to work again. "It's time he taught himself to control his emotions. But he *is* a good, kind boy." When she bent away from him Neil could see a half inch of pink slip under her skirt.

She didn't turn round as she said: "He can bring the kitten here —if it'll stay and if the old man or the police say it's all right. He's been on at me for months about having an animal and I'm worn down. He'll have to make arrangements about its feeding when he goes to boarding-school, because I'm so often out."

"It'll be settled by then."

She turned round again and straightened up.

"It's much simpler to arrange things for other people than for one-self, isn't it, Mr. Carter?"

"Yes." He grinned, eventually making her smile back at him. "Can I tell him?"

"If it will please you. And now allow me to get on with my work. I have a meeting at four and I'm nowhere near my target."

His elation had worn off by the time he had passed the Red Lion and entered the far lane. For the first time, too, he wondered if he had had it somewhere in mind to buy back Tony's approbation. He didn't think so, but whether he had or not, remembering the boy's face when he had last seen it he knew that with or without his successful intercession for the cat he could have lost Tony's friendship.

There were no cars now outside the cottage. Neil went in at the gate and looked round the empty garden. He didn't call out, he wanted to come on the boy unawares so that at least he would see him. The front door was open but he went quietly round the side of the house, past the magnolia tree with the freshly turned earth behind it, and into the yard. Tony was sitting on the rustic seat with Timmy on his knee. Neil stopped instinctively, but the boy made no move to run away and there was no expression on his face as he stared at Neil. Neil slowly resumed his advance, and sat down. Tony remained motionless, and Neil thought of Annabel on the white seat in her father's garden, not making room for him. Maintaining his silence he stroked the cat's head.

"I'm sorry," mumbled Tony.

"What's that?"

He had heard, but he was so surprised he wanted to be sure of it.

"I'm sorry. It wasn't your fault. You were only doing your job. And you didn't know BB."

Neil was amused at his relief.

"That's very fair of you. It must have been awful. Like a nightmare. And I *was* in a sense betraying your confidence over the monkey. Only I had to."

"I know."

"That's all right, then?"

"If it is with you?"

"Of course." Neil rumpled Tony's hair, and thought the head butted against his arm. "Can you cope with the food for the animals?"

"Except on the financial side." The young cat struggled free and disappeared across the yard. "Could the police give me an allowance?"

"For the time being, until we see . . . I'm certain they could." He handed Tony a couple of pound notes. "That's to be going on with."

"Thanks!"

"There's something else." He was dismayed to sense the reflex flinch in the arm beside him.

"What?"

"I just saw your Aunt Helen now when I went to Wesley House to look for you. She told me you could take Timmy home. If Bedlington Byrne agrees. And if he can't, the police."

"Aunt Helen said!"

"She did."

"You persuaded her."

"Never! I don't think one could, anyway. She said she'd been coming round to the idea."

"I thought she never would. I'd given it up, but I've been worrying about Timmy. He needs company or he'll wander and get into trouble. Oh, that's terrific!"

"It might be tricky at first, he'll come back."

"I suppose so. But it isn't far and he's fond of me. He knows me."

"Would you like to go and see BB?"

"Could I, do you think?"

"If you come with me you could. I'm going now."

Neil helped Tony to renew the rabbit food and put meat and fresh milk out for the cats. Fortunately there was a cat flap on the back door. Then they went to the Red Lion and collected the car. Tony knew the way to the hospital. The constable at the bedside, after shaking his head at Neil, went to stand in the corridor while Neil and Tony were in the small single ward. The old man looked, to Neil's unmedical and unfamiliar eye, much as he had looked lying beside the altar in the morning, but Tony whispered, "His face has changed."

BB was on a drip. Tony touched the horny hand which was motionless on the coverlet. There was no response.

"It's not cold, though," said Tony. "BB," he said, to the blank dark face through which came a regular noisy breath to stir the luxuriant moustache and give a macabre illusion of mobility. "BB! I'm looking after the animals. It's all right. You'll see."

He only then remembered, staring down at his friend, what BB was supposed to have done. He still couldn't believe it. He had thought that perhaps, when he came into the hospital and looked at BB in the light of what he had been told, he would have believed it, but he didn't. He would have to mention to the detective, when they left, the alternative. It would be very difficult, but he would have to do it, even running the risk of Neil laughing at him.

"BB!"

There was still no response. It was clear the old man no longer had any way of seeing or hearing. Neil and Tony didn't speak until they had driven out of Latchford and Neil had stopped the car in a lay-by which gave a long view of pastoral countryside.

"They don't think he'll get better," said Neil.

"If he doesn't get better than that, I hope he'll die. I'm glad he doesn't know what people think."

"He certainly doesn't know that."

"Mr. Carter . . ." Tony was kicking his foot against the side of the car. The regular relentless sound could become irritating.

"What is it?"

"There's something else . . ." He felt Neil tense.

"Something you haven't told me?"

"Oh, not in *that* way. It's just . . ."

"Something you don't want to tell me?"

"Not if you're going to . . . But I have to tell you."

"Then for goodness' sake get on with it. I'm listening."

"It's something I've got to believe because I'm sure BB didn't do it. He couldn't have done it."

"What did happen, then?"

"A miracle," muttered Tony.

"What?"

"A miracle!" said Tony again, stoutly this time.

Neil understood what the vicar had meant when he had told him to think of the implication. Tony was looking at him.

"You don't think I'm crazy?"

"No," said Neil slowly. "No, I don't."

"Do you believe in miracles?"

"I don't disbelieve." It was like the Creed. He didn't disbelieve, and in the last few days he had sometimes thought he would like to believe. Yet his own image of himself would have been scornful. It was strange.

He said gently: "But your lone voice is the only one telling me there isn't a far easier thing to believe in than a miracle."

"Why should it be easy?" Tony glared defiantly. "And I know more than one person who might have wanted to kill the curate."

"You do?" Neil tucked the remark away.

"There was no reason why BB should want to."

"But he might have wanted to kill the vicar. Would he have known the vicar had asked the curate to take the service?"

The eyes dropped. "Probably not." Tony looked up again. "But the others would. Mr. Arkwright. Mr. Naylor." He glared defiantly at Neil. "And the vicar himself, of course."

"Of course," agreed Neil steadily. "And I've just thought of another thing. Perhaps BB knew who had done it, even if he hadn't done it himself. So that he would know the wine was poisoned. Either through being in league with someone, or through having seen something he shouldn't have done."

"You can forget about being in league with someone," said Tony positively. "BB couldn't have been. I mean, there isn't anyone. I suppose he just might have seen someone doing something sinister in the vestry, only I've never known him go in there unless he was going to get ready for the service, and then it's always at the last minute. And he couldn't have overheard anything, because he never goes anywhere where there'd be people talking and he's deaf anyway."

"If he'd seen something he mightn't have realized what it meant and the penny only dropped when he saw the curate about to drink. That's possible, isn't it?"

"It's possible, I suppose, but I *honestly* don't think . . ."

"You think it's a miracle, then?"

Tony considered, watching Neil, but no longer afraid he might be trying to hide amusement, taking his grave intent look at face value.

"I think I do," he decided at last, "because he didn't poison the wine, and I just can't believe he saw anyone else do it." He considered a further moment. "I'd rather you didn't say anything to anyone, Mr. Carter. I shan't."

"I won't and you needn't, of course. It isn't evidence."

"The police will want to talk to me, won't they?"

"Yes."

"Shall I stay off school tomorrow?"

"Not unless they ask you to."

"Will you ask about Timmy?"

"In the morning, if not tonight."

"I'm tired, somehow," said Tony.

"So am I."

Neil dropped Tony home, then lay on his bed through the early evening. At his request he and Annabel went to the Frog again. There was no dancing, as it was Sunday, but he was able to touch her because they sat side by side behind their small table. He had to ask her how she had felt that morning.

"Awful," she said.

"So did I. I saw the vicar and he talked about God's terrifying leniency."

"What a phrase."

"Yes. But I know what he means. Someone took the most terrible advantage . . ."

He stopped, surprised and belatedly wary. This was never the sort of thing Neil Carter thought about, let alone spoke of. But she was caught up elsewhere.

"Someone? You mean Bedlington Byrne!"

"Tony doesn't think so."

She stared at him in surprise.

"Are you considering that?"

"I'm not considering anything. Thank goodness it isn't my responsibility."

"But there's no alternative to that old man. He shouted a warning."

"Yes." He had no impulse to say anything further.

Later, in the dark glade, he thought he learned more about her relationship with the world, but he judged it to be of no use towards the apprehension of Benjamin Quillin. It felt like a long time since the Quillin case had been his first professional consideration.

When he drew up at Wesley House he told her about Tony's surprise at how easily Aunt Helen had agreed to let him have the cat.

"It's not so surprising," said Annabel. "I've been working on her for a long time, and she was about to give in."

"*You* have?"

"Dear Neil. None other."

She kissed him, laughing at him as she got out of the car. He hoped she was unaware of the extent of his surprise that she had interceded for her brother. Arrogantly, he had decided what she was like, and he was already proved wrong. As he parked outside the Red Lion he realized that he would never fathom her. He found her uniquely exciting and he couldn't think why he wasn't exclusively, madly, in love with her.

CHAPTER 8

I

A young man with a firm yet deferential salesman's smile stopped Neil about twelve noon next day as he loitered by the Big Green.

"Excuse me, sir . . ."

The man mentioned a national daily, then took a few steps back.

But Neil's thunderous brow was for his own naivety. He hadn't thought out how he would behave in the face of this inevitable hazard, and he should have done. Bunington was already a place of national interest.

"I believe you are a police officer from the Met," continued the young man, doggedly but not retracing his steps, "and that you were present—"

"I'm on holiday but come and sit down," said Neil resignedly. "Have a beer."

The other went a bit limp, at the unexpected end to resistance.

"Thanks."

"Look," said Neil, when they had been served by Jim Bates's thin-lipped part-time barmaid, "I just happened to be in Bunington yesterday."

"On holiday, you said?"

"Yes." He didn't say it too vehemently, because he didn't want to appear to be protesting too much. "I'll tell you what I saw, but for interpretation and all things official you must address yourself to the Latchford Detective-Inspector, John Oliver. He's around."

"Of course. But you were there."

Neil was going to say that Bedlington Byrne had had a stroke, and not mention his opportune shouting, but the young man already knew of it. Neil was not the first interviewee. He was glad when John and his sergeant arrived. More Pressmen followed them, and the small tables brought together made up into an informal Press conference. John said he hoped he could rely on them not to call on the vicar or the curate. He nodded to Neil as he said this, and then

Neil told all he could about the events of Sunday morning. John tried to wind up the proceedings by saying how fortunate his force had been that Detective-Inspector Carter was on holiday in Bunington and able to give so valuable a first-hand report, to say nothing of professional assistance at the time. Then there was, at last, a reference to the Quillin affair, at which Neil found himself feigning surprise and looking across at John.

John said easily, without a pause and as if the speaker had only just reminded him that Bunington now had two claims to notoriety, that life was full of coincidences. He assured the questioner that there were no more possible developments in the Quillin affair.

"I know that Bunington is familiar to many of you, from your visits to the unfortunate Mrs. Quillin and her family," he said mildly, looking round the attentive half-circle, "but I trust you will take my word for it that the unhappy lady has nothing further to offer you, either on her own situation or on this one."

A woman with eagle eyes asked Neil why he had chosen Bunington for his holiday and Neil answered steadily, staring into the dual beam, that the Chapmans were old friends of his family and had recommended it.

"To anticipate your next question," he went on. "No, I didn't advertise my status in Bunington, because I know how ready people are to put two and three together. The prospect was hardly fair to Mrs. Quillin."

There was the silence of set-back, and John Oliver rose smiling. "Well, ladies and gentlemen . . ."

The party broke up. Neil, John and the sergeant stood watching it disperse. Some of them got into cars and drove away, others looked as if they were not yet ready to depart.

"What do you know?" John whistled softly. "That was a very thorough and systematic alert."

"I'm groaning."

"We can only hope."

"I've been seen all over the place with Mrs. Quillin."

"So would many a man have been, if he was so lucky." John grinned at Neil encouragingly. "Any damage is done now, so don't run away. Sit down again and have a drink. Can we be overheard?"

"No." On the inside of the window behind them the neat empty dining-room would wait another half hour for custom.

"The monkey," said John, when Jim Bates had served them and

retired indoors, "died of potassium sodium cyanide poisoning. Administered in a banana."

Neil realized how little he had wanted to hear such a report.

"I'm glad you rather than I will be telling that to Tony Chapman. Have you seen him yet?"

"Not yet. But we'll be waiting when he gets home from school."

"Five o'clock," said Neil absently, thinking of Tony's naked face.
"I know."

Neil asked for, and received, John's permission for Timmy to be transferred to Wesley House. Also an undertaking that the police would make no attempt to regulate the other animal inmates of the cottage so long as Tony stuck to his intention of looking after them.

"He will."

"If the old man goes we'll have to think again, of course."

"How did you find out about the banana?"

"Under a rose bush by the front hedge we found the remains of almost a whole one. Being under the bush it had been protected from both the sun and that night of rain. The bitten end contained traces of the poison. The poor little wretch must have taken a bite, dropped the fruit and then staggered as far as the centre of the lawn, where it expired."

"Banana skin?"

"Peeled back to expose the lethal end."

"So it was put into its hand."

"It must have been."

"Tony says it used to sit on the gatepost and chatter at people. Well, he'll tell you. He'll also tell you, John, over and over again, that the old man couldn't have done it. He'll imply, if he doesn't actually say, that he was even less capable of killing his monkey than his curate. He was one of those types who prefer animals to people. But whoever did the one thing, tried to do the other."

"I think we can be certain of that, at least."

Neil stared angrily across the Big Green. A swan had come to the pond from somewhere unknown, he saw its neck gliding behind the willow fringe. A trio of mallards were preening on the bank, watched by a black and white cat which began to slink nearer across the grass. When it was half way over a woman burst out of a brilliant cottage garden, clapping her hands, and the cat, shaking its head, darted away. The woman went back into the garden and, unless he searched keenly, was lost in her floral dress among her flowers. It reminded him of cottage garden jigsaw puzzles. His thoughts since he had come to Bunington had tended towards innocent images. And now . . .

"Do you know when the poison was put into the jug?"

"Not during the service, that's for certain. It could only have been administered from a container, and there was nothing on the old man, or lying about anywhere. But the bottle of wine in the cupboard is clear, as I told you. So we can only conclude the deed was done when the wine was being prepared earlier in the morning, or while it was waiting after having been prepared, or when it was taken into the church, or during the short time it was waiting there. But as it really must have been the old man—*pace* your young friend —then I think the only real possibility is that the poison was put into the wine while the jug was waiting in the vestry. If it had been anyone not serving at the altar he or she might at least have been able to get far enough away to hide or dispose of the bottle. The old man wouldn't have had a chance, falling at the very altar steps."

"Anyone else . . ." Neil thought of Tony's dark hints. "For interest, who had access to the vestries?"

"Just about everybody in the parish, as far as we can see, through the protestations of security properly maintained. Actually, they do seem to lock up at night, at least. The churchwardens, the sacristans, and the lay reader have keys, and the vicar and the curate of course. And Mr. Adams the choir master and organist has the key to the choir vestry. So the only deterrent to going in for nefarious ends would be that if you weren't a habitué you would run the risk of being remembered."

"And the habitués include?"

"Those with keys, plus to a daytime extent sidesmen, choristers, servers, women doing flowers and cleaning, and so on. The verger's on holiday and the office of sexton is vacant. We must be thankful for small mercies. There's an architectural divide between the two vestries, as you know, but I gather the connecting door is virtually never locked. If it wasn't for that handy old man, one wouldn't know where to begin."

"Who prepared the bread and wine?"

"Different people. This Sunday it was the vicar, after he'd taken the early service. Wine is never left over from one service to another unless it's ritualistically reserved—forgive me, Neil, if you know this —so the fact that all was well at eight o'clock is significant. The lay reader John Arkwright took it through into the church. Mightn't someone have been expected to notice the smell?"

"Not necessarily. Especially not with the lid. I did when I got very near, but I'm trained to recognize it and I was looking—sniffing —for it. Nothing in the cottage?"

"Nothing."

The swan drifted back.

"I hope there isn't anything in the pond."

"Neil, there hasn't been a fatality, as they say, except for that wretched ape, but this is the nastiest case I've ever been concerned in."

"Is your Super wanting to play a leading role?" Neil asked John.

"Not so far. If something could only happen one way or the other with the old man before he starts to get the bit between his teeth . . ."

"No change?"

"Sergeant Benson was there for a while this morning." John nodded to the sergeant.

"There was no change at all, sir, for the worse or for the better. Constable Berkeley said he'd groaned once or twice in the night and made sounds, but there was no sense to them. Constable Kelly's with him now."

"When I was small," said John Oliver, unfolding his considerable length against the façade of the Red Lion, "my sister and I used to play an interminable game which consisted of thinking in turn of a noun and adjective phrase which rhymed—like hell's bells, or narrow barrow—and giving the other a non-rhyming version of it—the longer and more pompous the better—then inviting him or her to guess."

"What on earth did you offer for hell's bells?"

"Underground tintinnabulation, as a matter of history. And now I must return to my ecclesiastical pursuit."

"I give it up." Neil rose too, reluctant to lose the company of Detective-Inspector Oliver.

"Church search. Come along, Sergeant."

II

Two gentlemen and one lady of the Press lunched at the Red Lion. The lady and one gentleman left Neil alone, but the second followed him into the garden afterwards and sat down beside him under his parasol. He asked Neil if he would be interested in forming the focal point of a "think piece" entitled "Behind the smiling face," speculating on the two recent unpleasant events for which Bunington had been the setting.

"Not even if I had my Chief's permission," said Neil agreeably, ordering coffee for two. "If there was any connection it might be interesting, but not as things are. I can't believe you're so short of potential material. I wasn't involved in the Quillin case, and you know about the other one, so let's talk about the weather. I see that for today certain records have been broken."

"I gather you've made a particular friend of Tony Chapman," said the reporter sadly. He had a long nose and a permanently melancholy expression.

"Yes. He was the only member of the family I didn't really know already, so I suppose I made an effort." Village life! Who had been talking? And whoever had talked, perhaps not one but several, wouldn't have stopped short at the brother.

"Tony Chapman is the brother of Annabel Quillin, and the only friend, one gathers, of the old man who poisoned the wine." The reporter looked as if he might burst into tears at any moment.

"Both those statements are true, but two truths don't necessarily make a connection. Although I admit that they can do, such as you are almost becoming tedious and I am growing restive. To save time: I have consolidated my friendship with Mrs. Quillin. I am a bachelor on holiday."

"Mrs. Quillin is a very attractive lady."

"You bear me out."

"And no doubt a lonely one."

"I shouldn't go too far. If you want to know anything about the Quillin case you must ask Scotland Yard, and be put in touch with those people who were involved with it. I'm not one of them."

All at once Neil was furious with his Chief. It was all his Chief's fault, being too clever by half, that he found himself wriggling and scheming and dreading encounters with everyone except John Oliver. A fine holiday! He forced himself to smile at his unwelcome companion.

"Sorry to disappoint you. I'm not saying I'd deliver if I could, but the point's academic. I can't."

It was impossible to know what impression he had made. The reporter drained his cup and stood up.

"Thank you for the coffee."

"Don't mention it."

By the time the man was outside the shade of the parasol Neil had decided he would go back to London. The man limped badly, and by the time he was disappearing back into the Red Lion Neil had decided to see the second week out. Because of Annabel and Tony and the appearance of things, selfish and unselfish motives pointing the same way. As far as his Chief's request was concerned, he was now certain the idea was a dud. But he would leave Bunington for a day, just to breathe. Funny, that just a week earlier he had thought that was one reason he was leaving London.

Neil walked slowly up the garden, through the bar and out again into the hot sun. He turned down towards the shops. Outside the greengrocer's was a pile of cherries and, thinking of Tony's enthusiasm, he went inside. Behind the counter was Janet Arkwright. She was talking animatedly into a group of bunched female heads, and the breathy drone of her voice was punctuated by shrill bursts of laughter. None of them saw Neil and he watched them, listening vainly, until they dispersed in a flurry at the disapproving thunder of the word "Janet!"

Neil swung round. John Arkwright stood dark and disdainful in the doorway which led from the back of his shop. His apron, his arms full of lettuces, detracted in no way from his authority. The girls ran out, and Janet said sulkily to Neil:

"Yes?"

"I'll have half a pound of cherries, please, Janet. Good afternoon, Mr. Arkwright."

"Inspector Carter."

"I hope you haven't been troubled by the Press," said Neil pleasantly, as Janet went to serve him.

"They have made their approaches."

"I've had a sticky time," said Neil. "The Press just don't believe in coincidences. It was obvious someone had been confiding in them." He was watching Janet carefully, and saw her hand jerk over the scale.

"God is not mocked," said John Arkwright, disposing skilfully of the lettuces into an eye-catching arrangement on the sloping counter. "You'll be leaving us I expect now, Mr. Carter."

"You make it sound as if I'd got what I came for!" said Neil in good-humoured protest. "No. I shall stay, as I intended, for a further week."

Mr. Arkwright straightened up, commanding Neil's attention. "I did not mean that, Mr. Carter. I meant that I would not expect anyone to stay voluntarily in the midst of such wickedness."

"Wickedness?"

"Evil is like an iceberg, Mr. Carter. The world sees only the tip."

"From the evidence of my own work, Mr. Arkwright, I would agree with you."

The greengrocer had turned round to his shelves, and Neil looked towards Janet. She was staring at him as she held out the bag. Amused at a sensation of having been dismissed, Neil went out into the sunshine. Having decided on two or three probably useful things to do, he walked quickly back to the pub and knocked on Jim Bates's sitting-room door. Invited in, he found the landlord working on some accounts.

"Bad luck, sir." Jim Bates looked commiseratingly at Neil. He was a man who caught on with the minimum of explanation. "Coincidence is a dirty word in Fleet Street."

Jim's eyes were very keen. Neil pulled a face. "Have you the slightest idea who could have got on to the Press? Or why?"

"Just couldn't tell you on either count, sir, but there's an awful lot of folks who like the limelight. And now they're here, I reckon there's most people that'll be talking to 'em."

"Yes. I'll just have to ride it. I'm not going to be driven away before I'm ready to go."

"That's the spirit, sir. Care to relax in that chair a while?"

"Yes, Jim. But I've things to do despite my unofficial position."

Neil reluctantly left the snug, over-heated, over-furnished room which smelled of its owner, and shut himself into the telephone box. He reversed a call to the Chief and told him the events of the hour.

"I really want your guidance, Governor," he concluded. "I must have been seen around, by most of the villagers, with Mrs. Quillin. Funny if I stop seeing her now."

"Very funny, especially as you're an old friend of the family. Carry on as usual, Neil. Even, I should say, be a little publicly affectionate. The greater danger dims the less."

The Chief really was a stoic. Neil was sure he had sent him to Bunington off his own bat, and he must be worried that it was all going to rocket out of control.

"That's what I thought you'd say. Although of course we'll ensure a feature on how the lovely hapless Annabel Quillin is finding solace."

"The family connection is the net to hold that up."

Neil didn't really anticipate his own next words. "I find myself glad that my parents are dead. At least they can't be sought out and questioned about the family friendship with the Chapmans."

"Neil."

"I'm sorry, Governor." He wasn't really sorry, because in two sentences he had purged his resentment of the Chief. "I thought I'd take Mrs. Quillin to Bristol tomorrow if she's willing. And I might run up to town on Wednesday."

"I wouldn't take Mrs. Quillin *that* far."

"I wasn't intending to. I want to water my window-boxes and it's a very private operation."

"All right, Neil, so long as you're seen to be still staying at the Red Lion."

"Shall I look in on Wednesday?"

"No need, as things stand so far."

"I could take the brother to London, I suppose?"

"I can't see why not."

III

He was half way round the Small Green before he realized that the Chapman family, too, would inevitably have had some parrying to do, and that he might not be the most welcome of guests, at least so far as the senior members of the family were concerned. He was cravenly relieved when Annabel answered the door.

She led him, as on that first day, into the cool drawing-room.

"Tell me the worst," he asked her.

This time they sat side by side on the sofa, holding hands.

"Luckily I was here when the first one called, so that set the pattern for when Aunt Helen had to cope on her own. She swallowed a bit hard on agreeing that the association between you and me was— 'purely social' was one of the phrases offered, I think, another was of course 'romantic'—but she saw the sense of it. I rang Father and warned him, in case they went for him in Latchford. Luckily at that stage they hadn't."

"It's all my fault," said Neil contritely.

"You were only doing what that Chief of yours told you."

"Thank you. Will you come to Bristol tomorrow? That Chief of mine has just told me on the telephone that we would be wise to continue being social. Better that you should be billed as finding solace than as still helping the police with their inquiries. Will you come?

I've just got to get out of Bunington for a few hours. I feel I can't breathe."

"I feel rather the same. Yes, I'll come. Now, would you like to see my etchings? I have them in a little room on the ground floor with a key and a venetian blind."

"More than anything in the world. But it must be just a glimpse, because the Latchford police intend to be *in situ* here at Wesley House by five p.m., to question Tony when he gets home from school."

Neil asked Annabel to tell Tony he would be in the garden at the Red Lion when his interview was over, if he felt like coming. Tony ran through the bar soon after six, rosy-faced and with heaving breast. Neil had the Coke on the table. They didn't talk while Tony subsided and took several long swallows.

"Inspector Oliver's all right, isn't he?" ventured Neil at last.

"Yes. I keep thinking of Beppo putting his hand out and taking that banana. Trusting whoever it was. And they think it was BB!"

"If *you* don't think it was," said Neil, rather to his own surprise, "then you shouldn't feel so badly about it. They're not certain. They can't be." It was strange, after all these years, to talk about the police as though he was a member of the public.

"They think they are." Tony pushed her hair back from his damp forehead. "But Inspector Oliver *is* nice. He told me BB had made some noises but hasn't said anything anyone can understand."

"I know. Have you heard about the Press coming down in force?"

"Annabel told me. How did they get to know?"

"I was going to ask you if you had any ideas on that. Have you?"

"No. I'll think about it. Do they know why you're down here?"

"I hope not. The thing is not to be intimidated. I'm taking Annabel to Bristol tomorrow. We both of us feel we can't breathe." Tony shot him a suspicious glance. "If I stop seeing her now, or the rest of you, or go away from Bunington, as in a way I'd like to," pursued Neil steadily, "then the Press will think there's something up."

"Yes, I suppose so." Tony saw the sense of it, but an awareness of opportunities which might pass and not recur made him say, to his own immediate consternation, "I wish you'd take me to London!"

"I will," said Neil, cutting across the attempts to back-pedal. "On Wednesday, as ever is."

"School!" groaned Tony.

"Well . . . when do you break up?"

"Friday!"

"Leave it with me. In the circumstances . . . The Press . . . I'd thought of coming round tonight to see your father and your aunt to offer my apologies. Are they likely to be at home?"

"Both of them, I think."

"I hope your aunt will let me in. When you leave here, by the way, you can go straight round and collect Timmy."

Jim Bates was coming down the garden, grinning like a goblin. He slapped the local evening paper on to the table. A large photograph of a girl stared up at them. It was under a headline which read:

CURATE SAVED BY ELEVENTH-HOUR REPENTANCE.

Under the photograph, in quotes, were the words: "A wonderful man."

"Yuk!" said Tony.

"Her old man won't like it!" said Jim Bates.

Neil, reading quickly through the article whose facts were glossed by the reactions of Janet Arkwright, thought of that dark, proud face. "One version or another will be all over the nationals tomorrow," said Jim Bates.

Neil took the paper with him when he called on the Chapmans after dinner. George Chapman already had a copy. Neil was relieved and pleased to be asked in and given a whisky. Annabel was there, and he felt one of his rare pangs of pity for her, paying the additional penalty of so quiet and isolated a life. Tony had Timmy on his lap. George Chapman's fulminations were now divided evenly between the clot who had returned the cyanide to the church shed, and the other unknown who had alerted the Press.

"There was no crime," he said testily. "We might have got away without any publicity."

"I doubt it," said Neil.

George Chapman slapped at the paper on his knee.

"It'll be all over the nationals tomorrow!"

"With Tony figuring rather more prominently," said Neil.

"How do you make that out?" George Chapman's neck was as dark a red as his face.

"One persistent chappie followed me into the pub garden after lunch and pointed out that I'd made a particular friend of the brother of Annabel Quillin, who was a particular friend of the old man in this latest Bunington affair. Trying to make out a connection. I denied it of course, as lightly as I could. But Tony is, after all,

Bedlington Byrne's only friend—to leave aside Annabel's troubles."

"Annabel will figure again, too," said Helen Chapman.

"Yes, but she doesn't have to run the gauntlet of school fellows."

"When do you break up?" George Chapman asked his son.

"Friday. I break up for good on Friday, Dad."

"I think in the circumstances you'd better consider yourself broken up now." Neil thought George Chapman almost managed to elevate annoyance to the status of rage. "I'm right in thinking you don't want to be the focal point of your peers for such a reason?"

"Oh, no!"

"Very well."

Tony looked gratefully at Neil, and tried to hold on to his glance. He had his fingers crossed down the side of the chair, and was praying. Timmy leapt off his lap but flopped down contentedly enough on the floor.

"I'm going to London on Wednesday," said Neil, sharing the observation between George and Helen Chapman, "not to the office as I really am on holiday. Just to see that the flat's all right and, candidly, to get out of Bunington for a few hours. Might I take Tony with me? The more I'm seen with any of you, now, the more ordinary things will seem."

Helen said, "I don't see why not," and George said, "It mightn't be a bad thing," at the same moment, and Tony gave inward vent to his suspended thanksgiving.

"And I'm going with him to Bristol tomorrow," said Annabel without enthusiasm.

"Making amends or compounding my felony," said Neil, spreading his arms in mock bewilderment and bringing to bear the full strength of his rueful smile.

Tony, following with his eyes the almost tangible beam, was surprised to see the extent of the adult response.

CHAPTER 9

I

Neil woke up next morning into the realization that to be in Bunington was stifling rather than cosy. The good realization, now, was that today he was getting out of it. On this recall he opened his eyes and stared through the uncurtained open window. The sky was still unclouded blue, the sun lying where it had lain each morning since his arrival in the village, across the twin points of his feet. Beyond them, *The Times* protruded under his uneven door.

Neil jumped out of bed, pulled the paper through, and got back under the sheet with it. On the Home News page was a short factual item setting out, accurately, what had happened in St. Leonard's on Sunday. Neither his name nor his role was mentioned. The last paragraph stated merely that Bunington was the parental home of Mrs. Benjamin Quillin, whose husband was wanted in connection with the multi-million pound bank raid, and who was thought to have gone abroad.

This was undoubtedly the best first. As he dressed Neil steeled himself against the revelations of the tabloids. Jim Bates did not disappoint his expectations: all the national dailies were stacked beside his breakfast place. He grimaced at the hovering Jim as he sat down.

"Well?"

"Much as you'd expect, I suppose. This is the worst."

It was the inevitable article, in one of the tabloids, about him and Annabel. The headline was SOLACE FOR AN UNLUCKY LADY?, and the article gave a résumé of the Quillin case, of Sunday's event in Bunington with Neil's part in it, and a few vague references to him and Annabel going about together. It ended with the paragraph:

Coincidence enough that the little village of Bunington should be the setting for two events of unhappy national interest, bridged by the figure of 12-year-old schoolboy Tony Chapman, brother of Mrs. Quillin and only friend of the old man stricken in church.

Isn't it expecting a bit too much of fate that an inspector from Scotland Yard should be present in Bunington too?

All this, of course, was in addition to a lurid and blackly head-lined news account of the incident in the church, with Neil's role given its due place. There were other suggestions, in other papers, during the course of their items on the outrage, of an association be-tween him and (in four papers out of five) "the unhappy Mrs. Quillin," but no other speculation that Neil was more than a holi-day-maker, and he hoped that the one reference was the melancholy reporter doing his worst. Also that no aspiring free-lance would pick up the suggestion in that last paragraph about his reason for being in Bunington . . .

There was nothing he could do about it. By the time his bacon and eggs had given way to toast and marmalade Neil had also pushed the papers to one side and was enjoying his breakfast. He felt better still when John Oliver walked in in time to join him for his second cup of coffee. After bringing a fresh pot, Jim Bates with-drew.

"That man is a marvel," said Neil to John. "I've been grateful be-fore at the way wretched events throw up characters to compensate. Have you seen the papers?"

"Yes. Not so good for you, Neil."

Neil's euphoria was persisting. "All isn't lost, so long as no one takes up the challenge. It's rotten luck for the Chapmans though. They're being very decent, agreeing that I go on seeing Annabel."

"I think they'd prefer the idea to get round that she was consort-ing with the police socially rather than professionally—after all, it's a sort of seal on her disengagement, as it were."

"I suppose so. Anyway, I'm taking her to Bristol today."

"That'll be nice for you both. Good to get away from the village."

John smiled encouragingly at Neil, who had no idea whether or not his fellow inspector thought he and Annabel really were socially inclined. But John would never ask him, or indicate an opinion.

"How's Jill?"

"She bears up. This business has upset her."

"It must have done. How did you get on with Tony?"

"All right I think."

"He thought you were all right. Did he still persist that the old man couldn't have done it?"

"Yes, but not obstructively. Answered questions of fact readily enough. I suspect he's a bit too sensitive for his own comfort."

Before he could answer Neil saw the movement in the doorway.
"Hello, Tony!"

Tony came forward.

"What are you going to do today?" Neil asked him.

"I'm going to town with Dad. One of the office juniors is on holiday. I won't be wanted all day, though. I can go to the library and the baths. Just thought I'd let you know."

He switched his glance hastily from Neil to John.

"That was thoughtful," said John. "Have a good time, and don't worry about anything."

"No . . . Mr. Carter, do you think you could go to the cottage before you leave for Bristol and if all the food and milk and lettuce have gone—put out a bit more? It's in the larder."

"I think I could."

"Thanks!" The day shone before Tony now as an unclouded attraction. Almost. "How's BB?"

"There's still no change," said John.

"So he's no worse?"

"No."

Tony looked from John to the table to Neil. "Do you want that piece of toast?"

"Help yourself."

Tony took the remaining piece of toast and spread it quickly with generous coatings of butter and marmalade.

"There's still a policeman by him all the time," John told him, "in case he says anything. But it looks as if his brain has gone."

"What's so awfully unfair," said Tony, through the last large mouthful, "is that he'll be called a murderer for ever and ever."

"But he isn't," reminded Neil. "Nobody is, thank heaven."

"Your Dad's waiting!" called Jim Bates from outside.

"Gosh, I'd forgotten, I said I'd only be a minute. Thanks for the toast. What time tomorrow?" asked Tony, poised for flight.

"Be here at half past nine."

"We're still drawing a complete blank on bottle and contents," said John, when he and Neil were alone again.

"Fingerprints," said Neil. "I only thought about that for the first time last night. Funny how you don't think of things when you don't have to."

"We dusted the jug, of course, and we took the old man's dabs in hospital. No one else's. Despite what the lad thinks, it just wasn't called for. The old man's fingerprints were all over the jug of course. But nothing else verifiable."

"Can you slack off a bit now? I mean, go back to Latchford and get on with other things?"

"Up to a point. The men are still searching. I think we can take it that the poison bottle *was* put in the unlocked shed when the wasps had been seen to. Can you come to dinner again?"

"Thursday?"

"We'll look forward to it."

II

Annabel wore the water-coloured dress she had had on the first time Neil had seen her. That seemed an awfully long time ago. The anticipated exhilaration of being outside Bunington and district of course didn't come, because there was no magic line beyond which the Press couldn't follow them. Not that he saw any suspected persons in the village before collecting Annabel and setting off, or anything untoward in his driving mirror. But it could be. It could even be that the mysterious unofficial Press agent had heard him mention the word "Bristol" somewhere or other, and had again given the alert.

"I think we must remain public all the hours of today," he said regretfully, in his awareness of her beauty and mystery beside him. "After all, we are demonstrating, for both our sakes, a sort of innocent togetherness."

"As you say."

He could never quite decide whether he was more deflated or intrigued by her indifference. "I rather look forward to being in Bristol again," he said, switching his thoughts out of the car. "I came when I was small with my parents, and had one of those marvellous very young days which seem to last a whole summer."

Bristol, in fact, with its towering and prosperous new buildings, was not remotely as it had impressed itself on him as a child, except for some green space by the river. But he caught a glimpse of that early, indefinable excitement when Annabel, on an errand for her father in connection with his motor-mower, directed him to a small factory at the heart of an as yet undisturbed minute-scaled maze of workshops and tenements. It hummed with gentle machinery noises, and gave at the back on to a thin garden with a herbaceous border, baby clothes drying on a line, an infant asleep in a pram and a woman sunbathing on the steps of a narrow three-storey building with trailing window-boxes. When Annabel was invited through into an inner office, Neil went outside where he could be seen. He put his arm across Annabel's shoulder as they left the building, and again, later, when they walked by the river.

"It does feel better, being away," he said to her, "whether or not anybody's looking."

"Yes."

"The perversity of human nature, perhaps, but I have never more urgently wished to be utterly alone with you."

He was able to read her half smile, now, as mild approval.

They bought cold chicken, crisp rolls and canned beer, and had lunch by the river. Afterwards, as they lay back in municipal deck-chairs, Neil tried to ask her a few official questions, in which she appeared to co-operate, but there was no useful result. At least the exercise helped him to get his thoughts on his own role back into proportion, and to feel he had earned the unexpected pleasure of accompanying her round the shops. They ended up in a hotel for drinks and a good dinner. Neil even sang in the car on the way home.

"So you don't wish you hadn't gone back to Bristol?"

"On the contrary. One memory complements another. Life is rich."

He didn't sense any signs of outside interest the next day, either, when he took Tony to London. It was still hot and bright, and London seized them in a sweaty embrace.

"What would you particularly like to do?" Neil asked, turning to Tony in one of the many traffic standstills.

"I'd like to go to Parliament but I know you need an introduction for that so could we go to the zoo in Regent's Park? If there's time? What have you got to do?"

"Absolutely nothing." Neil got into gear and inched forward. "So we'll go straight to the flat and out again for lunch provisions, take our time over lunch, then to the park. We'll have an early dinner in town."

"I like travelling by public transport in London."

"That's just as well because when—if—we eventually get to the flat I intend to put the car in the garage and leave it there until we're ready to quit."

Tony didn't remember when he had last felt so cheerful, despite the undertow of depression which surrounded thoughts of BB and his animals and his struggle to stay alive. But the new images helped to keep these at bay. He received his first setback of the day on the landing outside the flat, while Neil was feeling for his key. A small blonde figure burst out of the door opposite, crying "Neil!"

Tony's jealous pang blurred his vision and it was several seconds before he realized that the newcomer, despite its jeans and smallness of stature, was not another twelve-year-old boy but a young woman. Neil turned round with a comradely smile.

"Hello, Cathy!"

"I got your note," she said, breathless with pleasure and, thought Neil in mild affection, laughing at herself for it. "You'll find the petunias have borne up. Is your holiday over?"

"Not quite. I'm just here for the day. This is Tony Chapman. Tony, meet Cathy McVeigh."

"Hello." Cathy put her hand out and Tony took it. Neil smiled to himself at how alike they were with their minute hips and open-necked shirts and caps of shining fair hair. He felt quite pleased to see his neighbour Cathy. Her devotion, after the ambiguities of Bunington, was now refreshing rather than boring. He opened the door and looked at the two hesitant figures. They were exactly of a height.

"We thought we'd have a picnic in the flat," he told Cathy, then turned to Tony. "Shall we ask her to join us?"

Tony didn't have to try to be obliging. "Yes, of course." This would have been a more satisfactory kind of sister than Annabel. Cathy had a brown face seemingly devoid of make-up and a slightly snub nose. Her eyes were very large and brown.

"Have you got anything to eat?" she asked them.

"Not yet." A sense of reassurance was stealing over Neil, which amused him as he recognized it. He always liked to think of himself as independent of home and possessions, but there was no doubt he was feeling a renewal of confidence, standing in his little hallway, looking at a favourite print.

"I'll go out and get things!" announced Cathy happily. "But you'll have to give me some money, I'm broke till tomorrow."

"What happens tomorrow?"

They followed him into the sitting-room. He pushed the window open, glancing at the obviously healthy window-box.

"I get paid for a portrait. And my salary goes in."

"Everything all right?" asked Neil, on a belated qualm. He recalled Cathy's father, encountered on the landing when she moved in a few months ago, asking him only half facetiously to keep his policeman's eye on her.

"Oh, yes. I'm glad to see you though. Tell me what to get."

"I've read a few things in the papers," said Cathy, an hour or so later, when they were relaxed in chairs beside the open window, eating bread and pâté and drinking beer and lemonade. She kept her eyes down over her plate. "And about you," she said to Tony, looking up at him and smiling.

"You know all about what happened in Bunington on Sunday, then," said Neil.

"Yes." She looked at him now. "How absolutely awful."

"I think," said Tony, "that somebody on Sunday ought to—well—vet the wine before the services. I really think they should."

"That's up to John Oliver."

"But he won't, will he, Mr. Carter?"

"Probably not."

"Well, I think he should."

"I'll mention it. Now," said Neil, "I think you could drop the Mr. Carter and start calling me Neil. Like Cathy here. Especially if the three of us are going to the zoo."

Neil turned away from the happiness that leapt in the girl's eyes. Not that Tony's were any less expressive. Tony was thinking how well Neil timed things as far as he was concerned. He had just started to be reluctant to say "Mr. Carter." Probably since the advent of Cathy, who said "Neil" at least once in every sentence.

That afternoon the innocence Neil had lost in Bunington flowered again in the centre of London. He was even, for the first time that he could remember, able just to conceive how it might be good to be part of a family. They took a bus to Regent's Park to please Cathy and Neil, on the promise to take a tube away from it to please Tony. They wandered in the bright sunshine, among the crowds, following the keepers round as they brought food to the animals, easily amusing one another, neither Neil nor Tony, at least, stopping to think about what he was going to say before saying it, completely relaxed even if consciously postponing problems. Eventually they went back into the park and found deckchairs. The weather was continuing on its unEnglish way of being warm in the evenings.

"Will you have supper with us?" Neil asked Cathy lazily.

He was aware of her shifting in her chair. "I'd love to but I can't. I'm going out for supper."

"Break it?"

"No. Not when people have catered."

"You're quite right. She always is," Neil told Tony.

"Have you two decided where you're going to eat?" Cathy asked them.

"For some inscrutable reason Tony wants to go to a certain Chinese restaurant which looks down on Piccadilly Circus. So that's where we'll eat." Squinting through the low dazzle of sunshine Neil noticed again how alike were the two sprawling figures. Except that Cathy's small breasts jutted against her shirt. Neil felt an unfamiliar sensation as he looked at Cathy's breasts, nothing like the normal sensation from such a sight, something perhaps akin to the feeling which had underlain his professional reaction when he saw Tony in the doorway of Bedlington Byrne's cottage, holding the cat and looking defiance at the gathered policemen. There were a lot of odd sensations of late.

Cathy yawned and sat up. "Are you going back to the flat first?"

"We'll take you."

"Don't be ridiculous." She shook her hair away from her face. Tony thought she was extremely attractive, and had found himself during the afternoon wishing Neil did too, wanting Neil to put his arm round her or take her hand, and not look on her, as he obviously did, as if she really was another twelve-year-old boy.

So they parted underground, on the Bakerloo Line, when Cathy went north and Neil and Tony went south to Piccadilly Circus. They got their table in the window of the restaurant overlooking Eros, a huge table on a bright turkey carpet, and both ate a hearty meal.

"I'll arrange for the Houses of Parliament," said Neil.

"Thanks. Is Cathy a good painter?"

"I'm afraid I don't know."

"But you've got that little picture she gave you!"

"I know. I like it. I don't know if she's really good."

"What does she get a salary for?"

"Teaching art. I suppose they must have broken up."

The tube journey back to St. John's Wood was too quick and easy for Tony, but they were on the road again by eight and it was only ten when they reached the outskirts of Latchford.

Neil turned to Tony on an impulse.

"Shall we call and see BB?"

"Yes," said Tony. He heard his voice strained, partly because he somehow didn't want to, partly because for several hours now he had entirely ceased to think about his old friend and felt ashamed.

The constable was in the corridor.

"The vicar's with him," he said.

"Any change? Has he said anything?"

"There doesn't seem to be any change, sir, and he's only grunted now and again, like he's done all along."

"D'you think we could go in?" Neil asked Tony.

"Yes."

The vicar made such a hasty, jerky effort to rise from his knees beside the bed that Neil wasn't sure afterwards whether he had seen him motionless there for a second or two before he was aware of them, or had imagined it. Mr. Groome lost his balance and clutched at the coverlet so as not to fall completely to the floor. Tony had to try not to laugh and it was ghastly when in that moment the vicar said:

"I'm afraid he's gone."

"No!" Tony turned away, and then was at once ashamed and turned back, but Neil hadn't noticed. After calling to the constable to get a doctor, he was going over to the bed. The old man still looked no different, except that the rhythmic sound had finished and the moustache was still. The eyes had been closed already. The vicar now was sitting in the chair by the bed, pressing his temples with a handkerchief.

"What happened?" Neil asked, drawing up another chair, while Tony came over to the bed, touched BB's dead hand, then went out of the room as steadily as he could manage.

"I came about fifteen minutes ago—as I've come twice before—and this time . . . I said a sort of absolution for him. Something I extemporized, of course, I wasn't in contact with him and he made no confession. It wasn't really so much an absolution, Mr. Carter, as a—a request for mercy. It was a few seconds after I'd finished, and was praying silently, that I realized—there was no more breathing. It was entirely peaceful."

The vicar looked steadily into Neil's eyes, and then the doctor bustled in and Neil remembered Tony. He found him in the corridor, staring intently out of a window that looked on to a well. Neil asked the vicar to drive him back to Bunington while he waited for a Latchford police officer.

III

Neil went looking for Tony next morning and came upon him at his second try, in the sitting-room of Bedlington Byrne's cottage, using the telephone. He was saying goodbye to someone and slammed the receiver down when he saw Neil.

"Hello," he said, a new expression on his face so far as Neil was concerned. A sort of closed look.

"Hello. Everything all right last night?"

"Yes, thanks. The vicar dropped me here, so I could take Timmy home."

Neil was going to sit on one of the numerous dilapidated chairs, but on inspection thought better of it.

"Come outside." They sat down on the bench in the yard. "Look . . ." What he had to say had occurred to him in the early morning, depriving him of his last hour of sleep.

"Yes?"

Searching the face which turned to him, Neil thought Tony had been crying. Tony didn't care any more if Neil noticed.

"About the animals. Not Timmy, of course," Neil said hastily, "but the other two cats. And the rabbits. Now BB's not coming back . . ."

"Don't worry about them," said Tony, looking away. "BB told me what to do if anything happened to him. The old cats, that is. I've just rung the vet."

"Tony . . ."

"He'll come and put them to sleep here. That was what BB wanted." He swallowed angrily on a sob. In the still painfully confined space of his mouth he bit his tongue, bringing tears back to his eyes. "They wouldn't settle anywhere else, they're too old. He told me to give the rabbits away if I could. Well, I can do that easily. Ginger and David Edwards between them . . ."

Neil's reaction of surprise was familiar to him, before he remembered that he had also underestimated the sister.

"We'll just have to ask the police," he said gently, "in case there's a will, and anything in it about the animals."

"I know, the vet told me that. Actually, he won't come until he gets the all clear. I hope it won't be long. Of course I'll look after them until . . . There *is* a will, Neil, one copy in his desk—he showed me once, I mean he showed me the outside of it, that it was there—and one with my father's partner."

When he had walked Tony home Neil rang Latchford to tell John Oliver, and asked him about it that night when he went to dinner. Knowing he was engaged for the evening he had taken Annabel out of Bunington for the afternoon, and had not wanted to bring her back. So it took the Olivers all of ten minutes to clear his irritability. Only Jill, with a mischievous look as Neil relaxed, showed she was aware of it. They sat in the garden again before dinner, the two older children flitting about on their last games of the day.

"We found the will," John told him. "And Bertram Hughes—Chapman's partner—has a copy, and there was nothing ever more straightforward in the world than the fact that the cottage and its garden have been left to your young friend Tony."

Neil's shock of pleased surprise was succeeded by a mental picture of Aunt Helen, saying what should be done with the legacy.

"Who are the trustees?"

"George Chapman and partner. An older will was superseded just twelve months ago. I suppose Tony Chapman had been visiting for a year or so."

"Anything about the animals?"

"Only by implication. Everything of which I die possessed."

Neil had got up to leave before he remembered one thing Tony had said.

"You're assuming now, I suppose, that there's no danger in the church?"

"You mean . . . ?"

"At the altar."

"Heavens, Neil, we are. Assuming there's no danger. The case is closed, which never was a case, my Super has said so. And if we were to—examine things tomorrow, we'd have to go on examining them until kingdom come!"

"Yes, I suppose so. Well, I'm only drawing your attention to the doubts of young Chapman, as he almost asked me to do." Neil hoped John wouldn't ask him if he had any doubts, he wouldn't know how to answer, and John didn't.

They stood in the lane outside the cottage for several moments, savouring the summer-scented warmth.

"Everyone's slightly slowed down," said Jill eventually. "Have you noticed? Even the people, like me, who are usually nearly always cold, don't have to bustle any more to keep their circulations going. And the balls of fire aren't bouncing quite so high."

Neil thought he had never felt less like a ball of fire. He was slowed down uncharacteristically, for a start, by not being quite sure what he felt about a number of things. Next day he took Tony out for lunch. The vet was at the cottage and it was an emotional occasion, Tony swinging between a wretched little boy and a first-time property owner. Neil tried to boost an unhysterical opposition to Aunt Helen's determination that the cottage should be sold as soon as probate was granted. He took Annabel out for dinner. He took her out on Saturday evening too, at the end of a day in which his pleasure in Bunington was restored, through the restoration of his uneventful routine, to the extent that he felt glad again to be staying on until Monday.

On Saturday night he dreamed he was under fire in a hot climate, and woke to the centre of a noisy storm. Rain was blowing across the room and lightning turned night to day as he staggered out of bed and closed the window. Thunder cracking overhead kept him awake for a further hour. He thought it was thunder which wakened him the next time, when he opened his eyes on to a grey square of window. It took him a few seconds to realize that the knocking was on his bedroom door and that the clock beside him said almost half past eight. When he eventually called out, Alec Naylor came into the room and stood at the foot of the bed, staring at him and noticeably trembling. Neil shut his eyes, in order to wake up properly, but when he opened them again his visitor was still there. With the second sight of him, clearly present in the flesh, apprehension flooded through his body and then his limbs, in a physical stream.

"I'm sorry." He struggled to sit up. "After being kept awake by the storm I then went heavily to sleep. What is it, Mr. Naylor?"

The little man came round the side of the bed with uncertain steps. His eyes sparkled strangely.

"Mr. Carter," he began, but his voice was so husky he had to clear his throat and start again. "Mr. Carter, I've just come from the church where I was on duty at early Communion. Malcolm Darcy—the curate—was taking the service. He drank the wine—as he must do first, forgive me if you know this . . ."

The man evidently couldn't quicken up his thoughts or his speech even for a crisis. Neil already knew it was a crisis.

"Yes, Mr. Naylor?"

"And he—he died. In a *minute*, Mr. Carter. There's no doubt about it."

Neil found himself at the other side of the bed, pulling on his trousers.

"Have you got in touch with the Latchford police?"

"I've done nothing but come to you, Mr. Carter, you were so near. And leave instructions that nothing must be touched."

"Hurrah for that, at any rate."

"I haven't rung the hospital or anything because—well, there's nothing to be done for Mr. Darcy."

Neil really noticed Alec Naylor for the first time since the church-warden had come to his bedside. He saw with compunction that he looked sick.

"Would you like to stay here and recover?" he asked as he moved swiftly about the room. "There's nothing more for you to do at the moment."

"Thank you, that's very kind of you, but no. I'll get back home—to my wife." Something in his voice made Neil look at him again, but his face was as expressionless as ever.

"I think," said Neil, "it might be a good idea if you stayed around. The Latchford police will be here in no time and will want to speak to you eventually. Ring your wife as soon as I've used the telephone."

"Yes, of course. Perhaps I will just sit here for a moment." Alec Naylor lowered himself gingerly on to the edge of Neil's bed.

"Get full length, for heaven's sake, man! Come along back to the church if you're up to it in fifteen minutes or so, but if you aren't, the police will come up to you here."

"Thank you." Mr. Naylor lay slowly back, then sat quickly upright.

"The clergy, Mr. Carter! They must be above reproach!"

"Steady on!" said Neil, stopping still for a moment in his surprise. "You can't blame even a priest for getting murdered!"

"No, of course not." Mr. Naylor was now propped on an elbow, staring at him. "Mr. Carter . . ." He moistened his lips, and Neil was reminded of their other curious encounter, at dead of night in the vicarage gateway.

"Yes?"

"Mr. Carter. I should like to say a word to you about my . . . my . . ."

Neil was ready to leave the room, ring John Oliver and then get over to the church. He heard the impatience in his voice as he turned back in the doorway.

"Yes, Mr. Naylor, what is it?"

Mr. Naylor's lips primmed even as Neil regretted his lack of response.

"What is it?" he asked again, more gently and taking his hand off the door knob.

But the churchwarden firmly shook his head. "Nothing, it's nothing. I was only . . . you must hurry, I know. The Latchford police . . . will do what they should."

Neil chastized himself as he ran downstairs, for having shut the man up. But there was no time to go on thinking about it. As he nodded at Jim Bates through the closed telephone door he realized that somewhere at the back of his mind was a grim sense of thanks that John would let him be too busy really to think about what had happened. The heavy rain quickly soaked him through as he left the Red Lion, and he was glad.

CHAPTER 10

I

He had never in his life entered a building so reluctantly. At first the church seemed to be empty and Neil was half way down the aisle before he realized that his destination was the tiny lady chapel at the end of the south transept. The first person he saw, to his reassurance, was Helen Chapman. She was in the opening of the carved screen which marked the entrance to the chapel, and stood aside in silence as he came through.

There were three shallow steps up to the altar, and the tall man lay spread-eagled across them. Neil confirmed that he was dead, glancing only once at the face, frozen in struggle. He put his nose near the chalice which lay on its side by the curate's bandaged hand, its contents burning their way in a dark narrow stream down the carpeted stairs. The tray of wafers was on the altar, and the book, pallidly lit from the small side window. The silver jug was with the water carafe in the niche in the south wall.

"I've written down the names of those who were at the service."

Helen Chapman was behind him when he turned round. She must have performed that useful office on a reflex, all the competence had gone out of her face, it looked uncertain and unbelieving. For a weird second, when he heard the strangled sob, he thought she had uttered it, but she gestured to the back of the chapel. A small fat boy wearing an alb was huddled in the last of the half-dozen pews.

"He seemed too shocked to go home," said Helen quietly, "and anyway, I thought it best . . ."

She broke off as she walked towards the boy.

"This is Inspector Carter, Michael," she said gently, putting her hand on his shoulder, "a real inspector from Scotland Yard." The short tufts of the boy's hair stood out against the grey window behind him. He lifted his red tear-stained face and stared at Neil.

"This is Michael Gordon," said Miss Chapman. "The poor boy was serving." She walked a little way down the aisle again and Neil followed. "He had hysterics, but I'm afraid that was after the event, and not in time to prevent it."

He turned to her. "Do you know who prepared the wine? And when?"

She stared at him, fear in her eyes.

"The vicar prepared it last night," she said slowly. He noticed that her hand where it rested on the knob of a pew gave a convulsive twitch. "But he hasn't been here this morning. It's his early morning off."

"Who was here first this morning?"

She didn't take her eyes off him.

"As a matter of fact Alec Naylor and I arrived simultaneously. I brought the Elements through from the vestry, and I was back in the vestry while he was arranging them in here. It's difficult, isn't it, Mr. Carter?"

"Very difficult," said Neil. "I'm afraid there's an unhappy time ahead for everyone connected with St. Leonard's."

"Where will it end?" she murmured.

"It must end here. Miss Chapman, do you mind staying with the boy until the Latchford police arrive? You know not to touch anything, of course."

"Of course."

She was herself again. Calm. Competent. She sat down in the pew in front of Michael Gordon, and turned round to watch him. Neil went out of the chapel, across the church and into the main vestry. Everything was as it had been the time before, and again he let his hand fall before it reached the cupboard door. The outside doors of both vestries were unlocked, but the keys were there and he turned them.

When he came back into the chapel, Helen Chapman had squeezed in beside the boy and had her arm round his shoulders. Neil walked past them, touching her arm as he went by, and sat down in a front pew.

As he sat there he felt nothing. It was as if his outrage had been expended the first time, and he had gone beyond it. Like a reaction to war, which recoils in horror from the early skirmishes, and then has nothing left with which to deplore the real encounter. It was only when he began to think of the repercussions that feeling flowed again. Pity and dread. Pity for the vicar denied mercy, dread of the poison which would trickle on round the village. But the curate's body so close in front of him, the blasphemed wine, might have lain on a stage.

There was another thing, which he realized through the silent moments of waiting. While he dreaded seeing the vicar, dreaded seeing the extent of the damage to that sturdy tree, at the same time he wanted the vicar to tell him the worst, to tell him if this outrage-beyond-outrage really was too much.

Too much? Too much for what? What did he mean? It had happened. Did he mean, had it shaken something—fatally? *I am the Rock*. He wanted to hear the vicar say that, knowing what had happened. But he didn't want to think so fundamentally, it made the draught blow again which he had noticed at Evensong, during the space for private prayers. He began to pray, sitting with bent head, that he might be spared such thoughts . . .

He got up when he heard sounds in the church, and met John in the entrance to the chapel.

"Miss Chapman made a list of the people who came to the service. The boy was serving the Elements, poor little sod. Alec Naylor was on duty and came to tell me, as I said on the phone. If he's not around here, he's lying on my bed."

John had a look at the body, then directed his team up the steps.

"What can I best be doing for you?" asked Neil.

John looked rueful. It was a way he tended to look, unless it was

simply that circumstances since he and Neil had met had been con-
ducive to it.

"You'll probably be doing it all officially before long," said John.
"But now—if you can just *talk* to people. Such as your friend Tony
Chapman. I'll come and see you as soon as I can."

"Does the vicar know?"

"He will do by now. I sent Sergeant Benson."

Neil was ashamed of his relief, at the same time as he somewhere
regretted the loss of a reason for going to see the vicar.

"Mr. Carter . . ."

Alec Naylor was beside them. He looked restored, although without his customary smile.

"Thanks for coming back," Neil said to him. "Will you excuse us
for a moment?"

He encouraged John along the aisle, out of earshot. "I think he
was going to say something when he was in my room, but I was a
bit short with him, feeling in a hurry, and he thought better of it.
He just said something, as I left, about the police 'doing what they
should.' Thought I'd mention it."

"Thanks, Neil, I'll keep it in mind."

"Good luck."

Neil went out into the rain and walked slowly back to the forecourt of the Red Lion, where he stood looking across the Big Green.
He was glad the world reflected his mood and what must soon be
the mood of the village—bleak, uncomfortable and cold. The sky
now was low and grey and without feature, one great stretch of
cloud. Even the abundant flowers, the glossy feathers of the mallard
drakes, were drained of brilliance. Neil felt as if a spell had been
broken. He went on standing there with the rain falling on him,
aware of freedom as no more than a broken-down door. He went inside only when Jim Bates came out to fetch him.

II

After a breakfast of coffee Neil telephoned his Chief and was told,
as he had hoped and feared, to extend his booking at the Red Lion
for a further week.

By half past ten it had stopped raining, although water drops
hung in the air. Neil left the pub again, and walked along Church
Lane. Police cars were drawn up at the church gate and the vicar,

wearing a surplice, stood in the porch with his hands raised. The stillness of the little group of people in front of him told Neil that he was giving them a blessing. Neil stood short of the churchyard, partly screened by the hedge, and watched as the people came silently away, averted faces passing questing faces at the gate. When the next group reached the vicar he saw him speak to them for a few moments before raising his hands again. Policemen were walking among the tombstones, coming and going round by the vestry doors. When the second group of people had gone away the vicar was alone and although Neil was too far off to read the expression in his face he stood firm enough, looking steadily towards the gate and beckoning another handful of parishioners towards him. Neil walked on and stopped at the gate as the vicar for the third time raised his hands. He felt that Mr. Groome was aware of him and he remained with bent head in the gateway, hearing the unheeding voices of the police where he was unable to hear the vicar, until the feet of the people came in sight down the path.

As he walked on his sense of relief was not entirely for the vicar of Bunington. Absurd as it seemed to him, it was partly for himself. He found he had dredged up a memory of indignation and dismay felt as a small boy when his mother had suggested removing from his bedroom a large old wardrobe which held everybody's best clothes. He didn't make any use of it but he liked to think it was there. That just about summed up his attitude to the Church. Not much of an attitude, yet capable of being shaken. He recalled his relief when his mother, bewildered by his show of feeling, had given in and allowed the wardrobe to stay where it was . . .

He had crossed the Small Green and was going up the path of Wesley House. His shoes were wet and dirty and he dried them on the mat as he rang the bell. Helen let him in. He had known even before he met her smile that the vigil they had shared in the church had killed the earlier possibility of hostility between them.

"Come in."

He followed her into the drawing-room. Her brother and Annabel were there. Annabel was pouring out coffee from a tall jug. She raised her head for a moment and looked at him with slight curiosity. George Chapman was walking about. His restlessness filled the long quiet room, transforming it.

"You'll join us for coffee?"

Miss Chapman's words were for Neil, but their calm firm tone, he thought, was for her brother.

"Yes, of course," said George Chapman irritably, pausing.

"Please. I'm living on it just now."

Annabel slid out of the room.

"Sit down," said Helen to Neil, putting her hand on her brother's arm. George sat down simultaneously with Neil, but remained leaning forward in his chair, his hands twisting between his knees. Annabel came back with a cup and saucer and poured Neil some coffee. They curled their little fingers together as he took it from her.

"Where's Tony?" he asked.

"On his estate, of course," said Helen.

She spoke without sarcasm but her brother said furiously, "Even at a time like this!" He leaned back in his chair as if he had temporarily relaxed himself, by letting off a little squib of annoyance.

"He couldn't do anything by staying here," remarked Annabel.

George Chapman leaned forward again, towards Neil.

"Mr. Carter, I have faced the fact that we are all potential suspects!"

"All?" queried Annabel. "Well, yes, I suppose we are, in the physical sense that anyone can enter unlocked doors. But I, for instance, would have run a grave risk of being remembered had I been seen in the vestry."

Her father looked at her in annoyance for a moment, but his principal concern was to complete his say. He got to his feet again and resumed his pacing.

"There are a number of people," he pronounced, "whose presence in the vestry would be unremarked. Helen. Myself. Agnes Catchpole. John Arkwright. Christopher Corrigan. Alec Naylor. Michael Adams."

"Very much myself and Miss Catchpole," said Helen.

"The vicar and Mrs. Groome," said Annabel, and although she was speaking, Neil was sure, to provoke her father, he experienced a chill which made him shift in his chair.

Her father, after swallowing hard and with deepening colour, said "Certainly!", looking sternly at Annabel, and Tony burst into the room, slowing down, lowering his eyes, only when he had got inside the door and recalled the prevailing mood. Neil was briefly mystified, and then realized that Bedlington Byrne had been declared innocent.

Tony had run off to his cottage to conceal his joy. Pleasure flashed across his eyes when he saw Neil, but he said good morning sedately, and sat down on a pouffe.

"Get a cup if you want some coffee," said Annabel.

"It's all right, thanks." Neil guessed he had been getting into Bedlington Byrne's—his—cache of Cokes.

"The Divisional police are at work, I take it?" asked George Chapman.

"Yes. And have been since nine o'clock."

"I'm not on duty this weekend. What about the services?"

"There aren't any. The police are all over the place, but when I came past the church the vicar was in the porch—telling people, I presume, and—blessing them. I saw him raise his hands."

"That's a fine thing!" said Helen, her colour flooding briefly back.

"I said, didn't I?" exclaimed Tony. "I said they ought to vet the wine!"

"Tony!" thundered his father, and Helen said, on an unnerved-laugh, "George, for goodness' sake don't be upset by that! Now!"

George Chapman flopped forward in his chair, dropping his face into his hands. When he looked up he was calmer than he had been since Neil's arrival. He looked solemnly at the detective-inspector.

"The police have a terrible task," he told him.

"I know, sir." Neil was glad to find he had slipped without emotional protest back into his professional role. He felt as if he had always known that eventually it would be from this stance that he would have to consider the inhabitants of Bunington. He must suspect them all, every one of them, in order to help John, help him make sure this terrible thing did end here, as in the lady chapel he had assured Helen Chapman that it would. But perhaps the timing of the end was in Helen's hands. Or her brother's. Or . . . Everyone, in his mind now, must be guilty.

"I've no official role today," he said, getting to his feet, "any more than I had one yesterday. But I'm perhaps a bit more at home in the village than any of the Latchford men. In this house for instance . . ." He turned on the full persuasive power of his eyes, smiling. For the second time Tony, noting the response of his father and his aunt, found himself almost looking for a physical thread between them and Neil.

"Of course," they both murmured.

"I'm afraid you've all got long uncomfortable interviews in front of you, there's no point my pretending otherwise. But the sooner the guilty one is found, the less of that there will be." He had never been more glad of his ability to watch without looking watchful. Not that he was noticing anything he could consider significant. "Tony is exceptionally observant, and well able to describe what he sees. I'd like to take him out in the car this afternoon and have him talk to me about Bunington and its population."

He looked at the elder brother and sister, at his most persuasive. But there was no opposition to overcome. Either they had nothing to fear from Tony's acumen, or considered they had been clever enough to disregard it. He had to keep thinking things like that about them, about everyone, to remain continuously receptive to what might be available.

"Tonight—please," he said to Annabel at the gate.

"No glade," she reminded him, shaking some water drops over them from a lilac bush and smiling.

"We don't have to have a glade," he responded glibly, immediately wondering for how long that would be true. She was still smiling when he looked back from the edge of the Green.

III

From opening time onwards Neil stationed himself at the front of the Red Lion, behind a pint. Although it still wasn't actually raining this was not an appealing spot in which to sit since the night's storm; it was damp and chilly. But his mood continued to welcome the slight discomfort, and he hoped he might encourage anyone within eyeshot of so focal a point, by his air of relaxation and availability. For a time there was no one about at all except for Jim Bates, the gardens were empty and the front doors shut. Jim was able to fill in some of the village time which had elapsed while Neil was at Wesley House: Alec Naylor had driven by, presumably on his way home; John Arkwright had passed the pub in the other direction, no doubt from his home opposite the shop; a police car had driven young Michael Gordon back to his home beyond the shops, and hadn't yet returned. But of course, if it had no further business in Bunington it would go back to Latchford without repassing the Red Lion . . .

Neil was glad to see Sergeant Benson, approaching the pub from Church Lane.

"Sir." The sergeant nodded to Neil, then turned to Jim Bates.

"Inspector Oliver would like a ham sandwich and a pint of beer in half an hour, please, Mr. Bates. He hopes you will join him, sir," he said to Neil.

"Thank you. Have you happened to notice if the vicar has gone back home, Sergeant?"

"I beg your pardon, sir?"

Sergeant Benson leant towards him, because of the noise of the siren on the vehicle grinding up the lane from the shops. Neil's gesture told him not to bother, and the three men watched as, still screaming, it came into sight. It was an ambulance. Siren and engine stopped at the same moment, and the mate leaned out.

"Nine the High Street?"

Jim Bates stepped forward.

"You've passed it, it's behind you. Above the greengrocer's."

"Thanks." The man started to roll up his window.

"Just a moment!"

Jim Bates turned round and said rapidly to Neil and Sergeant Benson,

"Nine the High Street. That's where Mr. Arkwright lives."

"Is it?" Neil was on his feet. "Why don't you go aboard, Sergeant?"

"Hold on," said Sergeant Benson, to the ambulance men. He had a murmured word into his radio, listened, spoke again.

"I'm coming with you," he said to them, as he tucked the set away.

The mate shrugged and moved up on the bench seat. "It's an emergency," he said conversationally, as Sergeant Benson squeezed in beside him. The ambulance just managed to turn in one, and bore down the hill out of sight, screeching anew. Neil and Jim Bates stared at one another. John Arkwright . . . *God is not mocked* . . .

"Must be a bit hard on you," said Jim, "not being able to do anything."

"It is, Jim, it is. Although Inspector Oliver makes it as painless as he can."

John tore by a very few minutes later, smiling ruefully at Neil out of the window of the police car.

"They went that-a-way!" shouted Jim Bates to the back of the car as it disappeared down the lane. "What do you suppose, sir?"

"I don't, Jim, I mustn't. But I can't help hoping that it's the end."

John was back long before he had dared to expect him. The police car dropped him outside the Red Lion and went on down Church Lane. John, as he folded into a chair beside Neil and was served instantly by Jim Bates, had no expression on his face, but it was as if he was holding it there carefully, like a species of mask.

"Neil," he said, after a long swallow, "when this obnoxious day has drawn to its close I might, I just might, have a hysterical laugh on the shoulder of my understanding wife. Or I might cry."

A raindrop made a tiny splash in Neil's beer, and was followed by more, and larger. Jim Bates came out to them again.

"The cottage pie is ready," he said respectfully to John Oliver. "Better for you today, sir, than sandwiches. There's no one in the dining-room."

The two inspectors got up and followed him inside. He put their cottage pie in front of them as soon as they sat down, and left them. The rain now was streaming down the dining-room window, blotting out the garden.

"I really am terribly curious," said Neil, disturbing the mound in front of him so that he felt the steam on his face.

"And I'm a bit nervous about telling you, in case I have the hysteria here and now. Which wouldn't do at all." John ate two quick mouthfuls. "Neil, you may or may not know that Mr. Arkwright's daughter—Janet—had a crush on the curate."

"I had deduced it."

"Of course. Well, when she received the news, this morning, of his demise, she ran blindly out to the nearest of her father's greenhouses, and downed what she thought was half a bottle of paraquat. She came staggering back into the house, shouting out what she had done, and of course the parents rang nine-nine-nine ambulance."

"Of course."

"When the ambulance and Sergeant Benson got there just now, they were met by a very sheepish family. They ought to be shot, because they *do* keep paraquat in lemonade bottles. But the father had gone down to investigate and found that the bottle his daughter had swigged from was in fact his wife's homemade, unlabelled lemonade with which, being teetotal, he had been refreshing himself while last working in that greenhouse. The paraquat bottle was there all right, just less immediately to hand."

The two men struggled silently for a few moments, concentrating on their plates. Neil was going to eat all of his meal, today.

"I gave them a lecture, I can tell you," said John eventually, "and personally superintended the removal of all that paraquat in lemonade clothing. And the ambulance has taken the girl off to Latchford hospital, in any event. She needs supervision for a night or two."

"Was any family ever luckier than it deserved?" The danger was over and Neil was able to meet John's eye. He hoped Jim Bates would receive the news from another source. "This crush the girl had. Was it reciprocated?"

"Those I've spoken to so far outside the family say no. The father maintains a proud silence. I rather think still waters run deep in Arkwright. The mother can't believe that it was. Have you any idea what he was *like*, the Reverend Malcolm Darcy?"

"He was very noticeable. Commanding presence. Resounding voice. And yet . . ."

"Nobody is saying much more than that about him. A curiously shadowy figure, for one so positive."

"You must be finding out *something?*"

"Externals, yes, of course. Parents live in Manchester. Rented a flat between Bunington and Little B. Twenty-eight years old. No regular girl friend."

"I had a strange sort of surrealistic hour on Tuesday night," said Neil slowly. "I was walking round the village before going to bed—some time after midnight, I suppose. It was a marvellous night. Well, they all are just now. I stopped by the church gate, and a light went on in the vicarage and I saw Mrs. Groome drawing the curtains. And just then Alec Naylor nosed out of the vicarage gates in his car, telling me he'd been putting something in the vicar's letterbox. He seemed—well, a bit ill at ease."

"How rather strange."

"It's not all. I then went for a walk round the Big Green, from right to left when you come out of the pub. When I was almost round I saw Janet Arkwright come up Church Lane and go home—only I didn't know who she was, either, at that point. She was breathing rather distressfully so I fell discreetly in behind her and followed her until she disappeared among the shops."

"Unfortunately," said John with a sigh, "we can't afford to pass up on the unlikeliest sources of information. Will you say it all again officially to the sergeant afterwards?"

"Of course. I don't suppose it contributes anything. But the girl at least doesn't know I saw her. What of the Gordon boy?"

"We had to search his person, of course, and the environs of the lady chapel while he was still around, and I gather that when he was taken home he whined to his father and there was a quite unpleasant scene for my Sergeant Amery. Nothing was found, but Mr. Gordon is a sidesman and felt his Christian character was being impugned. Hey ho!"

"Miss Catchpole might be a useful source of information. That is, if she didn't do it herself, of course."

"I've spoken to her and she is, in several directions. Including the old boy Corrigan who you observantly told me didn't usually drink whisky in public at lunch-time. I gather the companion he had for most of his life until the man died a year or two ago held the place of a wife."

"Is that how Miss Catchpole put it?"

John grinned. "The first time round, yes. When I asked her to be more explicit, she was. Now, she also told me that the curate took tea with Mr. Corrigan a couple of weeks ago."

"The sole invitee?"

"So far as she knows and I haven't pursued this line anywhere else yet. He was visiting her and the conversation came round to Corrigan Hall and the beauty of the gardens, and the curate said he was about to have an opportunity to judge them for himself because . . ."

"And I suppose even then Miss Catchpole couldn't help wondering . . ."

"Well, she knew what she knew. And the curate was a golden boy, undeniably. Which isn't to say of course, for five minutes . . ."

"Of course not. And your interest in the senior churchwarden would be if the curate was asked to play and *didn't* . . ."

"Just so. The wine in the cupboard is still clear, by the way," said John. "Only the jug contaminated, as last time. The cyanide bottle hasn't come to light. No recognizable fingerprints, except for the lad's and the curate's, on the jug. The expected melange on cupboard door and table."

"I gather the vicar prepared the Elements last night."

"Yes. I'm off to see him when I leave you."

Jim Bates came to remove their plates. Neil looked at him carefully, hoping he was deliberately keeping his face averted.

"Heard about the Arkwright girl, Jim?"

"Yes, sir."

Jim Bates left the room still without looking at them. Neil and John grinned at one another.

"We must take all the solace we can get," said John.

"When will you have finished in the church?"

"By tonight, I hope."

"Won't there have to be a reconsecration, or whatever? And before the old man's funeral?"

"You're right." John smiled at him admiringly, perhaps with a touch of curiosity. "The bishop's being brought quietly in this evening and the proceedings won't be advertised. We were glad to go along with the vicar on that!"

"But you'll be there?"

"Yes. Because one or two of our *dramatis personae* will be. I'm sorry, Neil, but I don't see how I can ask you—"

Neil cut in, hastily and truthfully disclaiming any idea of it.

"I thought of taking Tony Chapman for a drive this afternoon, if you're not wanting him."

"I shall want him, of course, but you'll do far more with him, and I'd like your commentary beforehand. Please do take him, Neil. And now I'd like to hand you over to Sergeant Amery."

The two men were just getting to their feet when Jim Bates announced a visitor for Inspector Oliver. In the doorway they met a small man with a small dry wrinkled face, Neil thought like an amiable toad. John introduced his superior, Superintendent Crosby. The superintendent looked keenly at Neil as they shook hands. His hand, wrinkled and dry, reinforced the toad image.

"Inspector Oliver has explained to you," he said to Neil. "We are neither too proud nor too provincial to disdain any help you can give us."

"As a matter of fact, sir, I'm about to make a short statement to your sergeant."

"I shall be pleased to sit in on it." The superintendent's eyes flickered across at the table the inspectors had left, then fastened on John.

"Where were you making for, Oliver, after your working lunch?"

Neil didn't know whether toads normally bit, but thought this one had just done so.

"I'm going to see the vicar, sir."

"You can wait while Inspector Carter makes his statement, and I'll come with you."

When the Latchford men had left it was still too early to go for Tony, and the now familiar frustration of Neil's curious role abruptly descended. He mooched into the hall. From there he heard the voices in the bar, and remembered that, during English licencing hours at least, there was always something potentially useful he could do. He went reluctantly through, and spent the next hour at the scant mercy of a voluble family from Bristol on a day in the country. He sat where he could see the whole room, but no one from Bunington came into the bar. It could be that at last something had happened in the village bad enough to silence every adult tongue.

CHAPTER 11

I

"Tell me all you can about people," said Neil, having stopped the car where there was a long and consoling view.

He opened his window. The rain no longer threatened and the air smelled sweet. The sky had retreated and pale straggles of light attested to the thinning of the cloud.

"And so that we don't feel embarrassed with one another," he went on, "or not so embarrassed as we might, I'll say right away that by asking you that, I'm asking you about your father and your aunt. I'm sorry, Tony. Perhaps we should get them over first." He realized the enormity of it. "Heavens, this is awful."

"No," said Tony earnestly. "Well, I mean, it is, of course, but you have to ask me, I'm your only real contact in Bunington. Except for Annabel," he added grudgingly, "and she wouldn't be any good on things like this, she doesn't notice people, especially not people in Bunington."

"There you are, you see, *you* notice things *and* people. You're our first hope—the Latchford police and maybe Scotland Yard eventually —and I'm taking advantage of you. You're feeling better anyway, aren't you, because of BB?"

Tony felt his face flush.

"Did it show?"

"To me."

"It's stuffy in here. Can we go in the field? It won't be too wet under the trees."

"I was going to suggest it. Grab that ground sheet on the back seat."

There was a gate, and a very narrow path. It led straight along beside barley to the crest of a field, then disappeared, with the declining slope of the land, before the far horizon. They sat down in its first green enclave, under the branches of a hedgerow tree.

"I *knew* BB hadn't done that," said Tony, flopping full length on the ground sheet. "As if he could have poisoned Beppo! I suppose whoever did do it, did poison him?"

"I think we must assume that."

"Well." Tony rolled over on to his stomach and propped his face in his hands. "I couldn't bear to think that Dad or Aunt Helen had done either thing, but I honestly can't believe that they did. I mean, I can't help feeling that if they had—I'd have felt something. *Something*. They'd have been—different in some way. Well, they haven't been. Oh, they've been upset of course, especially Aunt Helen, but otherwise they've been just the same as always.

"There's been nothing to do with the clergy?" pursued Neil reluctantly, thinking of Helen Chapman's face and hands. "I mean— there haven't been any—problems with the vicar or the curate in any way, nothing unusual's happened which might throw some light on things?"

"Gosh, no!" Tony sat upright. "Aunt Helen works awfully hard in the parish, and the vicar's always saying how marvellous she is."

"She gets on well with him, then? And with Mrs. Groome?"

"She and Mrs. Groome run the Church Women's Fellowship together, and . . . and . . . she goes to the Bible Study meetings at the vicarage, and—"

"Yes, of course."

"When I think about Beppo," said Tony, "then I just can't think that *anyone* . . . oh!"

"What is it?" asked Neil quickly.

A huge furry bumble bee hung on the lowest pink flower of a hedgerow plant, making it swing. They both watched it.

"Only . . ." Tony passed a finger lightly over the velvet back of the bee. "Mr. Arkwright suggested once to BB that he should make some money out of his rabbits by killing them and selling them for meat and fur. I remember it because BB was so furious. He nearly went mad."

"That doesn't make Mr. Arkwright a potential monkey-poisoner. A large number of people see rabbits in that light."

"I know," muttered Tony, tossing over on to his back and lying looking up at the tangle of branches. "Mike Adams shoots them."

"Can you think of anyone who positively wouldn't shoot animals or bring about their deaths for any reason? Apart from yourself?"

"No," said Tony dispiritedly, after a moment's pause. "Not to be sure they wouldn't." He sat up again. His heart was so loud he wondered Neil didn't remark on it. "There's something else I ought to tell you about Mr. Arkwright."

"Yes?" Neil was aware of the tension.

"He's very strict with Janet."

"How old is she?"

"I think she's seventeen." Tony flopped down again and twisted over on to his stomach. "I looked out of the window the other night . . . the night you were . . . Tuesday. About half past twelve. I saw Janet Arkwright on our garden seat. I went out to her," said Tony, "cos she seemed . . . well, she was sort of strange. Her father had hit her because of her being in love with the curate. She showed me the bruises. On her arm and shoulder. They were *bleeding!*"

"What was she doing in your garden?" asked Neil, as matter-of-factly as he could manage.

"I asked her that, and she said it didn't matter where she was, and she'd just seen the seat."

"What happened then?"

"She just—got up and said she was going home. I saw her go round the Green and then I went to bed."

"You saw blood on her arm?"

"Yes. It looked black but it was blood all right. Everything was black and white because of the moon. There were two big bruises, and sort of cuts in the middle of them."

"Has she ever come into your garden at night before?"

"I've never seen her there before."

"But you often look out of the window during the night?"

Tony felt himself recoil, before a snake-like stranger. Neil saw the reaction, and reproved himself. He said quickly,

"Or was it just that you heard a noise or something?"

"No. I was just awake, and the moon was so bright." He hesitated, then went on. "I've heard Janet boast about going out at night when she's supposed to be in bed." To his annoyance he felt himself blushing. It was hearing Janet boast that had given him the idea for his infrequent rambles in the summer dusk. But Neil didn't seem to have noticed anything.

"What's *your* opinion of Mr. Arkwright, Tony?"

"He always looks rather cross I think, but I only know about him really from what other people say. Dad says he's very stubborn about church and village things. Well, Dad is too I suppose. Dad's got a bit of a bad temper, I expect you've noticed."

"I have, yes."

"But I just can't imagine him doing anything wicked . . ."

"And poisoning is very wicked. And the crime of a cool head. No. And anyway, we've exonerated your father and Aunt Helen." He hadn't of course, he couldn't, certainly not Helen, although Tony's sense of continuing normality at Wesley House was very persuasive. "Go on about Mr. Arkwright."

"I remember Janet saying once that he took a whole fortnight to forgive her when she missed the last bus home and got in an hour later than she'd said she would. He'll be furious about her writing that article. The choir have a joke about him. He preaches sometimes, and he always brings in about the righteous wrath of God. So he gets called the righteous wrath."

"Um. But Mr. Arkwright can take vengeance into his own hands. Mrs. Arkwright?"

"She's nice. Always the same. Another thing about Mr. Arkwright."

"Yes?"

"He could have been the one who saw the curate and Mrs. Groome in the vestry."

"Who—what?"

"Gosh," said Tony, flooded by a mixture of relief and amazement. "I was wondering how I could tell you—I knew I ought to—and then I told you without noticing."

"You haven't told me anything yet."

"It was after church the Sunday before you came. I was going to see BB and then I remembered I'd left my plate"—Tony bared his teeth in explanation—"on the washstand in the choir vestry. I came back for it and as I was putting it in I saw—the connecting door was open—I saw"—he dived in—"Mrs. Groome and the curate and the curate put his hands round her face and I thought he was going to cry and she was smiling—sort of not bothered and she took his hands and sort of brought them down and held them out in front of her and then I heard someone sort of shriek in the church—the other side of the vestry door—and Mrs. Groome heard it too and a shadow moved and I ran away."

Tony tore up a handful of grasses and scattered them, not looking at Neil.

"A sort of shriek?"

"Well, yes. It was beastly."

"A shadow moved?"

"The door into the church was open. Whoever it was must have been there."

"The sun from the south, yes. You didn't see who it was?"

"No. The way the door goes—you can't see from the choir vestry."

"But you heard. Male or female?"

"I don't know. Honestly, I don't know. I've tried to think since but it was just—a shriek."

"Um. Anger?"

Tony considered. "I suppose so. Sort of agonized. Anyway, it made me scared."

"You've no reason for thinking it was Mr. Arkwright?"

"No!" Tony spoke with sudden eagerness, seeing a chance to even things up. "It could have been Mr. Naylor!"

"Mr. Naylor?"

"Well, he's in love with Mrs. Groome. He might have been upset if he was watching."

"Oh, Tony!" Neil saw the little churchwarden in his mind's eye, nervously licking his lips on the way out of the vicarage in the very early morning.

"Well, you asked me to tell you . . ." Tony, beginning to feel obscurely scared again, took refuge in resentment.

"Of course I did," said Neil quickly. "Thank goodness you use your eyes and ears." Mrs. Groome's sharp golden image was blurring all over his mind, fuzzing the edges of the villagers, threatening her husband. "Mrs. Groome," he said. "How do you know Mr. Naylor's in love with her?"

"He always goes red when he sees her, or trips over something, or something. Oh, it's only Ginger and me," said Tony hastily. "I mean, I've never heard anybody say . . . And of course she would never—"

"And the curate?"

"I didn't know anything about that. I mean . . . everybody's keen on Mrs. Groome. She's super. But sort of like—well, like a goddess."

Tony stopped, shaking his head, furious that tears were threatening. Neil waited while he blew his nose.

"What's Mr. Naylor like?" he asked, when Tony had stowed his handkerchief away.

"He's OK." To Tony's relief his voice came normally. "My father says he's very conscientious. 'Pulls his weight' is what Dad says about him. His wife is sort of funny. She always looks in a panic."

"I thought so too." Neil hesitated for a moment, but his professional self drove him on. "What about the other churchwarden?"

"Old Corrigan? Gosh, I wouldn't put anything past *him!* I shouldn't say that, should I?"

"No, but go on."

"Well, I haven't really got any reason—except he's so proud and stuck up. He's—was—BB's cousin. I told you that, didn't I?"

"Yes."

"He's got pots of money, but he never did anything for BB. Even sat at the other end of the pew from him in church."

"BB might have had something to do with that."

"Well, yes, I suppose so . . . BB was very cheesed though about Mr. Corrigan."

"Did he talk to you about him?"

"Sometimes. Only to say things like that he came from the same stock, but *he* didn't need to be stuck up. And that Mr. Corrigan had no charity. 'No charity, boy, no charity.' He didn't mean for himself, I don't think, I think he meant it in the New Testament sort of way. Faith, hope and charity, you know—"

"Yes, I know." Neil steeled himself. "Tony, did you—ever have anything to do with Mr. Corrigan?"

Tony looked at him, puzzled. "To do with him?"

"I mean—did you ever visit him, ever go to his house like you went to BB's?"

Tony's surprise exploded in amusement, without his eyes leaving Neil's. "Gosh, no! Oh, I've been to Corrigan Hall of course, at least to the gardens. Once with Aunt Helen when she was collecting for something, and once on my own for my father, but I never got invited in. I don't think he likes boys."

It was Neil's turn to be amused, but he hid it.

"I'll tell you where information does seem to be a bit short, Tony, and that's on the curate. What on earth sort of a man was he?"

"I don't really know. It's funny, he's the hardest one of all to answer questions about."

"Why?" For the first time since they had pitched their camp Neil moved, finding that the blood had left one of his legs.

"He wasn't a very thoughtful sort of person," said Tony slowly, flopping down on his back and at last lying motionless, "if you know what I mean."

"I think I do."

"He was sort of on jolly terms with everyone, but I don't think there was anyone he knew very well."

"Janet Arkwright?"

"No, the curate *looked* super—well, you saw him yourself . . ."

"I did."

"I think with Janet it was like being keen on someone on TV. I don't suppose she ever had more than the odd word with him. I don't think anyone did. It's funny, but I can't sort of imagine him being—well, important enough for anyone to want to kill him. Oh!" Tony sat up and leaned over his knees, hugging them.

"What is it?"

"I've just realized . . ." His voice didn't come out properly and he tried to clear his throat. "Whoever it was who saw him in the vestry . . . could have . . ."

"They could have."

"Mr. Arkwright," said Tony huskily. "Mr. Naylor . . ."

Miss Chapman, added Neil in his head. Christopher Corrigan. "Did you say anything to anyone about what you saw? When you got home, for instance?"

Tony shook his head. He blew his nose again. "There was nobody in when I got home."

"The vicar could have seen the curate and Mrs. Groome," said Tony.

"Yes," agreed Neil, through suddenly stiff lips.

"His wife . . ."

"I see what you mean." He felt out of breath. "I take it that the churchwardens and the sacristans—and the lay reader—would have known that the curate was going to take those two services, and so was going to drink the wine first."

"Oh, yes."

"But other people wouldn't?"

"No, they wouldn't, I don't suppose."

"So someone might have wanted to kill the vicar?"

Tony considered. "Yes, they might have done, he has views on things that people mightn't like—I don't think the curate did, so much—but it could be tricky, going into the vestry, for anyone who didn't have to go—"

"But anybody *could* have gone?"

"I suppose so, yes. But they're locked at night. I think it must have been someone with a key. Aunt Helen's got a key, but I don't think—"

"Now, stop thinking about Aunt Helen."

"I can't, even when I try. She's a chief suspect, isn't she?"

"She's a suspect, along with Miss Catchpole. And the churchwardens. And the lay reader. And . . . What's Miss Catchpole like?"

"I think people are a bit scared of her. She always seems to be on her own."

"Poor Miss Catchpole."

"Oh. Yes, I suppose so." Tony felt surprised. It had never occurred to him to feel sorry for Miss Catchpole.

"Does she have any sort of a quarrel with anyone that you know of?"

"Not that I know of. Her family's lived in Bunington for centuries. She's the last one. She often told you that."

"When I saw her at the Summer Fair she prophesied that a peaceful phase of my life would come to a violent end. She said, 'I see red.'"

"Gosh, did she?"

"D'you think she could have seen something?"

"I don't know. She said when the river was going to flood last spring and it did. Only no one took her seriously so there was a lot of damage. The women in her family have always been sacristans. Like the men in Mr. Corrigan's have always been churchwardens."

"Thank you," said Neil. There was a silence, broken by the serene fluting of a blackbird. "You've told me everything you possibly could, have you, Tony?"

Tony thought for a moment, then nodded.

"You'll have to repeat it all to Inspector Oliver." Tony hugged his knees again, drooping his head over them. Neil sat silent beside him, repossessed of that sourness he had shed the first morning in Bunington, when he had marched down the lane and run his fingers along the hedgerow leaves. "It's important," he said at last, gently. "You'll have to be strong about it, but you'll be surprised how much easier it will be the second time. Anyway, I'll have spoken to Inspector Oliver by then, and he'll know what you have to tell him."

Tony said, his face still over his knees, "Perhaps I shouldn't have told you some things. I mean, Mr. Naylor is only Ginger and me . . ."

"I know. But you're right to tell us everything which might have something to do with what's happened."

"One thing," muttered Tony to his knees.

"Yes?"

"BB shouting. It looks as if it *was* a miracle."

Neil was aware of something lightening. "So it does."

"Not that it seems to have got anyone anywhere."

"We don't know that."

"Well, it didn't save Mr. Darcy, in the end."

"We don't know how these things work. Let's go back."

"Can we run round a bit first?" Tony lifted an ominously distressed face.

"Heavens, yes! What can I be thinking of! We'll have tea."

They found an ideal rustic tea shop and talked about the Yard, animals, and Tony's new school. Neil kept them off the subject of Bunington. When he had dropped Tony at Wesley House he managed to get hold of John and passed on everything he could remember that Tony had told him.

"Mutual comments when I've seen him," said John.

II

Neil found it far less of an ordeal, in the evening, to ask Annabel if she felt her father or her aunt was capable of committing one of the most horrible crimes he had ever come up against. She turned to him, half smiling.

"What does Tony say? I presume you've asked him the question."

"I'm afraid I have. He said something I found indicative, although it hadn't any facts to it."

"What was that?"

It was warm again, but with the restored warmth had come the rain. They sat at an open window in the Frog, watching it gleam on leaves, hearing it splash on slate and stone.

"He said he felt sure he'd have sensed something in the house if either of them had—done anything like that."

"Only if they were mad, I suppose," said Annabel musingly. If he was with her, Neil would always have to be looking at her. Her beauty made even the lovely Mrs. Groome seem overdone. "I think

Tony's right, I think even I, self-absorbed as I am, would have noticed something was different." She turned to him. "It hasn't been."

"Thank you. Is your aunt . . ."

"In love with the vicar? Madly." She laughed at him. "You're funny when you're put out. One thing Tony hadn't noticed?"

"No. And he underestimated *your* powers of observation."

"I see either what I want to see, or what I can't avoid. I can't tell you anything about it, except that I can't think there is anything *to* tell. I doubt if Aunt Helen is even aware of how she feels."

"The vicar's marriage," said Neil. "It seems—unlikely."

"Naomi was the poor little rich girl," said Annabel with glib indifference. "Her father's Sir somebody or other in plastics. It's a very vague legend in Bunington, except in Aunt Helen's book."

"Yes?"

"You're interested?"

"Heavens, I must be."

"Apparently she spent her first youth in London, being always on the edge of marrying someone glamorous. Poor Ernest was always in the background, being some sort of distant cousin of hers—and stayed in the background because of her money and so on, he belonging to a less pecunious branch of the family. The legend has it that she got tired of the glamour and her showy suitors, recognized Ernest's true worth, and in the end proposed to him. They lived happily ever after." Annabel yawned. Neil thought she might be feeling envy of Naomi Groome's latterday certainty. "Aunt Helen's still not quite convinced Naomi's entirely *persona grata*."

"Is she?"

"Oh, I would say so. It's Aunt Helen's excessive concern for Ernest."

"And children?"

"A boy at boarding-school. Neil, they're not your worry. I'm your worry."

He laughed, and was conscious of relaxing. He put his hand over hers on the bench seat they shared. It tensed.

"How much longer are you staying in Bunington?" asked Annabel.

"At least over this next week."

"I'm going to the seaside on Tuesday," she said casually, "but you'll know that."

"I'll what? Why should I know it?" He laughed again, to hide his surprise and disappointment, this time without enjoyment.

"Well," she said. She twisted her hand round under the pressure of his and interlaced his fingers. "Because of the policemen who are watching me."

He stared at her.

"Oh, don't pretend, Neil. I've seen them."

"Perhaps you have. But not for a week or two now, if you think."

"Really?"

"Really. What are you going to do at the seaside?"

He was so constituted that jealousy was a reflex action when his woman, however temporary, proposed activity from which he was to be excluded.

"I'm going to visit a girl-friend. And get a change of scene. I've earned it, Neil!" She pulled gently at his fingers. "I didn't tell you," she said, "but I should have gone last week and I put it off. I put it off until this week, when I thought your holiday would be over."

"My holiday is over. Thank you for putting it off. Of course you can't put it off again."

Even when the first wave of jealousy ebbed, it was difficult to know what it left behind on the tangled shore of his emotions.

CHAPTER 12

I

It rained again on Monday morning, for Bedlington Byrne's funeral. At nine o'clock the superintendent and John Oliver called on Tony, with a sergeant, and the four of them spent an hour in the drawing-room. Inspector Oliver asked most of the questions and, as Neil had said, it wasn't quite so bad the second time, particularly as the inspector already knew about the things Tony had told Neil. Immediately the police had left he ran to the cottage through the rain, Timmy accompanying him but, catlike, choosing to weave a primrose path behind hedges and through ditches and across gardens and the corners of fields. Tony saw him when they left, and again when they arrived.

He couldn't remember ever before having such mixed feelings. He was churned up to begin with, feeling guilty about the Arkwrights and the Naylors and above and beyond all Mrs. Groome, so that he was perhaps even more affected than he might have been by the magnolia tree and the empty hutches and the cat flap, BB's old canvas chair and the table beside it marked with glass rings. But the elation of ownership was at the same time tremendous. He opened the front door with the key Aunt Helen had given him after only one murmur of support from Annabel. Mrs. Halliwell, now that the property was in the family and the stench non-recurrent, had consented to come in and clean, and the slight smell which remained did no more than remind Tony of his old friend.

He wandered through the rooms, upstairs and down. Timmy, vaguely following him, played shipwreck over the shabby furniture. Aunt Helen had already arranged for a man from Sotheby's to come and look for hidden treasure. Tony was trying to maintain a calm solid front against her determination that the cottage be sold and had been rewarded by an injunction from his father, whom as trustee she could not oppose, that nothing was to be done in a hurry.

He pulled out drawers here and there. The lower ones tended to be empty of all but the odd button or stud—Aunt Helen had immediately and personally supervised the removal of clothing to farflung charities—but the small upper drawers contained snapshots and note books and other papers which he would eventually examine. They looked unexpectedly tidy, probably because the police had already been through them and put them back in some semblance of order. Tony had turned on Aunt Helen in a reflex of fury when she had suggested that the contents of these drawers also should be removed, and she had not suggested it a second time.

Walking about the cottage and being aesthetically depressed by the appearance of its interior, Tony wondered yet again about his mother, who a short while before his birth had devised the interior of Wesley House which so charmed him. He wondered how much of her he had inherited. As always, from whatever direction he approached the thought of her, he came upon his favourite photograph full length and alive, smiling at him, putting out a hand, edged head and body with a dazzling angelic light. Although his intellect now told him that this image was unlikely to be accurate he continued to see his mother as an angel. He didn't really know anything about her, anyway, except that if his father and Aunt Helen were to be depressed by the interior of the cottage, it would be in a different way from him and her . . .

BB's bedroom had an enormous sagging bed. The window looked over the garden. Tony opened it and stood staring out on the steady rain. He had never been upstairs in BB's house while BB was alive and it was funny to see familiar things from slightly different angles, especially in this village of high hedges. For instance, he saw that the house opposite was extending its barn and that there was a pony in the field beyond . . .

Ginger was at the gate, his jacket shoulders dark with rain, his red hair soaked brown. Tony called out proudly, "Come in and have a drink!"

As Ginger sprinted across the grass he bounded cheerfully downstairs, Timmy appearing and overtaking him. He let Ginger in through the front door.

"Come into the sitting-room. Take your jacket off."

Ginger followed him and he took two cans of Coke out of the cupboard, and two glasses. There were still about a dozen cans left. BB must have got them in for him, anticipating visits. That was the sort of thing which still made his eyes swim. He hoped he would be all right in church. Ginger would be the first to notice if he wasn't.

"Gosh," he said, handing Ginger his glass and his can, "I'd forgotten that we'd be in church this morning."

"There's plenty of time." Ginger went on looking round while he spoke, and stopped only to open his can and pour out his drink. Tony was gratified to see that Ginger was impressed, despite his attempts to appear to be taking it for granted. In the end, after they had said "Cheers!" and raised their glasses, Ginger was forced to ask for confirmation that it all belonged to Tony.

"Yes," said Tony, playing cool, "only Aunt Helen thinks I'd be wise to sell."

"You wouldn't want to do that, would you? I mean . . ."

"I haven't decided yet," said Tony airily.

"I wouldn't want to sell. I mean . . . your own house!"

The pretence of indifference vanished on both sides.

"It is rather super. I don't think I want to sell, really. I don't suppose there are many boys of our age who have their own house."

"I don't suppose so," agreed Ginger humbly, in an admission of Tony's unique position which the householder found himself wanting to reward.

"You can come here whenever you like," said Tony. "Use the garden if I'm not here to let you in." It was a defiance of Aunt Helen, too. "I shan't say that to anyone else."

"Gosh, thanks."

They lounged in their uncomfortable chairs, drinking Coke. As they gazed contentedly at one another, parish events slowly took precedence in their minds. Tony saw his change of mood reflected in Ginger's face. A sense of discomfort hung in the air.

"You know about Mr. Byrne's grave?" inquired Ginger, after an uneasy pause.

"No?" Tony leaned eagerly forward, his relief at the distraction stronger than his pang at Ginger's words.

"Wait for it." Ginger also leaned forward, blinking his orange lashes. "It's in the Corrigan compound!"

"Never!" Tony's disbelief was shot through with a hope that Ginger might not be teasing.

"Yes it is. Mr. Corrigan went to the vicar and told him."

"How d'you know?"

"I was in the hall when Mrs. Groome was talking to Mum."

This was plausible. Ginger's mastery of events depended largely on a talent for being in the right place at the right time.

"What did she say exactly?"

"I can't remember exactly. Don't be greedy. She said Mr. Corrigan had been to see the vicar and had—insisted, that was what she said, insisted—that Mr. Byrne should be buried in the family vault."

It was the generation of choristers before Tony and Ginger who had coined the phrase "Corrigan compound" to describe the elaborate Victorian mausoleum with its angel and trumpet and open stone book inside its own grass plot and iron railings, which housed Corrigan remains.

"Fancy old Corrigan. I'm glad, though."

"Mr. Byrne's parents aren't in there, are they?"

"I think his father's buried in India somewhere. He showed me his mother's grave once. No, it isn't in there. That's why he showed it to me, really. He was—angry, that day, that it wasn't." BB had wept drunken tears at the graveside, because a woman born Corrigan, and his mother to boot, had been buried in the open. It was almost, when BB was in those moods, as if she had been put in unconsecrated ground. "Why on earth, though?"

"I don't know why," said Ginger, a bit irritably. "You'll have to ask your detective friend."

"Yes, I expect Neil'll find out. He's asked me lots of questions."

"He's not in charge of the case."

"I know he's not, but he *is* Scotland Yard. And he might be called in, in the end, if the Latchford police can't solve the crime. He told me."

"Your aunt or your father might have done it," stated Ginger, looking with interest for Tony's reaction. Tony hoped he was disappointed that he didn't show one.

"I know. That's what Neil said. I said I didn't think so."

"You don't know."

"I don't know, clever. But I'd have felt *something* if either of them had done anything like *that*. Anybody could have done it, anyway. Your father could of." Ginger jumped, and Tony was satisfied. "I'm sure he didn't though, of course."

"I think it's Mr. Arkwright," said Ginger. Tony tried to keep his face free of expression.

"Any reason?"

"He's always so *angry*. I bet he beat Janet over that article in the paper. I bet that was why she tried to drink that poison, not because of Mr. Darcy."

Normally Tony would have told Ginger about the beating which ended in bleeding. But somehow, telling the police had sort of sealed off what he knew so that he couldn't tell anyone else.

He said, simply and truthfully, "I shouldn't be surprised."

"She's still in hospital. The lemonade must have gone up her nose."

"I wanted to laugh about that," said Tony, above Ginger's guffaws. "But there was no one to laugh with and it sort of got past it."

Nevertheless he managed to catch Ginger's mood sufficiently to snigger with him for a few moments. Both boys stopped abruptly and stared at one another, shocked.

II

Drama, thought Neil, drama.

About half the people who hung about the gate of St. Leonard's were members of the Press. He recognized most of them as he recognized most of the villagers, because they had been there so recently. He could see the tabloid articles before they were written. "While the victim of the mysterious killer lay awaiting burial, the only suspect was lowered into his grave . . ." The weather continued to accord with the general mood. The sky had come down again, draining the colour from even the hectic summer shirts of some of the Press people. Those who were the more soberly and formally dressed were detaching themselves from the group at the gate, moving up the path to the church door. Neil joined them, beside John Oliver and Sergeant Benson. John Arkwright, just inside the doorway, handed each of them a service sheet. They sat in the back pew so as to see as much as possible, as many people, movements, inter-reactions. Christopher Corrigan was already in his place in the front pew, in sole possession of its polished length. The Chapmans and Annabel were settling in just behind him, Mr. and Mrs. Naylor on a level with the three policemen across the aisle. Neil, glancing sideways, thought he caught Mrs. Naylor's restless eye, but it moved swiftly on.

There was a stout middle-aged woman on her own behind the Chapmans. When she turned round Neil saw she had a kind face on which her look of deep anxiety seemed unaccustomed. Miss Catchpole came out of the vestry, genuflected, then took her solitary place. Mr. Gordon (whispered and indicated John), and his attractive much younger wife. Mrs. Mason, whom Neil already knew by sight, her handkerchief to her mouth. He wondered, before he could tell himself not to be frivolous, if she had held it thus when she had taken her cake offerings into Bedlington Byrne's cottage. Jim Bates plumping heavily into the pew in front of them, within smelling distance. Mrs. Groome coming in through the little north door which led direct from the vicarage, poignantly subdued but inevitably radiant as she crossed in front of Mr. Corrigan, made brief obeisance, and sat down half way up the church beside the aisle. One or two people Neil didn't know, already there or still arriving. Finally feet dragging, moving with difficulty, and Bedlington Byrne's coffin coming up the nave, on the shoulders of four young men to whom Neil couldn't give names, causing the congregation to rise. As the coffin was set down before the chancel steps a diminished choir appeared, the vicar bringing up the rear. From where Neil sat, the organ didn't quite drown the sounds of altercation at the door behind them, which must be Mr. Arkwright denying admission to the Press. It ended with the door closing reverberatively and Mr. Arkwright striding up the aisle and into the pew beside the middle-aged woman with the kind face. Well, yes, he might have guessed from what Tony had said. Neil was on the left of the nave this time, and could see Tony in the chancel, looking at the left front pew with its single occupant, then hanging his head.

Recent events in Neil's life both professional and private had sent him to funerals, and the service was more familiar to him than the Eucharist or Evensong had been when he had arrived in Bunington. The vicar preached for about ten minutes, speaking of Bedlington Byrne's long connection with church and village, his love of animals, his "gruff honesty." The vicar's bearing was as usual, quietly confident, no jot different, thought Neil, narrowly observing him. He knew he did this less as a detective than as a man, but today he was not inclined to consider the implications. It was difficult, with someone who never looked really well, to assess the toll of strain. From the vicar's voice, Neil thought he was withstanding it.

There was nobody at all in the front of the church except Christopher Corrigan and the four young men who had separated to right and left in the third pews. Neil felt less uncomfortable than he generally did at funerals, because there was no family with that pinched-nostril, physically battered look with which people withstand exposure of their grief and bewilderment and which always made him feel an intruder. But when Christopher Corrigan followed the coffin on its way out, there was something in his face which made Neil turn away. The old man, amazingly, was suffering, and Neil thought he recognized the familiar suffering of the bereaved. It was a minute or two before he began to wonder if it might be caused by more than the normal sense of loss . . .

It was still raining as they walked to the mausoleum, but with less force. There was nothing now that even John Arkwright could do but glare as the Press formed a loose circle round the mourners. Christopher Corrigan stood beside the vicar, his eyes cast down. Mrs. Mason sobbed, intermittently audible. Tony slipped through the outer ring and came to stand beside Neil and they glanced once at each other in understanding. A blackbird fluted tranquilly nearby and water drops fell with slow regularity off the end of the angel's copper trumpet. Annabel and Mrs. Groome, standing next to each other, summed up all female beauty; Neil noticed that even John Oliver was distracted by the sight of them. Beyond them, he spotted the melancholy countenance of the reporter who had tackled him in the pub garden, and his heart sank.

Earth to earth, ashes to ashes, dust to dust.

It must have been old Corrigan who had insisted on the Prayer Book service. But no soil rattled on Bedlington Byrne's coffin: it was carried inside the Corrigan vault. As it was lifted for its last short journey the old man Corrigan looked up, then swiftly down. Neil sent his eyes flickering rapidly round the inner circle of those who had known, but not necessarily loved, Bedlington Byrne: John Arkwright, thunder-browed beside his sweet-faced wife; Mike Adams, pale and intense; George and Helen Chapman, the high colour of each receded to no more than a tangle of veins in the cheeks; Miss Catchpole, her small face smaller than ever under the mushroom of a huge black hat; Alec Naylor without a smile; Mrs. Naylor, her panic barely contained until her husband, not seeming to look at her, put out a hand; Mrs. Groome gazing through the mausoleum and beyond it; Annabel a picture of modesty. And behind them, that other, more restless circle, its cameras ready for action . . .

Neil's scourge was beside him almost as soon as the vicar had given his blessing and walked slowly away, his wife at his side.

"Good morning, Inspector. The old fellow shouting out before his stroke was at first thought to be a last-minute repentance. What's the explanation for it now?"

"Just a minute," said Neil. He turned to Tony. "I'll see you soon. Excuse me now."

Tony, after glaring at the reporter, ran off. John Oliver was raising his voice from the pathway.

"Ladies and gentlemen of the Press," he said, and the ladies and gentlemen of Bunington, too, stopped to listen. "If you would like to follow me out of the church grounds."

John was good at implied rebukes. The Press accompanied the mourners into the lane. Some showed signs of clinging to various local people, but by the time John and Sergeant Benson were standing in the doorway of the Red Lion, the inhabitants of the village had been allowed to go their ways, with or without promises of later co-operation. Neil's interlocutor kept pace with him, despite walking with a pronounced limp, and wasn't shaken off until Neil slipped literally under John's arm and into the bar.

Jim Bates was already back in place, ready to serve him a double whisky. The rain had ceased and John remained in the doorway and the Press on the forecourt. Neil, as he drank, could hear John speak to them.

"I appreciate," said John, "that you haven't travelled to Bunington to attend a funeral. You are here because of the death of the curate of this parish, the Reverend Malcolm Darcy, through drinking poison which had found its way into the wine prepared for the early morning service of Holy Communion. Those are the simple facts." Neil thought Jim Bates was swearing under his breath. "The investigation of this death," went on John, "is at an early stage and has so far yielded only negative results. You will be kept informed of positive developments. In the meantime, it will be very much appreciated if you go easily on the inhabitants of Bunington, and, in particular, refrain from calling on the vicar. I can't think what questions you could have at this stage, but if there are any I'll try to answer them."

Neil listened for a certain set of lugubrious tones, and heard them. He came out of the bar with his glass in his hand, and stood noticeably behind John.

The reporter was repeating his question word for word and when he had finished John said:

"A man can cry out against the smothering hand of a heart attack. Protest with his last muster of breath, to put it melodramatically. The follow-up to Mr. Byrne's cry was such that the cry was taken for the cause, the heart attack as the effect. Now that it appears Mr. Byrne had after all nothing to do with the first contamination of the wine, the attack is seen as the cause of the cry, which in normal circumstances would have been apparent right away."

Neil experienced the sensations of relief and disappointment in about equal measure.

III

"You did well over the old man's shouting," he commended John a little later, upstairs in his room whither Jim Bates bore them beer and a ploughman's lunch. "D'you think that's the true explanation?"

"Neil, I don't want them to start speculating on Bedlington Byrne having been an accessory or an inadvertent witness of something he understood only at the eleventh hour. Any one of those explanations is possible, although both my Super and I are inclined to rule out the accessory idea. What's the matter?"

"Nothing. A goose over my grave." Neil had shaken himself inwardly, first, at hearing John's explanation of the shouting, because he had been so uncharacteristically obsessed by the possibility of a miracle that he hadn't really considered the alternatives. Then, seeing in his mind's eye the vicar rising with nervous haste from beside

Bedlington Byrne's death bed, he had shivered so that John had noticed.

"Could the old man's death have been hastened, actually?" he asked John.

"Actually, I suppose it could. Why do you ask?"

Neil felt his eyes sliding away from John's. "Oh, just to confound confusion. Have you any ideas yet?"

"Too many."

"Have you seen all the principals?"

"I've seen Mr. Naylor who said he left the vicar in the vestry on Saturday night, preparing the Communion for early next morning, and the vicar who said, yes, that's right. I've seen George and Helen Chapman, and Agnes Catchpole who said she'd foreseen it but couldn't—or wouldn't—give me the solution. I've seen John Arkwright who looks as if he could take on any enemy of the Lord single-handed but who doesn't admit to ideological differences with the curate, and Christopher Corrigan who was taken queer during the interview and rang for his manservant. I'll have to see him again. Heavens, I'll have to see all of them again, or my Super will. These were only preliminary canters, a quick scout to see if there was anything obvious enough to give me a short cut. There wasn't."

"Not even the monkey business?"

"Neil, all of them could have given that monkey the banana. Miss Catchpole goes for long solitary walks in the dark. Arkwright goes about the village on foot at all hours. Even the Naylors were in Bunington that night. George Chapman came home late from a dinner party. The vicar was summoned to a sick bed very late indeed. And that ape apparently used to sit gibbering on the gatepost half the night, came in and out of the cottage via the cat flap. And everybody knew it and some people didn't like the creature because of its unbeguiling habit of alighting on passing heads. And someone put the banana into its outstretched hand."

"You're far enough on, though, to list the front runners?"

"I suppose so, if we ignore the fact that anyone, from inside or outside Bunington, could have done it. Thanks to young Tony Chapman, and yourself, we have motives; and thanks to circumstances, we have greater ease of opportunity for the principals, which ties in with the possible motives."

"Will you specify?"

John pulled a piece of paper out of his pocket and spread it out on the broad window ledge beside his chair. "There are," he said, "in no significant order, the following: Alec Naylor. Has strong ideas of how the clergy ought to conduct themselves."

"He's a convert."

"I know. And thought to be in love with the vicar's wife."

"By two little boys. Observant—but two little boys."

"Also by Agnes Catchpole. No facts, admittedly, but corroborative observation. And you saw Naylor driving out of the vicar's gateway at 12.30 one morning, when the vicar's wife was manifestly still up and about. He could have seen her with the curate in the vestry because his car was outside the Red Lion until one o'clock that Sunday. His wife wasn't with him, but he tells me he went alone on his usual post-service Bunington 'ramble.' Can't be proved or disproved. Then there's—"

"John, tell me about the Groomes—if you can and will."

"Of course. We went straight to the vicarage when we left Tony this morning. Mrs. Groome didn't hedge at all. Yes, the curate had declared himself to her in the vestry that Sunday morning and, yes, she had been kind to him. The vicar was present while we talked to her, apparently all serene. He as well as his wife had forgiven the curate his trespass. But he prepared the Elements on both the poisoned Sundays, and he could have seen his wife and the curate and not been so happy about the situation as he now appears. Mrs. Groome herself could easily have done it, Neil, and I needn't spell out her possible motives."

"I feel like Tony felt about Bedlington Byrne."

"Why, particularly?"

"I suppose—I want to admire the Groomes. They seem so admirable." He couldn't explain to John, because he couldn't properly explain to himself, what a long way back it went.

"John Arkwright," said John. "We rang the hospital, and indeed there were bruises on the daughter where the skin was broken. I haven't seen Arkwright since I saw Tony Chapman, but he offered me the information last night that he had tried to 'beat sense into the girl,' and had also 'chastized her' (I quote in each case) for that interview she gave the Press. I asked him if he considered the curate to have been in any way involved in how Janet felt about him and he said, 'Because it has happened, he is involved.' He wouldn't amplify, however many different ways I tried to put it, but there's a good enough motive, anyway. And his wife told me he didn't get home until just before one that vestry day, so he could have been the one to see the encounter between Mr. Darcy and Mrs. Groome.

Janet Arkwright's coming home tomorrow, by the way, her mother told me. Apparently she regrets what she tried to do—it was sheer impulse—and the doctors are satisfied she won't try it again."

"Not much to come home to?"

"The mother's a nice woman. And not so much weak I suspect as realistic. Arkwright admits, incidentally, to being the one who bought the poison—well, his signature appears on behalf of the church in the Latchford poison book. No one of course admits to returning it to the shed."

"Christopher Corrigan?"

"Ah, yes. I spoke of his deceased friend, and then hard on the heels of that I said I believed he had had the curate to tea recently, and that was the point at which he came over peculiar and had to ring for his valet. There's a piece of suspicious behaviour, if you like. Might also have observed the scene in the vestry—no one seems able to confirm his story that he went home promptly after the service that Sunday."

"And Mr. Darcy was in love with a woman."

"So it would appear."

"And Helen Chapman and Miss Catchpole had keys."

"And Miss Catchpole, again without supporting facts, spoke of Miss Chapman's attachment to the vicar. She wasn't in the house when young Tony ran home after the vestry scene. The devotion of a woman of that type could well take the form of devotion to the wife as well, in the sense that she was vital to the loved one's reputation and peace of mind. Also she was alone with the Elements the second, fatal, time. As indeed was Naylor."

"Miss Catchpole?"

"She has a key to the vestry, as you say, but I can't add anything to that as yet. And she appears to feel rather like Tony Chapman over the poisoning of the monkey—if not of the curate!"

"So that's one, two, three, four, five, possibly six prime suspects, followed by an extravagant chorus of bucks, blades, and professional bridesmaids. And there's the fact that the *incognoscenti* would expect the vicar to be the victim, rather than the curate. I'm sorry for you, John."

"You may be sorry for yourself before you've done."

"I hope not, for both our sakes. By the way, there's something funny about Naylor's wife."

"I thought so too. I'd like to know if there's any history of instability."

"Still no sign of the poison bottle?"

"Still no sign. If it was buried, whoever it was has had the rain to help them. Soil everywhere looks churned up. We're investigating the environs of the church, but we can't dig up every smallest plot in Bunington and beyond, or look into every cupboard. Not yet, at any rate."

Neil got up and pushed his window wider by a notch. The rain had stopped again but the horizon hills were still shrouded.

"Something's bothering me, John. There was a point at which I felt—disturbed—and I can't remember when it was. I know it wasn't at any of the big moments, when I could have expected it." Neil turned back from the window. "The reporter who asked the question about Bedlington Byrne is the fellow who picked on me in the garden here last time. He certainly has the knack of putting his finger on it. Do you know anything about him?"

"Nothing. I've never seen him before. I mean, before last week."

"Do you really think they'll keep off the vicar?"

"They might. At least they may keep off actually ringing his doorbell."

The knock coming at Neil's door just at that moment made him and John grin at one another, and John look briefly boyish again.

Neil went across and opened the door, and John's Super stood there. He looked lingeringly at the plates and glasses.

"Good afternoon, Inspector Carter. John, the landlord has given me a room. Would you be ready to come down?"

The superintendent nodded to Neil as he and John went out. In a sudden access of gratitude for his own situation Neil went downstairs too, and telephoned his Chief.

CHAPTER 13

I

Miss Catchpole lived in the lane which wound thinly from a corner of the Small Green. Neil knew, from his walks, that it petered out on a field and a long view of more fields darkly defined by hedges, rising gradually to a horizon of hills. Miss Catchpole's small house, which Tony had pointed out to him, was half way down the lane and this time, after walking to the end and staring towards the invisible slopes, Neil loitered outside its gate. He had the sure feeling that Miss Catchpole would see him and, if she wanted to be seen, would come out and speak to him. He didn't think, if she failed to appear, that he would ring the bell.

She came almost at once, round the side of the house but looking at him without surprise, already knowing he was there. She crossed her little front garden and leaned on the gate.

"Good afternoon, Mr. Carter, I've been expecting you." Her thin grey hair was pressed unbecomingly flat, as if she had taken off the black mushroom hat without looking in a mirror. She stared at him over the gate, the suspicion of a smile about her mouth.

"May I talk to you?" asked Neil, when he had realized that she would wait for him to break the silence.

"Of course. Come in." She looked behind her, along the lane, as she opened the gate, warily, so that Neil looked too, and raked the empty rainwashed Green with sudden anxiety. Afterwards, he decided it was at that moment that the body on the altar steps became real to him.

He followed Miss Catchpole up the neat path, into a neat hall. He was somehow surprised at the cleanliness and order of the house. Witches were notorious for living in a muddle . . . Was he thinking of Miss Catchpole as a witch? A witch who looked after Christian vessels and vestments?

Reproving himself, he followed her into the sitting-room. It was comfortable and attractively but simply furnished, set about with a host of small treasures: dark frames clustered on the walls with tiny pictures at their hearts, tables with glass tops and small objects on velvet beneath the glass, sepia photographs, china figures and animals.

"All these," said Miss Catchpole, gesturing round at the photographs, "are dead. Family and friends. Sit down, Mr. Carter."

"Thank you."

Miss Catchpole sat facing him. Her legs were so thin they appeared wasted. He felt she would jeer at him if he offered a conventionally commiserative response to the admission of solitude she had so conversationally made.

"You're helping Inspector Oliver with his inquiries," said Miss Catchpole, after a pause in which she openly examined him. Her smile at her joke was a grimace, as was Neil's. "You don't find Bunington quite so delightful as you did."

"No. I look forward to leaving, now, and I'm sorry."

"I can tell you," said Miss Catchpole, leaning forward and speaking with intensity, "there is as much suffering to come as has already been endured."

"Can you—or will you—be more specific?"

She leaned back in her chair, looking weary.

"Mr. Carter, I sense the propensities of men and women, the good and evil in them and how it will move and interact. It is not a specific gift. I sensed that something bad would happen in Bunington, and when I saw you the first time I knew you would be concerned in it, and that it would affect you beyond its outcome." Neil jerked protestingly in his chair and she said, with her grimace of a smile, "You don't want to hear me say that, probably because you already suspect it to be true. Can you smell coffee?"

"Yes. It's a good smell."

"Would you like some?"

"Please."

She was out of the room a very few moments. Disturbed as he was by her presence and by what she had said to him, he was unable to make his surroundings feel sinister or, indeed, anything but friendly. There was an enormous Bible on a stand in a corner, and a palm cross curling at an angle behind one of the pictures. There was a collection of china dogs and two bowls of roses.

The coffee was as good as any coffee he remembered tasting. He said, as it warmed his chest, "How will I be affected by events in Bunington?"

He was surprised to hear himself ask such a question. She said gravely: "I know that it will be within yourself that you will be affected, not merely in the extra dimension of new contacts. You are already inwardly affected, of course: when you first came here you would not have asked me such a question."

"I knew that as soon as I'd asked it!"

"That is all I am certain of. Beyond is speculation, which I might or might not get right, but which I consider immoral to put into words. So don't ask me anything further of that order."

"I don't think I want to." The airiness of his manner was a cover for unfamiliar discomfort. "Anyway, I really should be remembering that I'm a police officer, albeit in an unofficial capacity and with no power to demand answers to questions. It's obviously occurred to

you, Miss Catchpole, that you yourself must be one of the chief suspects in this murder."

He felt he was breathing fast, as if he had just been running to
get away from something.

"By virtue of my office and my key," she murmured. "I don't
think I have any obvious motive." She grinned at him again. "But I
realize it is of no significance to state that I am a Christian, seeing
this is a plea which can be put forward by each person who is under
suspicion."

"In your opinion, would they all be telling the truth?"

"You know I shan't answer that." She lifted the coffee-pot and he
held out his cup and saucer. "I will tell you only what I am certain
of."

"And you really are certain of nothing else?"

A look of exhaustion passed over her face.

"Of nothing else, Mr. Carter. Except that people disguise their
motives, even from themselves." She sat forward again, he thought
by an effort. "Now, you can question me, if you wish, as you would
question my fellow sacristan, or the churchwardens, or—others
closely involved in the activities of the vestries. I suspect, however,
that Inspector Oliver has already made you privy to my statement."

"In general, yes. What did you think of the old man's monkey?"

Her face was full of pity.

"It was as God made it. I despise no member of the animal kingdom, excepting—I admit it—certain human beings. I have three cats
which are at present all sitting in the garden apparently enjoying
the sensation of damp grass beneath their bottoms. They are all
black—appropriate pets for the village witch, even if she is a white
one, and worships before the Cross at its proper angle." Grinning at
him, she rose and straightened the palm cross askew behind the picture.

Village life, thought Neil.

II

One of Miss Catchpole's cats had come round to the front of the
house, and watched him from the porch as he walked away. He
went the length of the lane again, because she had told him there
was a way into the first field and a continuation of narrow paths beside other fields which would eventually bring him round to the

Corrigan acres and thence back into the village via the Big Green.

Perhaps it was a sense of fatality engendered by Miss Catchpole's firm statement of her certainties, but his feeling of wariness, of unfamiliarity with himself and his reactions, seemed to have grown and settled into a steady state of mind, rather than lunging at him, as it had lately been doing, in a series of stabs. He felt less disturbed as he left the cottage, surer of his uncertainty, and once more ready for a lonely walk.

He was aware again of his surroundings. When he reached the end of the lane he saw that the sky had lifted to reveal, in blue-grey outline, the furthest hills. Tentative rays of sun had brought some pastel colour into the landscape. Made wise by Miss Catchpole, he found the start of the overgrown field path and set out steadily along it, not so much thinking as being passively aware of how he felt.

He began to think only after he had walked for about half an hour and sat down on an old wooden seat where the path crossed a lane, and then his thoughts were of Annabel. He realized as he leaned back to watch pale sunshine on the ripening wheatfield in front of him that he and she were about to spend their last evening together.

He examined the realization as it came to him. He thought she would be prepared to come to London to see him, to stay at the flat, she could even be expected to welcome it, but he wasn't going to ask her.

Looking round him, hearing the small disconnected sounds of insects and birds, he was unable to say why. She was beautiful, desirable, intelligent, she would relish what he relished of London. Despite his injunction to himself not to try and teach God his job, he didn't feel guilty about her. He simply felt, for no reason at all which he could see, that she belonged to his Bunington experience, and would end for him when that did. And that would end, whatever Miss Catchpole had said.

At the same time he found it extraordinary, to have discovered such a woman, and to wish to make no effort to retain her company, not to be madly in love with her.

Was Annabel in love with him?

Ah, thought Neil, ah, perhaps this is it. He didn't know. He suspected that she might never be in love with anyone. And there were times in the past when he had found himself wanting to be on the safe side, to be sure of getting out first. A cold, egotistical trait . . .

But, for whatever reason, tonight—tomorrow, on Latchford station

—he would say *au revoir* to Annabel Quillin and think goodbye, placing her in his memory as the most perfect thing of its kind that he had ever encountered, intact in the midst of surrounding imperfections, like Miss Catchpole's jewelled pictures in their dark frames. He wouldn't, he couldn't, let himself so much as imagine what it would be like if they were absorbed in one another . . . He had thought before, with distaste, that he had an outsize instinct for self-preservation . . .

A robin was singing, out of a bush not much above the level of his head. A thing he liked about robins was the way they so often sang from an accessible level, so that one could watch the bulging throat, the tiny opening gorge. When the robin stopped he could hear the drone of a bee. Then a fresh sound, fine stalks snapping, a brushing noise, behind him and getting louder.

Neil turned round as the sad face of the long-nosed reporter came through the bushes which screened the exit from the field behind him. He limped round and sat down on the seat beside Neil, with a sigh.

"Good afternoon, Inspector Carter."

"It is less of a good afternoon," observed Neil, "than it was just now."

But the man was there, so he turned to look at him. Nose really dominant in profile, long chin, pale blue eyes drooping at the corners, brows rising, brown hair lank and flat, white hands with long fingers. The whole person, thought Neil, betokening gentle inquiry.

Where had the word gentle come from? But one could be gentle, and still implacably determined.

"What have you in mind this time?" asked Neil, hearing a note in his voice he sometimes heard when questioning a persistently uncommunicative suspect. "Perhaps you think I am Svengali to Mrs. Quillin's Trilby, and that I willed her into the crime too horrible to name. Or perhaps—"

"Please, Mr. Carter."

It was unexpected, how such lack-lustre tones could be so insistent.

"Please what, Mr. . . . ?"

"Barnes. Humphrey Barnes." The sad eyes turned to look at him. "Of course, you're not a bit pleased to see me. Any more than you were this morning."

"Why follow me, then?" Despite his annoyance, Neil found he was curious to know.

"It's hard to explain. I relish strange connections. I'm not a bread-and-butter newsman, Mr. Carter."

"Meaning?"

"I don't make a living from it, or try to. I've got a little business, with a small trustworthy staff, so when something especially intrigues me, I pursue it. Sometimes I sell things to newspapers or magazines. But that's not why I follow my nose."

He touched the organ with a long white finger, ruefully. Neil thought there was a smile somewhere about, although he couldn't actually see it. He was feeling less and less hostile, but he wasn't going to let that show, either.

"And what beckoned this time?"

"By utter coincidence I was with a legitimate newspaper friend of mine when the news of the first black Sunday was telephoned through."

Neil felt himself zooming into professional focus.

"Telephoned through. By whom?"

"As an earnest of good faith, I'll tell you. By an unknown woman. By which I mean she didn't give her name. I didn't speak to her, of course, but I heard the recipient of the call ask her for her credentials, and fail to get them."

"Did he—she—say anything about the voice?"

"Only that there really wasn't anything to say. It was without expression, as if it was reading a prepared statement."

"What did it say?"

"I gather it said simply that in the parish church of St. Leonard in Bunington the Eucharist had been poisoned, and that each time a question was asked, it repeated those words. Like an answering service. Do you believe me?" The long face turned to Neil again, inquiringly.

"Possibly. And what made you feel this was a situation which merited your presence?"

"I suppose I started to speculate on how anyone could do that. And then why. And then, after I'd come the first time, the coincidences, Inspector. Chief among them that Bunington was also the home of Mrs. Quillin, and that you, a detective from Scotland Yard, had been on hand to cope in the church. It was like holding a well-turned piece of furniture in my hands, the way the sections dovetailed."

"And now you could be exercising manic ingenuity, to get me to confess that, after all, there *is* a connection between my presence in Bunington and Mrs. Quillin as *cause* rather than *amie célèbre*. Did you sell your speculation on my presence here not being a coincidence? It appeared in one section of the Press."

"I haven't tried to sell anything, I'm still thinking. Put it down to one of the professionals."

"Disarmed or not, I will still tell you that I am here coincidentally and on holiday."

"Very likely, Mr. Carter, but I'm not thinking so much about that, now."

"About what, then?"

"I asked you a question, and then I asked Inspector Oliver, and he answered it."

"Well, then?"

"No mystery, possibly. But I am intrigued. Has no one, I wonder, had the thought that the old man shouting might have been a miracle?"

Neil laughed so harshly a flock of sparrows took off from the hedge in front of them.

"Inspector Carter?" Mr. Barnes showed surprise by a further upward thrust of his permanently surprised eyebrows.

"I'm sorry," said Neil eventually. "The boy Tony and I have thought about it, yes."

"Ah." Mr. Barnes drew his wide mouth out, unambiguously smiling. He had long ivory-coloured teeth. He pushed his hands down between his knees and rocked backwards and forwards on the seat.

"You don't ask any questions about the murder," observed Neil.

"I find it the least interesting part of things. My interest, really, is in ordinary human nature, especially when subject to unnatural pressures. A murderer, by definition, is extraordinary, a freak."

"Or an ordinary person, subject to unnatural pressures?"

Humphrey Barnes shrugged. "I'm still more interested in those who don't react to so rare an extent."

"You're fortunate in having the time to indulge your interest. What sort of business allows you to do that?"

"Printing. Small and specialized. Long-established family. I'm not the only brother involved."

Neil thought he was beginning to get a picture. But there were incompatible elements. "Why did you ask me that first time if I would fit into your think piece?"

"Because I thought I might write something."

"But you didn't?"

"No. And it wasn't really my motive. I wanted to know how you would react."

"Why?"

"Because you interest me."

"Are you lonely, or something?"

"Lonely sometimes, since my wife died, but not anything else, Mr. Carter."

"I'm sorry."

"That's all right. I suppose I ask for it."

"Are you going to write anything now?"

"I don't know. I think I could be serving a long apprenticeship as a writer. A real one, I mean. Not just hawking the odd choice piece of information or surmise."

"So you might say that this—whatever it is—is your hobby at the moment?"

"I might say just that, and it would be close to the mark. Some people go about the country looking for old steam engines. I go about looking for the more bizarre results of human behaviour."

"I'd rather, personally, that you didn't write anything about the idea of a miracle."

"So would I, at least as things are at the moment. It's just something, with other things, to think about."

"Are you a member of the Church?"

"No, but I might be."

"Really?"

"I might be a member some time of anything, or of nothing."

"It must be fascinating," said Neil, "to be so inconsistent—if it isn't disconcerting."

"Nevertheless, I find other people more interesting than I find myself, Mr. Carter."

"I can't think why you find *me* interesting."

"I find you interesting, I suppose, because you seem to be all over Bunington's mysterious courses, without apparently having anything to do with any of them." Neil laughed again. "You might as well be friends with me, Mr. Carter. I might help you at some time."

"All right. Have a shot at helping me now? How does this business strike anyone who isn't all over Bunington?"

"Oh, I keep getting schoolboy thoughts about Benjamin Quillin having a vendetta against the village, or something, because it never *really* released his wife to him."

"Wrong! Annabel Quillin never *really* belonged to Bunington." Neil saw interest drift across the pale eyes. "I'm afraid you're not going to be able to tie everything up so neatly as that."

"Ah, well. But I do so like to find connections where there seems to be merely coincidence."

"You couldn't connect a miracle to anything."

"I know, I know. I *am* inconsistent, as you just said. And I always find it hard to climb down off the fence. Even to get up off this bench."

Mr. Barnes rose to his feet, stiffly, and took a few limping steps in the lane before coming to a halt in front of Neil.

"What did you do to your leg?" asked Neil.

"Hurt it in the crash which killed my wife. Perhaps it affected my head as well." He smiled for the second time. "I don't frighten you any more, do I, Inspector?"

"You never did frighten me. But you would hardly expect me to be any less wary of you, simply from hearing you tell me how harmless you are."

"I suppose not." Mr. Barnes looked carefully at Neil, who allowed him a slight smile in return. "And now I must go back to London."

"Without asking me any more questions?"

"I've got plenty to think about for the moment. And contrary to appearances I do have work to do. I'll see you again."

"That won't surprise me."

"Goodbye, Mr. Carter."

"Goodbye, Mr. Barnes. Look where you're treading, with that leg of yours, the path's very uneven."

"As I discovered on my way here. I'll take care."

Listening to the sounds of Humphrey Barnes limping away, Neil found himself envying the man. If he was what he seemed, he must feel all the time the way he, Neil, had felt in the car on the way back from Bristol, when he had seen life as rich, and felt it so strongly he had had to tell Annabel. As he sat there on the seat in the lane he felt it again, and was elated.

III

When Neil emerged on to the Big Green more than an hour later his elation had been overlaid by his now habitual Bunington wariness, but it remained, underneath, transforming his current uncertainties into an exciting challenge. He felt agreeably, straightforwardly, tired and thirsty as he skirted the Green towards the Red Lion.

Jim Bates was just opening the bar.

"You've got good instincts, Mr. Carter!"

"Give me a pint, Jim, I've never been so ready."

"Afraid I'm going to be too busy for a while to talk to you." Jim Bates offered a fractional inclination of his head towards the hallway as he drew the ale.

"That's all right. I'll take it out front."

Neil looked round as he left the bar, and this time noticed the open door and John's reptilian superintendent sitting low behind a table serving as a desk, nothing moving but his eyes, observing all comers. Nodding and smiling, not waiting to see if his gestures were returned, Neil went out on to the forecourt.

The metal seats had dried off, and when he had replaced the sweater he had shed somewhere in the country he was warm enough to sit in his original seat by the porch, looking across the Big Green.

The sky now was higher, with blue lakes among the clouds. Mallards were disporting in and around the pond, and there was colour again in the gardens. Jim Bates's part-time barmaid came up from the shops and went in with a nod. Neil heard Jim grumbling at her for being late. A couple of young men came up from the same direction, in working clothes, and passed him, smiling. An old, exquisitely maintained Bentley bore slowly down Church Lane and stopped in the act of turning left beside the Green. It stood still while Neil counted twenty, then reversed and parked beside the pub. Christopher Corrigan got out and came to sit down beside him. Neil saw the same look in his face as he had seen on the way out of church that morning.

"Have a drink?" he suggested.

The old man rumbled what might have been a token protest at the idea of being treated.

"No, please. You look as if you could do with a Scotch."

Neil got up without waiting to see how his further suggestion had been received, and called his order through.

"Want to talk to you," said Christopher Corrigan, as he sat down again.

"It's really the Latchford police you should talk to," said Neil gently, uncomfortably aware of the superintendent nearby. The old man looked incredulous, then, as he took Neil's meaning, haughty.

"I am not about to confess to a murder," he said stiffly.

"I wasn't thinking you were, sir. Although I admit I *was* assuming it had something to do with Mr. Darcy's death. And I have to be careful, because I have no official position in the inquiry. But if there were anything else . . ."

He waited, watching, and the most noticeable thing was the sagging of the shoulders, which had straightened up as Christopher Corrigan took offence. But Neil was also aware of the change in the face, as the new look of suffering seeped back through the old look of pride, softening and blurring the features so that he was reminded of the cousin, Bedlington Byrne.

"Learned today," rasped Christopher Corrigan, his voice unmodified by the sorrow affecting his appearance and suiting strangely with his words, "what it is to be too late to put things right."

"Tell me?"

The barmaid appeared and set down the double whisky. Neil indicated his own empty glass.

"He was my cousin," said Christopher Corrigan, when they were alone again, "son of my father's sister."

He lapsed into silence and Neil waited, noticing with a lift of the heart that the swan was back, drifting intermittently visible beyond the willows. A mallard, preening on the edge of the Green, fluttered a few feet into the air, squawking, as a police car screamed with unnecessary efficiency to a stop beside the Bentley. But for all its occupants knew, thought Neil, the superintendent might have been standing in the doorway of the inn. The two uniformed men who got out of the car smiled automatically towards him as they went inside, through expressions of preoccupied anxiety.

". . . Aunt Laura made a foolish marriage." Neil jumped discreetly to attention. "Ran away against father's wishes. Eloping, they call it. Came back alone with the baby to the cottage. Father gave her the cottage. Saw her all right, but didn't see *her*. When she died, son stayed on. Bedlington. Worked in Latchford, retired. All right, you know, but—two old men, lonely, big house, plenty of money, no wife—never had a wife, either of us—damn ridiculous, never spoke, all that room . . . Shabby place, old women coming in, or not, not looked after, ill, drinking . . . Too late . . ."

Christopher Corrigan's features had been designed, and tempered through the years, to convey pride and confidence. Neil had to look away as they crumpled.

"Have a drink," he said to the table, as his own beer was set in

front of him. He buried his face in the froth. When he looked up
again the old man to his relief was much as he had been when he
had first sat down, except that there was a tear running down his
cheek.

"Damn ridiculous thing," he said, "all those years."

"Yes."

Not ridiculous, thought Neil, monstrous. Decades of father and
daughter under separate roofs nearby, maintaining a total lack of
contact. Decades of solitary cousins, each one without wife or child,
doing the same. Only of course this cousin, for most of those years,
had not been without a friend. Had Christopher Corrigan's companion been tall and fair?

"But you weren't alone," said Neil softly, "so what you did—or
didn't do—is understandable."

He had thought the face was as red as it could go, but it noticeably darkened, and the old man clutched the table top as a preliminary to rising.

"Finish your drink," Neil said quickly, laying a hand briefly on
the huge dark paw and holding the glaring eyes until the hostility
went out of them. "Did you ever try to approach your cousin?"

"No." Mr. Corrigan sat back in his seat but left his hand on the
table. Neil knew he was being assessed now as a man. "And it
would have to have come from me. Any approach. I was the one
who had things to offer."

"Even when you were little boys . . ."

"Wasn't allowed."

"Then you are not so much to blame. Other people decided how
you were to behave."

"Dammit, man, I came of age!"

Now there were two tears, one down each cheek. Neil was glad of
John, driving himself up from Latchford way, parking beside the
other police car and coming over to them. The old man continued to
stare at Neil, neither squaring his frame nor wiping his eyes. Evidently his remorse, or his confusion, was stronger even than his
inbred sense of what was due from him. Neil felt a pang of pity.

"All right?" enquired John, with his cheerful smile.

"All right." Neil tried to appear equally cheerful. "Mr. Corrigan
and I have just been having a chat. Will you join us? Your Super's
in," he added, *sotto voce*.

"Must be getting along," said Christopher Corrigan, rising to his
feet. Neil saw that imperceptibly he had restored his customary ap-

pearance and that only the two glistening tracks down his cheeks bore witness to his agitation. "Thanks for the drink," he mumbled.

"Thank you for joining me," said Neil, but he was talking to the old man's retreating back.

"What was all that about?" asked John, as they both watched the Bentley on its way.

"Not about afternoon tea with the curate, I'm afraid. Although I think I learned something . . . The old boy's apparently suffering remorse because he didn't do anything for his cousin. Heavens, John, because he didn't even speak to his cousin, throughout their lives."

"Of course, he wasn't alone for most of the time."

"That's what I said to him."

"You did! And the reaction?"

"Fury. He calmed down when I—brought my charm to bear. Poor old sod." He thought John looked severe. "Aren't you going to sit down?"

"Mustn't. Must go through. Will you be around later?"

"Not this evening. I'm taking Mrs. Quillin out to dinner. She goes away in the morning, and I'll be gone when she gets back."

"I see. I hope you have a good time."

Just occasionally Neil wondered, with John, where discretion ended and naivety began.

"Any developments?"

"Nothing. Nothing."

"It was only yesterday."

"Neil, you know as well as I do that on our time scale yesterday is a long way behind."

"Yes, I do. Good luck inside."

He took Annabel to dinner at the Frog. It had won over the Rose and Crown as the setting in which he would remember them together.

Their last outing had the special sweetness of their first. They enjoyed their food and drink, laughed, whispered in each other's ears on the dance floor. At no point during the evening did either of them mention the fact that their Bunington idyll, at last, was over, and Annabel mentioned it only implicitly at the end, by leading him into the dark silent house, into the little room on the ground floor with the key and the venetian blind.

Once, the only time in the time he had known her, he sensed her trying to memorize his face. Before he left he scribbled an endearment on one of his cards, and closed her hand over it.

"You already know where I live," she said in return.

It was as if something had been got out of the way.

"I'll pick you up at ten tomorrow," he said from the doorway, memorizing her in his turn, glowing palely in the lamplight. More disturbing than leaving her was Tony's face glimpsed for a second between the banisters.

CHAPTER 14

I

Tony next morning awaited Neil's arrival at Wesley House with slight anxiety. He had come out on to the landing in the night because he had wakened to the sound of voices downstairs and thought they might belong to burglars. When the figure in the hall had looked up and he had recognized Neil he had been so relieved he had taken a little too long to dart away. He didn't want Neil to think he had been spying, especially since he somehow no longer held views about him and Annabel.

Just before ten he went and hung about the gate. When Neil arrived he jumped into the passenger seat of the car. As they looked at one another mutual wariness faded into grins.

"I thought I heard burglars last night," said Tony hurriedly. "I've got into the car because I want to tell you something. Aunt Helen's changed her ideas. Now she wants the cottage done up, and let!"

"What does your father want?"

"He goes along with it."

"And you?"

"I think it's great. I'll be a landlord as well as a householder. And then I can live in it myself eventually. Annabel got Aunt Helen to promise that I could have the biggest say on what we do to the cottage. Annabel knows I've got good ideas about the insides of houses.

Like my mother, you know. Annabel does know things sometimes, that other people don't. Well, that Dad and Aunt Helen don't."

"Yes."

Neil turned away from Tony's flushed cheerful face. Annabel had come out of the house and was standing watching them. Neil opened the car door.

"I shall have to go back to London soon. Will you ask me to coffee in the cottage tomorrow morning?"

"Gosh, yes!"

"Get out, then, and bring Annabel's case."

It was a small case, matching the dressing case she kept in her hand. She had never looked more beautiful. Neil could not imagine that any man, ever, would be able to take the continuance of her favour for granted.

Tony and Aunt Helen waved them off. They didn't talk until they were almost in Latchford, and then Neil asked what train Annabel was catching. It was the only question he had asked her about her visit to the seaside.

"London. And then I go on from there. When will you go back to London?"

"Before the weekend. Of course, I could be back again, if the Latchford police ask for help."

It was the first time he had thought of this possibility in relation to himself and Annabel. Glancing at her composed face, he had no means of knowing whether or not she had thought of it or, if so, what the thought had meant to her. She said nothing and he went on, briefly uncomfortable,

"Of course, bureaucracy being what it is, I might not be the officer assigned to the case. Which way from here?"

"Left then right."

On Latchford station Neil became aware that the morning was damp. It hadn't rained since the night, but the platform gleamed and a moist wind sneaked across it. They talked, laughing a little, about the law of life which put railway platforms in the teeth of prevailing winds. They looked in at the waiting-room window, and after observing its serious-faced occupants and the pock- and graffiti-marked walls, walked up and down, lightly holding hands, until the train arrived. When he had stowed her case on the rack, pulled the window down and come back on to the platform there were only a few seconds in which to take her hand across the sill and kiss her.

"Thank you," he said, "Annabel," as the train began to move. To his surprise, as their fingertips yearned briefly, finally, he thought she looked wistful. "Have a good time."

"Thank you," she said sombrely. "Goodbye, Neil."

"Goodbye."

The line ran straight into the distance, and he watched the train as far as his eyes could see, even after the white blob of her had disappeared from the carriage window. As he drove back to Bunington his almost detached admiration of their sophisticated stance grew inadequate and he felt chilled and solitary, touched by that distaste for himself which was always waiting to pounce. Jim Bates in the doorway of the Red Lion was a warming sight.

But Jim said without preliminary, jerking his head towards the open door behind him, "They want you in there. They're waiting for you."

II

The superintendent was behind the makeshift desk, as Neil had seen him the day before. But now he was flanked by John Oliver and Sergeant Benson, and Alec Naylor sat opposite.

The superintendent indicated a chair at the side of the room, in neither camp. As he sat down Neil sensed an atmosphere which made him uneasy.

The superintendent turned his bright black eyes on John, who turned to Neil. Alec Naylor had his head down and was examining his knees.

"Inspector Carter," said John, "Mr. Naylor has come in to talk to us further, and in the light of what he's said, we hope you may be able to help us."

"I?" He caught Sergeant Benson's eye, and it slid away. The atmosphere, as yet impossible for Neil to define, was visibly affecting everyone in the room except the superintendent.

"Yes." John gave a brilliant insincere smile. "Mr. Naylor," he said gently, almost coaxingly, "will you tell Inspector Carter what you have just told us?"

Gradually Alec Naylor raised his head, and having done so looked Neil squarely, if deferentially, in the eye.

"I didn't want to say what I just said, Mr. Carter, I really didn't. I've got a very great respect for the ministry. I wasn't going to say anything, in fact, and then I thought about it again, and I decided, however I felt, it was my duty—"

"Just tell him, Mr. Naylor," said the superintendent softly.

"Yes, sir, of course, sir. I'm sorry." The churchwarden took a deep breath and expelled it slowly. "Well, Mr. Carter, you know I already told the police that I was in the vestry on Saturday night when the vicar was preparing the Elements. I came in while he was doing it, and I left while he was still there. I said that right away."

"Yes?" Neil's throat was dry.

"What I didn't say . . . what I felt I couldn't say, at first . . . when I went into the vestry—through the outside door and perhaps a bit hasty, a bit sudden—the vicar . . . he sort of jerked back from the table and I saw his hand go to his pocket—he was wearing an ordinary jacket, Mr. Carter—and the lid of the silver jug banged down. Of course I didn't think anything about it—then—I just said, 'I gave you a shock, Ernest,' or something like that, and he laughed, and said, 'Yes, you did.' And then I was just there for a moment, checking on a list as the superintendent knows—"

"Yes, I know," said the superintendent. "What is it, Mr. Carter?"

Neil had started, remembering the churchwarden's reproving words in his bedroom the morning of the curate's death. *The clergy, Mr. Carter, they must be above reproach!* He had thought Naylor was talking about the curate, but he wasn't, he was talking about the vicar. But what had he said then? Something about *wanting to talk to you about my . . . my . . .* Somehow Neil didn't think the churchwarden had still been on the same subject. There was something else . . .

"Nothing, sir," he said firmly to the superintendent, who, after staring at him thoughtfully for a moment, turned back to Mr. Naylor.

"Then I left," said Mr. Naylor. "And left the vicar there."

"What was he doing when you left?" asked Neil. He felt stiff and there was a cold lump in his chest. He was now able to interpret the mood of the room. It was embarrassment.

"Still pottering about by the table. Of course I wasn't really watching him, not thinking there was any reason—"

"Thank you, Mr. Naylor, you have been very helpful." The superintendent made Neil uneasy. The man never gave any indication of when he was going to speak. "Please don't talk of our conversation here to anyone."

"Of course not, Superintendent." There was a shade of reproach in Alec Naylor's flat slow voice. Under the superintendent's steady gaze he got to his feet and walked to the door.

"Good morning," said the superintendent, when he had reached it. Alec Naylor closed the door quietly behind him.

"Inspector Oliver," invited the superintendent at once.

"The night Bedlington Byrne died, Neil," said John, "you called at the hospital in Latchford on your way back from London with Tony Chapman. When you went into the ward Mr. Groome was with Byrne. It was he who told you the old man had died. We'd like you to think very carefully whether there was anything in the vicar's manner to indicate—alarm at your entry, or any unnatural sort of agitation."

"Anything," supplemented the superintendent, "which you would not have expected to see."

Neil's mental picture of the vicar jerking up from beside the bed, losing his footing, clutching at the coverlet to regain his balance, slotted vividly in.

"Yes," he said heavily, and told them.

"This is extremely unpleasant," said the superintendent, when he had finished, not looking as if it was anything to him personally.

"There are a number of apparent motives," Neil heard himself saying, "and of opportunities to match them."

"Certainly there are, Mr. Carter." The superintendent's soft confident voice roused irritation in Neil. "However, the vicar prepared the Communion wine on both occasions. On both occasions he had arranged for the curate to take the service, and therefore to drink first. He had a reaction to Mr. Naylor coming into the vestry which would be peculiar in anyone who had nothing to hide. He was alone when the old man died, and had a guilty reaction when you went in . . . Oh, we know it was expected that the old man could die at any time, but his end could have been hastened. Something held quite briefly over the nose and mouth would have been enough. There was no strength for a struggle. And his wife was receiving court from the curate."

"Which she admitted."

"Yes. But we do not know that she did not reciprocate."

"It's a formidable list." He had to make a real effort to hide his discomfort.

"Let us say," said the superintendent, "that it adds up to the advisability of putting the vicar ahead of the other suspects at this juncture."

The superintendent was on his feet, near the door collecting his coat off the coat stand. "I'll be back at two," he told John and the sergeant, "and we'll continue together. Inspector Carter." He went out.

"Continue what?" asked Neil, without vetting the question first to see if it was proper.

"Seeing the vicar again," explained John. "Look, I'm sorry I can't lunch today, I promised Jill I'd slip home."

"That's all right." He was glad not to have to make an excuse. He left the Red Lion a few minutes after John had driven away, and set off along Church Lane.

III

Mrs. Groome made Neil think of autumn, with her orange dress and dark gold hair. He found it appropriate. The events of the last weeks should have worn out any summer.

"May I see your husband? I'm not here officially, of course."

"Come in."

She was as serene as ever. She led him this time into another room, where the vicar was sitting behind a desk, writing. He got up as he saw Neil and indicated one of the armchairs. As Neil sat down he came round the desk and took the other.

"I'm glad to see you, Mr. Carter."

"Are you, Mr. Groome?"

He stared into the pale eyes, aware as always of the glow to each side of them, from the vicar's wet white temples. Even while he felt for his handkerchief and dabbed his forehead, the vicar held Neil's gaze.

"Are you unwell?" Neil asked him.

"I am never well physically. But I manage."

"I hope you are no worse because of what has happened."

Mr. Groome shrugged. "Perhaps. It's to be expected, with a weak heart."

"Heart in the other sense—courage—that hasn't been weak."

"My congregation has never needed it more."

"And you?"

"Nor I!"

"How in God's name do you do it?"

"In God's name, Mr. Carter! Just think for a moment what the

Church has had to bear through the centuries!" Mr. Groome bundled himself excitedly out of his chair and took a turn in the space between them. Neil saw him blink for a second as his leg came into sharp contact with the corner of his desk. He stood leaning against the desk, a faint colour in his cheeks, the only time Neil had seen it there. "Murder, war, intrigue, a man like Becket taken beside the altar, the Saviour hung up on a cross! There can be nothing worse than that, Mr. Carter, and that was the *beginning* of the Church, that was what the Church was founded on! Because of that, nothing subsequent has power to shake it, even hatred in its name. Antagonistic and indifferent people, corrupt priests, calumnies—"

"Mr. Groome!" Neil surprised himself by the urgent sound of his voice. The vicar sat down again and looked at him, waiting. "Corrupt priests," said Neil more gently. "Calumnies. A priest might be corrupt, or he might be calumniated. Two possible evils." He stared into the vicar's steady eyes. "You prepared the Elements for last Sunday and the Sunday before. On both occasions you gave the conduct of the service to Mr. Darcy. Alec Naylor has now told the police that you had a guilty reaction on Saturday night when he came on you in the vestry. You certainly had one when I joined you at Bedlington Byrne's death bed."

They stared at one another in silence. Neil was aware of a bee, droning its way up the window pane. Beyond the window rain was falling again, softly. The vicar said at last:

"I am, and always have been, a very clumsy man. With nervous reactions. There is never a time when I am not carrying bruises somewhere on my body. In a situation such as this I can only make the worst possible impression. Did you tell the police—the other police—what you had seen?"

"Yes. I didn't want to."

"Why not?"

"Because I was convinced—am convinced—you had merely been startled out of a state of prayer or contemplation."

"Were convinced. Or hoped?"

"Oh, yes, I hoped."

"Why?"

"Because of my observation of you. And admiration."

"And?"

The sense of insistence in the room was swinging back and forth between them, and now it was all in the eyes opposite.

"Yes, all right," said Neil, "because I was brought up to believe that you are the representative of God on earth."

"And therefore, can do no wrong?"

"Yes," said Neil reluctantly, "that's what I hoped."

The vicar got to his feet again and walked round the desk. He faced Neil across it.

"Mr. Carter," he said, "you are naive. For all your sophistication you are naive."

"That's not something I ever expected to hear." His attempt at casualness was, to himself at least, a painfully inadequate coverage of his shock.

"Naive people put too heavy a burden on corrupt priests."

"Don't talk like that!" Neil leapt to his feet and glared across the desk.

"Sit down!" commanded the vicar. "That was my bitter moment," he murmured, when Neil had obeyed him. "It has passed." Again he dabbed at his temples. "Mr. Carter, because suspicion is on me does not mean it is on the Church. The Church survives all its incompetent vessels."

"I came among my other reasons," said Neil, "to tell you that I don't regard you as an incompetent vessel. Or a corrupt one."

"Thank you. Whatever I say, whatever happens, I cherish your coming."

"Mr. Groome." With an effort he tried to pull the interview back into its intended shape. "The police will be arriving again at any time."

"So you came also to warn me?"

"I think so."

"And to try me. The devil's advocate."

"My own advocate. I came for my own sake, as well as yours." Having confessed it, he felt immediately lighter.

Mr. Groome made the motion of squaring his short fat figure.

"Well, Mr. Carter, I must meet what is ordained for me."

Neil found there was one other thing he had to say.

"If there was a first miracle, there could be a second."

"You're quite right. But there is no if about it. There was a first miracle."

"There was?"

"Yes. It was in Cana of Galilee. Now, if you will leave me, I will prepare for my next visitors."

"I can't deny you, Vicar."

"That's blasphemy, Mr. Carter!"

Neil got up, bent his head over the desk, heard his voice.

"Give me your blessing."

He felt the damp pressure of the vicar's hands. When they withdrew he went quickly out of the room without a look or a word. The hall was deserted and he let himself out of the house and turned down the lane away from the village.

IV

He walked for a long time, under the soft rain, down lanes and across fields where he had not yet been. As on his last Bunington walk he felt rather than thought, aware of the birds singing joyously and flocking along the hedges, the sheep and cows in the fields, the varied colour patterns of the crops. The vicar's words, "I must meet what is ordained for me," repeated themselves in his head like a refrain, against each scene as he passed it. He was neither happy nor sad, anxious nor comforted. He felt the rain soaking his shirt and jacket and at last even his trousers, the strength in his limbs as he moved. He had the sensation that, although he was treading the earth, vigorously, aware of the varying textures underfoot of turf and soil and pebble, he was in reality floating above the ground. When he found himself back in Church Lane he had no idea how long he had been away.

The door of the church was open and he walked up the path and looked inside.

The interior was dusky and silent, empty but for one figure which knelt near the front beside the aisle. As it shifted, jerkily, half turning its head, Neil saw that it was the vicar. With his lost sense of time he was unable to think whether Mr. Groome was still preparing for the visit of the Latchford police or recovering from it. For a few seconds he watched the now motionless figure, finding himself moved by the meekness of the priest kneeling in the congregation. Then, barely deciding he would do it, he moved quietly into the body of the church, entered a pew near the back, and himself knelt down. As he knelt there, still not thinking, the state of suspension in which he had roamed the countryside seemed to intensify and reveal itself as a state of prayer. Ever since his conscientious boyhood he had equated prayer with effort, and was astonished. Even the intensification of the feeling, now, was something outside and beyond his own conscious powers. He waited, not trying to put it into words, aware of himself only as the centre of a growing expectation. But as at that other time, when he had sat waiting in the lady chapel for John Oliver, he began to be afraid, and then he did seek words, asking to be spared such feeling . . .

He was relieved, released from awesome possibilities, when he heard the door creak, and then steps behind him. He looked up as they passed down the nave, and saw Mrs. Naylor walking towards the still motionless kneeling figure of the vicar. As she touched him on the shoulder and, starting awkwardly up from his knees, he turned towards her, Neil got up and went out.

The rain had stopped, but for the first time the damp clothes on his back felt uncomfortable. He didn't know what or how, but he knew something had begun to happen. He went quickly down the path and turned towards the Red Lion. Jim Bates was in the hall.

"I'm cold and wet, Jim."

As Jim put out a hand to feel his jacket, Neil's teeth began to chatter.

"For heaven's sake, man!"

Jim propelled him into his own room, where there was a small wood fire. He disappeared and came back in a moment with Neil's towel and dressing-gown. Perhaps the best thing about Jim Bates was the way he seemed to understand things without asking questions. He went out again and Neil took all his clothes off, rubbed himself down vigorously with the towel, donned the dressing-gown, and sat on the mat as close as possible to the fire. When Jim came back he was carrying a tray of tea and toast.

"This'll put you right," he said, as he set it on the table.

"I'm all right now, Jim." He was. Calm and unanxious and even happy. Suddenly, sharply, happy at the sight of Jim's tray-load and the thought of Jim's wise kind instincts. "But I'll be better still after that."

There was lemon cheese with the toast. Neil thought food had never tasted so good. Only when he had eaten three rounds and drunk two cups of tea did it occur to him that he hadn't spotted the open door or the superintendent. He stretched his legs out to the fire.

"It was very quiet in the hall, Jim."

"Yes. They're all out and about."

"I think I'll go and have a bath."

"That's a very good idea. Have a kip as well, until dinner. There's salmon tonight."

"I think I'll do that too. Even though this is a room I feel I never want to leave."

Neil gathered up his damp clothes. The hall was fresh and cool after Jim's sealed seasoned box. There was still no sign of police presence in the inn. He climbed slowly upstairs, spent a long time in a hot bath, then went back into his room, into bed and almost immediately to sleep, aware of the gently stirring curtains at the open window and his sense of well-being.

He was awakened by a knock on the door, and struggled up into renewed apprehension.

It was Jim Bates.

"Inspector Oliver's just rung for you. Can you go right away to the vicarage?"

CHAPTER 15

1

When Neil reached the vicarage Mrs. Groome was just showing a uniformed constable out of the front door. Her eyes told Neil nothing and she turned quickly away and led him into the room where she had taken him the first time he had called. He had the impression it was full of people, at first out of focus round the clear central figure of the vicar, sitting in his chair by the long window, the enclosed garden behind him lit by evening sunshine. Neil searched the vicar's face, but there were no more clues than there had ever been, and the handkerchief was still furtively at work. When Neil looked beyond the vicar he saw that the other people were the superintendent, John Oliver, Sergeant Benson with an open notebook, a young WPC, and Mrs. Naylor. Mrs. Naylor looked completely different, blazing-eyed and bold. John and the sergeant looked worried.

"Inspector Carter," said the superintendent, moving no more than the fingers of one small wrinkled hand, "please sit down."

Mrs. Groome put gentle pressure on his arm and he found himself joining John on the sofa. Mrs. Groome went and sat on the stool beside her husband's chair. Neil watched the superintendent's face, but even so had no warning of the thin dry voice.

"Inspector Oliver," said the superintendent, and the vicar pressed his handkerchief against his forehead, "since it is at your request that Inspector Carter has joined us, perhaps you will acquaint him of developments."

"Of course, sir."

The superintendent had a book between his hands. Neil could only think of the group in the makeshift office at the Red Lion, when it had been the husband present, and of how long ago that first encounter seemed, and how distant its pervasive embarrassment. Now the atmosphere seemed charged, excited.

"Inspector Carter . . ." began John, but Mrs. Naylor interrupted him.

"I've just killed my husband," she snapped, turning round on Neil. He had to blink against the brilliant certainty of her eyes.

"That is so," said the superintendent softly, riffling the pages of the book. Neil noticed that the contents were handwritten.

"He was in love with her!" said Mrs. Naylor indignantly. "And then after he'd killed the curate, out of jealousy, he tried to throw suspicion on the vicar."

Several people started to speak at once, but it was the vicar's quiet insistent tone which came through.

"I did—jump, Amy, when Alec came into the vestry. My thoughts were a long way off, and I came back abruptly. Alec was telling the truth."

He mopped his brow and she tossed her head away from him. Mrs. Groome sat motionless, staring down at her hands joined loosely in her lap. Neil didn't look at her again directly, but he felt her all the time like a golden mote in the corner of his eye.

"He killed Mr. Darcy because he was in love with her," said Mrs. Naylor aggressively to the yellow top of the superintendent's head, bent over the book, "and then he tried to throw suspicion on the vicar." She nodded with a significant look towards the book, then turned round on Neil again. "He left the book out," she told him, "and so I found it. The only time he's ever forgotten to lock it up. He wrote about her a lot." Her bright eyes clouded even as she stared triumphantly at Neil, and she looked bewildered, vaguely patting at her hair.

"Inspector Oliver!" pleaded Neil.

John and the superintendent started to speak on an instant, and John gave way.

"It is true, Mr. Carter," said the superintendent, still turning the pages of the book but now looking up at Neil. "Mrs. Naylor put paraquat in her husband's tea this afternoon, and it killed him."

"Yes, I managed better than Janet Arkwright," said Mrs. Naylor complacently.

"And it's all explained in the book," supplied Neil. The wave of relief flowing over him was so strong he had to make an effort to continue grave. He glanced now at the Groomes, and the vicar was watching him. Mrs. Groome was still unmoving in her little-girl attitude, her hands motionless on her knees.

"You could say that," answered the superintendent. At last he snapped the book shut, and looked across at Neil with a sigh. "Mr. Naylor kept a detailed daily diary of his thoughts and deeds. He was certainly much preoccupied with thoughts of—the vicar's wife. And with views on how the clergy should conduct themselves. He made no attempt to reconcile these opposing preoccupations, or even to remark on the paradox, but perhaps that is not surprising." Neil saw the superintendent's lips twist and wondered if he had bitten his tongue before he realized that he was smiling. "He had a third preoccupation," continued the superintendent.

"Yes, sir?" asked Neil, into the expectant stare.

"His wife."

Neil looked at Mrs. Naylor, and she was as still and downcast as the vicar's wife. Yet he felt that she was temporarily deaf to what went on around her, and he knew that the vicar's wife was an instrument bound to record every note which sounded in the room.

"His wife, sir?"

"He knew that his wife was not . . ." The superintendent also glanced at Mrs. Naylor, and appeared to come to Neil's conclusion. "He knew his wife was mentally unstable. He seemed, strangely, to fear that she might implicate him in some way in the investigations. He says at one point"—the superintendent looked down at the book again, and quickly found what he wanted—"'I tried to say something about Amy. Perhaps I should try again.'"

"In my room after the murder," said Neil. "That was it. He said 'My . . . my . . .' and didn't get any further."

"Yes, Mr. Carter?" pressed the superintendent.

"He obviously wanted to tell me something when he came up to my room after the murder, sir." Neil realized as he was speaking that John in a million years would never have let his Super know that his fellow inspector had cut a suspect short. "He talked about 'my . . . my . . . ,' but he couldn't get it out. When he came to you this morning"—he felt dizzy a moment as he realized that the other meeting was only a matter of hours behind them—"to tell you about—the vicar's reaction in the vestry—I thought at first it was *that* he was wanting to tell me about, but I really knew it wasn't. It was his wife."

Both wives still sat motionless, their eyes on their laps. The WPC had a red spot in the centre of each cheek.

"Yes, well, Mr. Carter, it seems that he had cause."

"And the murder, sir," said Neil, looking towards the book.

"The murder, Mr. Carter?"

"I suppose he killed the curate because he saw him—put his hand out to Mrs. Groome in the vestry that Sunday morning." Neil tried not to sound eager and made a point of not looking at the vicar or Mrs. Groome.

"I don't think he can have seen the curate with Mrs. Groome in the vestry, Mr. Carter." The superintendent stared expressionlessly at Neil. "I think he would have mentioned it in his diary." Neil stared back. "There *is* a relevant passage," said the superintendent. He bent his head, turned a few pages, and began to read. " 'Darcy speaks of his admiration for Naomi. Of her kindness to him. He says, "I am at the vicarage often, and she is always kind to me." Jealousy. It tears me. Blurs my sight.' That is all, Mr. Carter, on the subject of the curate vis-à-vis the vicar's wife."

The superintendent looked up at Neil and Mrs. Naylor said sharply, without moving, "He didn't call her Naomi to her face, of course. Oh, no!"

Even the superintendent turned his head. Mrs. Groome was still staring at her legs.

"And he murdered for that!" Neil broke the fascinated silence in which most of them were looking at Mrs. Naylor. "May I ask what he recorded of the murder, sir?"

"Nothing at all, Mr. Carter." The superintendent could have been smiling again, more sourly. "Naylor has turned merely from a live suspect into a dead one."

The superintendent was on his feet. His movement appeared to

bring Mrs. Naylor back to vague awareness. She lifted her eyes and
stared at him, passing a hand uncertainly across her head. "I never
combed my hair before coming out . . . I had to get the bus, of
course, and it was damp . . . What else is there, sir?"

"Nothing else, I don't think," said the superintendent.

"Can we go now?" Mrs. Naylor got to her feet, picked up her
handbag and clutched it against her. "He was in love with her," she
said, turning the renewed angry brilliance of her gaze on to Neil.
"That's why he did it. And then he tried to throw suspicion on the
vicar."

The WPC moved closer to Mrs. Naylor, and Mrs. Naylor turned
and stared at her. Neil saw the girl struggle to banish the look of
revulsion from her face, and succeed.

"WPC Roberts will look after you," said the superintendent to
Mrs. Naylor. "Go with you and Sergeant Benson to your house to
collect some things, and then bring you to the station at Latchford."

Mrs. Naylor shrugged. "She needn't touch me." She drew her
skirt away on the side nearer to the WPC.

The superintendent turned to the window. "Do you want to
speak to her, sir?" he asked the vicar.

"I don't think now . . . Go in peace, Amy," said the vicar wearily.
"Thank you for trying to help me. I will see you." The fingers of his
right hand formed a tiny cross close to his chest. Mrs. Naylor stared
at him. Mrs. Groome got slowly to her feet and raised her eyes, settling them tranquilly on the distance.

"Come along," said WPC Roberts. The red had spread from her
cheeks, all over her face.

Mrs. Naylor was in the centre of the small file as it left the room.
"I'll see you later, Neil," murmured John, the last to go.

Mrs. Groome followed them and Neil and the vicar stood alone.
Neil said, "I'm sorry," annoying himself, and the vicar murmured,
"Amy, oh, Amy."

When Mrs. Groome came back she passed Neil without acknowledgement and went up to her husband. They took hands and stood
gazing at one another. Neil watched them, unaware of himself as an
extra presence in the room until at the same moment, without releas-
ing hands, they turned towards him.

"Goodbye," he said then, going to the door. He felt an enervating
wave of oppression and disappointment. "Please don't bother to see
me out." He turned before going into the hall, and they hadn't

moved. "I'm sorry," he said again, and the vicar said, as he and his wife turned back to face one another, "Thank you, Mr. Carter."

II

The front door bell rang as he was about to open it. Janet Arkwright was on the step, smiling and holding out a wrapped package. Her smile changed when she saw Neil, becoming at the same time more guarded and more provocative. She let the package drop to her side, but held it out again when Mrs. Groome appeared beside him.

"From my father," she said, smiling as she had first smiled when Neil opened the door. "A bottle of his elderberry. I was to tell you it was especially for you, Mrs. Groome."

"Thank you, dear. That's very kind of your father." Mrs. Groome put the swathed bottle on the hall table.

"Goodbye again, then," said Neil, crossing the threshold. He put his arm across Janet's shoulders, to encourage her away from the vicarage. They walked to the gate together.

"I reckon my luck could be in today," said Janet, turning and facing him when they were in the lane.

"You do?"

She was more sure of herself than he had yet seen her, and for the first time he was more aware of her as a woman than as a schoolgirl. She was wearing a coarse cotton skirt and cheesecloth blouse and her hair was untidy. Her figure was very good. She carried a bulging canvas bag by a long frayed strap over her shoulder.

"I'm going to Latchford," she said, riveting his eyes.

"Yes?"

The game took the edge off his dissatisfaction.

"There isn't a bus for another ten minutes, and it's so slow anyway."

"You'd like me to run you there?"

"You'd be an angel."

He could tell she was trying not to show too much eagerness.

"I don't think I'd ever be that, but all right, I'll take you into Latchford."

He had a book in the car he'd promised to lend Jill Oliver, and he could drop it in at the Division.

"Thanks!" She set out, with long strides, and he walked beside her. She went straight up to his car on the forecourt of the Red Lion and stood expectantly beside it. When they were a mile or two out of the village he asked her what she was up to.

"I'm going to London, Mr. Policeman."

"Tonight? And where's your luggage?"

His hand was on the gear lever and she pushed a corner of the canvas bag under the spread of his fingers.

"I've got all I need in here for a week."

"You're going for a week?"

He felt her shrug, as he felt the close scrutiny of her gaze. He seemed unable to take his eyes off the road.

"I don't know. I just want to get away from my father." Fractionally she hesitated. "It's all right, Mr. Policeman, I'm going to stay with a friend. Anyway, I can take care of myself." He believed in her competence even as she relaxed, stretching out with a luxurious sigh, and he could see her legs and an arm out of the corner of his eye. "Away from Bunington," she murmured, "I can breathe." He thought of the young Annabel.

On the outskirts of Latchford the road divided, left to the railway station, right to the town. The Division was in town. As he swung right Janet sat up.

"You've gone the wrong way, Mr. Carter!"

"Yes, Janet, I'm going to the police station."

"Oh, no!"

"Oh, yes, Janet," he countered goodhumouredly, wondering at her insistence. The Division was just in sight, at the end of a long straight stretch of road.

"No, Mr. Carter, no!"

He felt pressure in his side and glanced down. He knew right away that the metal tube was a gun barrel. The knowledge pervaded him physically, to his toes and fingertips.

"If you stop," Janet said quickly and quietly, "if you slow down, I shall shoot you. I shan't kill you, but I really will hurt you, Mr. Policeman. If I shot you in the knee it might never be quite the same again. I really do mean it."

He turned his head slightly towards the Divisional building as, at a steady pace, he passed it.

"Keep left for the station," said Janet, holding the gun steady, "and stop short of it."

He did as he was told. He was reluctant to turn and face her, and when he did he was surprised that she didn't look intense, that she even grinned at him, almost playfully renewing his awareness of the gun in his side.

"You're awfully clever," she said admiringly.

He went to open the door of the car, and she flicked the safety catch.

"All right," he said, ostentatiously folding his hands in his lap. "Now, please make that gesture in reverse." She did so, quickly, not looking down at the gun. "You're at home with it, aren't you?"

She shrugged. "I taught myself. It's my father's service revolver. He has a licence, Mr. Policeman." She grinned at him again. "You're not quite so clever as you think, actually, are you?"

He had just enough of himself left over from the tension to wonder at her nerve, at the calm of her face.

"I'm not so clever as you think I am, Janet."

But already he felt he had known for a long time. He had, perhaps, known in his instincts.

"What do you mean?" For the first time since they had stopped and faced one another, her eyes narrowed.

"Why did you think I was going to the Divisional police?"

"To hand me in, of course. I don't know how you knew."

He glanced at her steady hands.

"I didn't know. I was going to the Division to hand in a book I promised to lend Inspector Oliver's wife." He nodded towards the glove compartment. Her hands, both of them on the gun, began to tremble slightly. He kept his face and his voice without expression. "Your nerve gave a bit too soon, Janet. You would have sat in the car a couple of minutes while you waited for me, then I would have brought you here and you would have got out of the car and gone to London."

Her face was cold now with anger, her hands steady again.

"I shall get out of the car and go to London, Mr. Policeman."

"What time's your train?" He knew she would slip the safety catch if he so much as let his eyes stray.

"Half an hour."

"You might as well tell me about it, then." She couldn't possibly grow any more alert, she could only drop her guard. Her narrative might yield a moment where anger or triumph made her careless. It was not the first time he had lived in the precise second passing and not one second beyond it, but familiarity with the indescribable sensation, knowledge that so far it had ended well, brought no reassurance.

She smiled at him. "I *would* like to tell you, Mr. Policeman, as we've got the time. I'll stay in the car until just before the train. I'm afraid I shall have to shoot you before I go, so that you won't be able to get out and follow me." Her eyes briefly left his face, travelled down his body. "I'll shoot you in the leg," she said. "The leg, not the knee, and it'll get better. I'm sorry about it, but I promise it'll only be in the leg."

"Leave it until the last minute," suggested Neil.

"Of course. I don't want to do it at all." She smiled at him again, but her face hardened as she went on speaking. "I hate my father, Mr. Policeman, he's always been beastly to me, always. You see, he's never been interested in me, I'm just a nuisance, unless he's enjoying himself being cruel to me."

"Janet."

"It's true!" For the first time she spoke passionately, and he saw tears in her eyes. She shook her hair back from her face. "I did it as much against my father as against Malcolm."

"Against your father . . ." He felt curiously unreal, as if he was dreaming. Only he wasn't foolhardy enough to pinch himself to make sure he was awake.

"You'll see . . . I'll tell you . . . Malcolm wasn't interested in me either. I thought he was at first but he wasn't. Then I thought, he isn't interested in anyone, anyway, and then I saw him in the vestry. With her . . ." Janet shook her head, more fiercely, and one tear began to run down her cheek. But there were no tears in her voice. "I thought I'd die, but I didn't—do anything—until the next Saturday. My father beat me on Friday night for being out late. But I was only walking about, I didn't want to go home . . . I made cuts in the bruises with a knife and I showed them to people . . . I heard my father tell my mother that Malcolm was going to take the service and I remembered that poison they'd had for the wasps. I said, "If it's in the shed I'll use it." I didn't really think it would be, but it was. I recognized it because I was with my father when he got it. It was tricky the first time." Neil wondered if his anaesthesia had turned to paralysis, he couldn't get even his little finger to move against his knees. "There wasn't much time," said Janet, shifting her body but not her hands, "between everyone leaving after the early service and coming back for the next one. Not that it really mattered all that much if anyone saw me in or around the vestries—my father's always getting me to do things for him. I was lucky, though. I got behind those bushes opposite the vestry doors—they're thick but there's space behind—and I saw the vicar come out and when I went in there was no one else there. I'd got gloves on and I just lifted the lid of the jug and let some of the stuff drop in. The second time it was dead easy. I took my father's key and went in the night. I buried the stuff back again each time because I knew it was dangerous."

"Did you mean to poison yourself? You'd succeeded in your aim. Mr. Darcy was dead."

Her eyes filled with tears again, but her hands remained steady.

"Yes, I did. I felt awful. I wanted to die too. And then when it didn't work—perhaps I was glad. I don't know . . . My father was still foul. I told them in the hospital how cruel he was. And they saw the bruises, and the cuts."

"You wanted the police to think your father had poisoned the wine."

"Right first time!"

Her eyes were furiously sad, making him realize how superficial had been his judgement of her apparent calm. Making him realize that the moment of personal disturbance he was unable to place had been when she was standing near the bran tub at the Summer Fair.

"And you got on to the Press."

"Yes. That was a bit sort of extra. Something to do while I waited for next Sunday. Honestly, I quite enjoyed that, and being interviewed, and knowing how clever I was. I *am* clever, Mr. Policeman, although my father's never thought so, he made me leave school and go into the shop. He always wanted a boy. He hates me and I hate him."

Neil thought the hands had started to tremble, but not enough for him to try anything.

"What about the monkey?"

Her face clouded. "I didn't like that. When I came to do it, I didn't like it." She shook her hair back. "I got the banana ready during the night, in the garden. Then I just went for a walk and gave it to it where it was sitting on the gatepost. I wanted to make sure the stuff worked. It held out its hand for it. I stood at the gate," she said sadly. "It was awfully quick."

Against his picture of Janet going about her terrible business, Neil saw an hourglass with the sand pouring away his separation from pain and immobility. A quarter of an hour must have passed.

"What will you do when you get to London, Janet?" He was amazed at the normality of his voice.

"Get lost," she said. "I know someone who can help me. I know lots more than people imagine . . . than my father imagines . . ."

"Your mother . . ."

She tossed her head again. "I'm sorry for my mother but she's got no spirit. She should have gone ages ago."

"Where's the poison bottle?" he asked. He was talking at random.

"It's buried at the back of the farthest greenhouse," said Janet. His heart smote him to see her hump her left wrist and look at her watch. "It's empty, or all but. That's why I used paraquat this last time."

"This last time . . ."

"Yes!" She was more triumphant than she had yet been, and there was no doubt now that her hands were trembling. "You heard me, Mr. Policeman. I told Mrs. Groome my father had sent it, especially for her."

"Mrs. Groome . . ."

"Malcolm was in love with her." Janet's face was suddenly blank. She took a gulping breath. "But you've spoiled it, it's all spoiled. I've done it all for nothing. They'd have believed it was my father, because of Malcolm and me. But now you'll tell them . . . You'll still tell them, with a broken leg. I *do* have to kill you, Mr. Policeman."

But she was indecisive, faltering, for the first time. She had just realized that the linchpin of her genius had been pulled away. And Neil's numbed brain was running a picture now of Mrs. Groome, picking up a wrapped bottle from her hall table. He didn't stop to consider any longer. He came down on the trembling wrists with the force of his lifetime, a fraction after Janet had thrown the gun on the floor at his feet, crying out that she couldn't kill him, and then crying out with pain. She flung herself against his chest and burst into tears.

III

When he had disengaged himself Neil locked the gun in the glove compartment and drove to the Division. Janet was a child, sunk down in the seat beside him, sulky-faced, silent, occasionally giving a shuddering sob. He took her by the arm and tore into the building. The half-minute before Mrs. Groome answered the telephone was the longest of his life. The superintendent was standing watching him when he rang off. Neil talked to him before leaving the Division. He broke his journey back to Bunington to sit for he didn't know how long in the car, trying to understand things, at a spot where he could see into the distance. He drove on eventually because he knew John would come looking for him as soon as he was able.

There was a police car outside the Arkwrights' shop, and John met him on foot from his third tour of the Big Green.

"They've been taken back to Latchford," said John as he and Neil sat down outside the Red Lion. John's face was unusually flushed.

Neil called through for drinks. "Mrs. Arkwright?"

"Frozen. He too, of course. All very simple as far as we were concerned. Are you all right?"

"Yes." But he was having to make an effort not to shiver.

They sat in silence drinking the whisky which Neil had ordered without reference to John. It was a glorious evening, the dusk pink from a cloudless sunset.

"What do you think it is with Janet Arkwright?" John asked at last.

"I don't know." Neil thought of what she had done, and of what she had finally not done. "I suspect she isn't crazy. Or even psychopathic. Temporary insanity perhaps. I think—she's too young and too old at the same time. Very clever. Very potentially loving. It must all have gone dreadfully wrong at the most vulnerable moment."

"Arkwright really does seem to have been a hard father."

"Oh, yes. But perhaps he was afraid there was an abnormal amount to subdue."

"He'll never tell us. He'll never justify himself. I hope the mother gets over it."

"One couldn't get over that."

"I do congratulate you, Neil." Neil thought John really was pleased, his amiable face clear of any shadow of envy or disappointment. "The ridiculous thing is," went on John, "she wasn't even on our list of suspects. And even now one can see why she wasn't."

When John left he and Neil said goodbye for the time being. Neil went immediately to the vicarage. Both Groomes came to the door when he rang. To his credit and Neil's surprise, the superintendent had telephoned.

Mrs. Groome took his hands and drew him into the hall. She held on to his hands and smiled at him. There was a definite and peculiar power, a sort of sublimated sensuality.

"Thank you, Mr. Carter," she said softly. "We never can, of course, but we want to say it."

"And for your prayers," said the vicar.

He felt inadequate again, vaguely guilty.

"They were unlike the ones I used to have . . . make . . . whatever one does with prayers."

He hadn't at all wanted to make a silly joke at that point. But the vicar accepted it.

"One offers them, I think, Mr. Carter." Neil realized he had offered none when he had been in danger of death. Mrs. Groome was still holding his hands. He fancied a current running into them from hers, too rich for his blood. Gently he disengaged. "Try not to let this be just an episode, Mr. Carter," said the vicar lightly.

"No." He would have liked to say that what had happened would remain more than an episode, but he didn't know, and with such a man, in such a situation, he could not be glib.

"Pray for Janet, if you will."

They both showed him out, both silent, smiling gravely, and his sense of inadequacy went with him up the lane and across the Small Green. Helen Chapman was collecting gardening tools together. He called her to the gate, and told her that Janet Arkwright had confessed to the poisoning. She listened in silence, her colour ebbing. As he finished he saw that all her weight was on the gate, and he opened it carefully and helped her up the garden to the seat. They both sat down.

"Ernest and Naomi," she said, gazing at him. "Thank heaven."

"Pray heaven for Mrs. Arkwright." Neil seemed to hear himself speaking, learning what he was going to say as he listened. "And the father."

"Mrs. Arkwright is a nice woman. Mr. Carter, that must be the worst thing that could possibly happen to a mother."

Sombrely he agreed. A thrush repeated itself indignantly nearby, defying the dusk.

"I'm glad it's been solved," said Helen. "For all the obvious reasons, and also because if it hadn't been, poor George would never have been quite sure about his sister."

"Mothers would have looked at their choirboy sons, and felt the same."

"Yes." She got to her feet with almost her usual decisiveness of movement. "You'll come in?"

"Not now. I'll leave you to tell your brother and Tony."

He told Jim Bates the same edited story over a belated supper, and then rang his Chief.

It was impossible to tell his Chief, unlike the others, without presenting himself in an interesting light. Yet somehow in his own mind, despite the thrust and ambition of his nature, he was taking it quietly for granted, his elation was for things quite different.

His Chief was probably pleased, but soon changed the subject.

"You saw Mrs. Quillin on to her train this morning?"

"It seems like last month that I did that, Governor, but—yes." There was a silence. "No, I can't tell you any more about her trip than I could yesterday. And you did say I was not required to press for information."

"I did, Neil, I just thought that perhaps . . ."

"No."

"You modern young men are so restrained."

"That's not the general opinion. And anyway, you assume too much."

"Do I? Do I, Neil? Well, that's something else again. It's quiet here, by the way. I'll see you on Thursday morning."

"Thank you very much, Governor."

"And Neil. Well done."

The phone rang as he put the receiver down. It was Tony.

"Gosh, it was you I wanted to speak to," he said unnecessarily. "Aunt Helen's told me . . . You're coming to the cottage in the morning?"

"Of course. We have a date. I'm going to bed now to get in shape for it."

But he sat up another couple of hours with Jim in his cosy foetid room, drinking and talking.

CHAPTER 16

I

The sunshine next morning, Neil's last in Bunington, was painfully bright and searching, even through the filter of the curtains. It took him a long time to dress, and after putting his suitcase on the bed and making a few ineffectual turns of the room, he decided to pack later.

"If you haven't started the egg yet," he said to Jim Bates as he sat carefully down at his breakfast table, "I'll just have toast this morning."

"Certainly, sir."

Jim's alert speed of movement enhanced Neil's sensation of frailty. Jim brought a larger pot of coffee than usual. Neil persuaded him to sit down and join him in a cup.

"Surely you'd feel better for one?" he suggested.

"I've had one, and I did," said Jim, pouring out. "But you ended your stay in the right and proper way. You've had a hell of a time. I'm sorry, sir."

"Have I?" Neil gazed out of the window, at the bright tranquil garden turning insubstantial as the steam from the coffee frosted its way up the glass. Did he hope that was how the whole Bunington experience would soon seem to him? "I feel as if I've been here all my life, Jim, d'you know?" Already, after two long swallows, it was easier to focus on his landlord's attentive face.

"Think I can understand that, sir. A lot's happened."

"Yes, Jim."

"A lot to a lot of people. Think you'll ever come and stay with me again?"

"I might."

"As time goes on," said Jim, getting to his feet, "you'll find only the best part of it has stuck. We're lucky that way. Although I reckon that's why so many people make the same mistake twice."

Jim poured him another cup of coffee before going about his business, and Neil sat on in the dining-room, slowly drinking it, until he felt strong enough to climb the stairs and fill his suitcase.

When he had finished it was still too early to present himself at Tony's cottage, and he strolled round the village, meeting no one but the self who had arrived in Bunington a long two weeks ago and taken an immediate tour of inspection. That self, in whose steps he followed and whose sensations he partially recalled, seemed to possess an ingenuous quality which his current self had shed even though he no longer believed his sophistication to be impenetrable. Perhaps it was the certainties in the mind of that recent, distant figure which made Neil think it was ingenuous . . .

It was a magical morning, the pale blue sky flecked with wisps of white cloud. The solitary swan was gliding across the pond and the ducks were preening. When Neil approached the cottage he saw Tony looking from an upstairs window but by the time he was through the gate his host was standing on the step.

"Do you want to be inside, or in the garden?"

"Inside, I think, as I haven't seen the place yet."

Tony showed him round, upstairs and down, full of ideas on alterations and improvements which struck Neil as interesting and here and there inspired.

"You could take it for a holiday," said Tony, as his guest followed him for the second time into the kitchen.

"What would Jim Bates say?"

"Well, then, wait until you get married, and take it for your wife for the summer."

"Ha!" said Neil. He had been going to ask Tony if they had heard from Annabel, but decided to wait until the context changed.

"Would you like it black?" Tony was measuring instant coffee into a jug.

"Yes, please, and yes, I did have rather a lot of whisky last night."

"I thought you looked it a bit. It was the reaction." Tony put the steaming jug on to a tray. "Aunt Helen started to cry at breakfast, because the strain was over. Let's go into the sitting-room." He called over his shoulder. "What d'you think made her own up? Gosh, when you think . . ."

"It's not my investigation."

"It's awful, though, isn't it? I mean, I've known her all my life."

"It is awful. Have you heard anything of Annabel?"

"No. You're not going back to London today, are you?"

"I'm afraid I am. I'm expected in the office tomorrow. Tony?"

"This is the last time I shall ever cry," announced Tony, in a small squeezed voice, his flushed face bent over the pot as he carefully poured out coffee.

"I shouldn't bank on it. Thanks."

Neil took his cup with a sigh, and wandered to the window. The fields and slopes behind Bunington had never looked more full of the promise of peace. They held too, he fancied for a moment, a sort of gentle reproof that he was leaving them. And Annabel. *We have left undone those things which we ought to have done.* The wording was out of date, even in the eyes of the Church. But they were the words he had been brought up on. It was infuriating, debilitating, ridiculous, when he knew he hadn't committed a crime, to wonder if he had committed a sin.

But he was going.

"Look," he said to Tony, as he sat down again, "you'll come and spend a weekend with me, won't you?"

Tony's face shot up, transformed. "Yes, of course! If you . . ."

"I'd like you to come. I'll write to you in a while to suggest a time."

"That'll be great. I didn't want to lose touch . . ."

"We won't."

"Will Cathy be there?"

"I presume so, unless she's moved."

"Oh, gosh, is she moving?"

"Not that I know of," said Neil, trying not to sound impatient, "but people do rather come and go in London."

"I suppose so. Do you think we could go to the Houses of Parliament?"

"Why not? I'll arrange it."

"Gosh."

II

It was three o'clock when he got away, what with saying goodbye to people and having a late lunch which Jim Bates insisted must be a good one, and then a brandy with Jim in his room.

"I'll let you know how people go on," said Jim, as Neil finally got to his feet. "I'll miss you," he added, abruptly and heavily, as Neil shut the car door. "There never was such a time."

Neil drove away past the Big Green and the Corrigan fields, as he had come. He found himself smiling over his surprise at the ease with which he was apparently leaving Bunington behind him. He enjoyed being alone in the car, his own company, as keenly as he had always enjoyed it, and was relieved. He turned on the radio and was aware of the summer countryside as he sped through it, singing where the programme invited him. He wasn't held up by traffic until he reached the beginnings of London and the rush hour.

He didn't mind. He didn't mind anything. He felt relaxed, refusing to be depressed by the squalid edges of the metropolis. He would go home and have a bath, stroll down to the delicatessen and replenish his food supply, probably call in at the Harp and have a drink and see who was there . . .

Once he had crossed the no-man's-land surrounding London the enforced crawl was more interesting. Familiar names, familiar buildings, small communities, people on pavements. There was a jingle going on the radio when he saw the news-stand and the *Evening Standard*, and its persistent phrase belonged ever afterwards to that moment. He saw the cover of the *Standard* because he was forced to a halt, in the line of traffic next to the pavement.

One photograph on the front page, two smiling faces side by side. Benjamin and Annabel Quillin.

The car behind him hooted and he edged forward. The hollow feeling in his inside was so unusual he examined it, as it slowly filled again with the usual matter. His temples, though, went on drumming. A pile of *Evening Standards* was set out on the next stand, but this time he saw no more than the already deeply familiar outline of the picture, as he had to keep moving. He thought, self-protectively, "an old photograph," but he knew it wasn't. It was extraordinary, what he knew just from that one short agonized glance.

Instead of turning north to the flat he went on into town, towards the office. He had other glances at evening papers, each one a painful corroboration of the first. Just short of the office he was stopped again, close enough to the news-stand to reach out with his money and receive a paper in exchange. He dropped it on the seat beside him and picked it up again when he had parked in his usual spot and switched off the engine. The caption said "Re-united in Buenos Aires," and Annabel and her husband had their faces touching. He had never seen Annabel smile as she was smiling, even through the blur of newspaper photography. She might have been wearing the clothes in which she had said goodbye to him on Latchford station. The article explained that Mrs. Quillin had not been in custody in the United Kingdom, although it was not thought the UK authorities were aware she had left the country. Nor was it thought she had arrived in the Argentine aboard a public flight.

Inside, the office was showing signs of the end of a working day. "Chief Inspector Larkin still at home?"

"I believe so, Governor."

The sergeant stared back at him unsmiling. But then, reflected Neil in the lift, he and the Chief were the only two who knew why he had gone to Bunington. The only two, at any rate, who were sure.

He was in the lift when he was hit by his own reaction of masculine rage. He had to hold the doors for a few seconds until it passed, until he remembered that, to himself at least, he had already called "enough."

In the outer offices he answered greetings without slowing up. The Chief had the *Evening News* on his desk and the photograph was smaller, but it was the same photograph. Neil dropped his *Standard* on top of it, and he and the Chief stared at one another without expression.

"I told you you assumed too much," said Neil at last.

"It's a good thing, Carter, that you went unofficially."

"It was the only way I could have gone." But he must not be too raw, or the Chief would think his inclinations had overcome his duty. He knew they never had. Telling Annabel that the vigilance had been called off, that hadn't been softness, it had been an error of judgement. To tell the Chief of it would be an act of masochism. Such a bird, some way, some time, would have flown.

"Sit down, Neil," said the Chief.

"I'm glad to see," said Neil as he obeyed, "how bravely you're taking it."

"Well, Neil, I'll tell you." The Chief leaned across his desk, confidentially. "You know I pride myself on my nose." Neil thought, in fleeting interested memory, of Humphrey Barnes. "I never felt really happy about Annabel Quillin. Can't tell you why. It was an instinct."

"Thank you."

"No, I didn't hold out on you. There was nothing in the file."

"But you were right. I was wrong. I thought she was a lady one could never fathom, but I had no feeling she was carrying that kind of secret."

"It's as well we kept it to ourselves."

"We didn't. Most people in Britain, if they care to remember, are aware that I escorted the lady. Was—affectionate with her in public."

"Because you knew the family of old and were on holiday. If you get ribbed, as you may do, you'll remind 'em about that. 'If I'd been on duty,' you'll say, 'you don't think—'"

"Yes, of course, Governor. But they'll go back to Bunington, and dig."

"And if they do. There's nothing to find. You were never connected with the Quillin inquiry."

The Chief looked steadily at Neil. Was he whistling in the dark? For that day, at any rate, Neil was too weary to care.

"I'm not going to ask you a lot of intimate questions," said the Chief, "either now, or tomorrow, or next week. Just the practical one—have you any idea how she might have made contact?"

"There's an address in Bristol which will have to be investigated. If I can remember where she directed me. A small manufacturer of lawnmowers. Probably clean, but she was out of my sight a few moments."

He thought with another gush of anger of his lulled, lyrical response to that gentle scene.

"See Sergeant Greaves on your way out. Better get them on to it right away."

"Of course." He made an effort. "I'm sorry, but I'm certain I couldn't have done any more. I'm certain no one could have done anything in the face of that—determination."

"I don't suppose they could. I'm sorry too." The Chief leaned back in his chair and a look of approbation spread grudgingly across his face. "You did solve another crime, Neil, and prevent a third."

III

It took about ten minutes to get the car out into the street again. And another half-hour to get home. Central London was sporting that rare and lovely summer mood when even commuters, under a mild blue evening sky, find themselves ambling towards bus or train. Neil observed it all as if he was seeing it on film. He was surprised when a truck driver with a big red face winked at him as they passed a few feet apart. He felt curiously contained, compact, as if occupying a very small space.

It took him a minute or two to sort out the whirlwind of Cathy, bursting through her door as he felt for his key.

"Neil!" She drew back. "Are you all right?"

"I'm fine." He made himself smile. "How are you?"

She pulled a face. The piece of hair which fell over her nose was streaked with blue paint. "Oh, I'm all right."

He went into his hallway, picking up the letters lying there, leaving the door open behind him.

"Are you back for good this time?"

"So far as I know."

She hovered in the doorway, and he idly remembered when she had been duplicated by Tony, hovering beside her. Nothing seemed of very much importance. He moved on into the sitting-room.

"You should have let me know, I'd have stocked your fridge with basics."

"It doesn't matter," he said absently, studying the envelopes. One of them was addressed in an unfamiliar neat hand, and he roughly opened it. He read the signature first, then the rest of it.

It was more than a smokescreen, Neil, believe me. But one must be where one belongs, and if there is no honest way of getting there one must use deceit. I shan't ever forget you.

Smokescreen. He shuddered. In denying the word, she had used it. For a few seconds he was blind and deaf with rage, and when it passed he was amazed to find that his abiding reaction was of envy. Not of Benjamin Quillin, which he might have expected, but of Annabel, for knowing where she belonged. She had known, all along, but he would have to embark on the peculiar task of redesigning his memories . . .

He remembered Cathy and went quickly out into the hall. She had gone, and his front door was shut. So was hers, when he looked out on to the landing. He left his door on the latch and rang her bell. She came and stood there in silence, gazing at him with a sort of grave doubtfulness. He could see the *Evening Standard* thrown down on the hall table behind her. He must begin, in all departments, as he meant to go on.

"Are you going out tonight?" he asked her.

"No."

"Busy at home?"

"Not especially."

"Well, then, as my fridge isn't stocked and yours presumably contains the essentials, would you feel like making me bacon and egg in due course? I can supply some wine."

"Neil, of course I would!"

She appeared to be the same simple creature she had always been. And if she questioned him later about the article in the paper, he was ready.

"That's great. Tony sends love, by the way. Give me a couple of hours."

The lift doors opened and he turned round into the questing melancholy countenance of Humphrey Barnes.

Neil stared at him. He didn't know yet, he couldn't know, if anything permanent had happened to him in Bunington, but he suddenly knew the one person he might be able to talk to about it was this man.

"They didn't show me the register at the Red Lion," said Barnes, "I just looked at it." There was no sign of an evening paper but he was carrying a briefcase. "I thought you might be back," he concluded with a sigh.

"About ten minutes ago."

"I'm sorry."

"Liar." Neil introduced him to Cathy. "I've no spirits and no beer," he told him, "come down to the pub."

"I'll see you around, then, Neil," said Cathy in a small brave voice.

"In a couple of hours," he said. "Two eggs if you've got them." He watched, touched, as the light came back into her eyes.

"Nice little girl," observed Humphrey Barnes as the lift doors closed on them. "Reminds me of that lad in Bunington, the brother of Annabel Quillin."